A TALENT FOR DESTRUCTION

MICAH EDWARDS

VELOX BOOKS
Published by arrangement with the author.

CONTENTS

GREY MICHAEL

It started out like any other workday. I had houses to sell and people who wanted to buy them. Honestly, I've always found being a realtor embarrassingly easy. People seek you out and ask you to sell them incredibly high-ticket items. I've done other sales jobs, and you always have to talk the buyers into extras, into upgrades, all for a tiny commission.

With houses, it's so much easier. Your customers walk in already prepared to sign their life away for the next thirty years, so it's easy to convince them to go for the nicer house, the better neighborhood, the higher price tag. The bigger commission, from my point of view.

Obviously it's not always completely smooth. I've had some real nightmare clients. Who hasn't? I've been yelled at, talked down to, insulted, even physically threatened on a couple of occasions. But 90% of my job was just about keeping a smile on my face and saying empty phrases like "Okay, I hear you" or "Let's keep looking!" Easy as pie.

So I didn't expect this day to be anything out of the ordinary. Houses had been selling well lately and I'd just gotten several new ones added to my roster. If I kept my numbers up, I was on track to have the most sales of the quarter, so I was pretty motivated to get out there and get folks into a new house.

I usually like to go do a walkthrough beforehand to make sure that there aren't any surprises, but I hadn't had a chance to do that with my upcoming afternoon showing. If I had, maybe it would have turned out a lot better for the Hubers. Then again, maybe it would have turned out a lot worse for me, so… I don't know.

The house looked fine from the outside. It was a California split-level, a little under two thousand square feet, a classy mix of brick and wood siding. The house and land were well-maintained, and I could see that Mrs. Huber, Marilyn, was already charmed by it. It was within their price range, in the school district they were looking for, and basically everything was just falling into place.

I could smell an easy sale. I was going to be able to knock this one off on day one, and then it'd just be a matter of paperwork. I refrained from rubbing my hands together in glee as I walked the Hubers up to the front door, but only barely. That's how good I was feeling about this.

Inside was great, too, at least at first. Hardwood floors in the entry hall, big windows letting the whole place glow in the afternoon sun, nice neutral colors on the walls and a pleasant smell in the air. It was picture-perfect staging, and the Hubers were eating it up. Irving was pointing out fancy features in the kitchen, Marilyn was talking about having people over for parties, and I just followed along pretending they needed me there. I didn't have to do a thing. The house was selling itself.

Everything went perfectly right up until we were leaving. We'd finished touring the top floor and they'd both gushed about how perfect the view from the master bedroom was. I was leading the way down the stairs, chatting over my shoulder with the Hubers and keeping one hand on the railing to guide myself along. I wasn't really paying much attention. How much attention does anyone ever pay to stairs? These were carpeted, they didn't squeak, and the wooden posts and railings were solid and attractive. They successfully connected the floors of the house. That's all you can really say about stairs.

Suddenly, Marilyn broke into my patter. "Sorry, this is a strange question, but… how many floors does this house have?"

"Three, including the finished basement," I told her, wondering why she was asking. We'd just finished walking through them all.

"Right, that's what I thought. Only… this is the second flight of stairs. And we're still heading to the front hallway."

I honestly had no idea what she meant at first. Obviously it wasn't the second flight of stairs, or we would be on our way to the basement. These weren't the basement stairs. Therefore, we hadn't gone down two flights.

I tried to think of a way to say "you have not successfully counted to one" that didn't sound patronizing or rude. Finding nothing, instead I said, "Well, we're here now, at least. We can—"

I stopped dead on a small landing where the stairs made a right turn. It should have been just a couple more stairs to the entryway. Instead, I was looking at the hallway leading to the bedrooms. The one on the top floor of the house.

I looked behind me. At the top of the stairs I could see the hallway we'd just left. My mind lurched, trying to find some sense to seize on. It was a three-level house. I was at the base of some stairs. I could see other stairs ahead of me, leading down. Therefore, I must be on the middle level, where the entryway was. It's just that I wasn't. I was on the top level. Having taken stairs down to get there.

"Something's wrong," I said stupidly. Irving and Marilyn reached out and held each other's hands. They looked around nervously. I realized that they were waiting for me to do something. I was in charge here, after all.

"Let's just… let's just take the stairs down," I suggested, suiting action to word. This time, I kept my eyes focused ahead, watching every step. I could hear the Hubers walking along behind me, their paired treads only a stair away. Ordinarily I would have been annoyed to have a client stepping on my heels like that, but right now I didn't blame them at all.

Eleven stairs down brought us to a right-turn landing. With trepidation, I made the turn, hoping that somehow I'd just misunderstood something before, that I'd somehow failed to use stairs correctly. My hopes were dashed as I stepped out into the same carpeted hallway leading to the bedrooms. The ground floor was still somehow below us.

The Hubers exchanged wide-eyed glances.

"I don't understand this," said Marilyn.

"Well, look," said Irving, trying to be reasonable. "If 'down' doesn't work, maybe 'up' will?"

He turned and began to walk back up the stairs. Struck by a sudden curiosity, I moved across the hall to look at the stairs leading down. Marilyn kept her position on the landing so she could see both of us.

When the stairs came into view, I saw exactly what I'd feared. Although Irving had gone up the stairs behind me, I was now ahead of him on the floor he was climbing to.

His face blanched when he saw me. "This—this is impossible."

He looked back at Marilyn below him. "How is this happening?"

"I can see you," Marilyn called weakly to me. "From both directions. I can see you at the top of the stairs—" She pointed. "—and at the bottom over here."

She turned her head and gestured. Suddenly feeling weak, I sat down against the wall, taking solace in its solidity. I closed my eyes and pressed my fingers to my temples, willing this all to be some sort of fever dream.

"Are you alright?" Irving called. I heard his footsteps start toward me. He was only four or five steps from the top. Somehow, though, they kept going.

I opened my eyes. Irving was climbing the stairs, a look of terror on his face. He scrambled faster and faster, yet he never moved forward. Marilyn screamed. I leapt to my feet. Behind Irving, the staircase was lengthening, adding a stair beneath his feet for every step he took.

I lunged forward, my hand extended for him to grab, but as I reached for him a dozen new stairs appeared, dragging him away from me.

"Go back down!" I shouted. Irving turned and tried to run, but it was too late. The stairs stretched away at a frightening rate, a corridor reaching out to infinity. Irving was reduced to a tiny speck somewhere in the middle, and although I could hear Marilyn screaming right behind me, I could also hear a tiny version echoing faintly up the walls of what had been the staircase in front of me.

Less than a second later, the staircase snapped back into place, the same eleven steps there should always have been. Irving was gone.

Marilyn was shrieking. She had collapsed onto the landing and was clinging to the railing like it was a lifeline. She sobbed Irving's name over and over, but there was no response.

Her total breakdown helped bring me back to myself. I took her by the arm and attempted to tug her to her feet.

"Mrs. Huber. Marilyn. Come on, please. We have to get out of here."

"How?" she wailed, a question for which I had no answer.

"I don't know. One of the rooms, maybe? There must be—" I opened the door to one of the bedrooms. Fear gripped my stomach.

The door now led to another set of stairs. Or, more probably, the same ones.

"Irving. Irving!"

"Come on! That isn't helping. Let's… I don't know, let's try going down the stairs with our eyes closed. Maybe it's an illusion." That didn't make any sense, but it was all I could come up with.

It was good enough for Marilyn, at least. She closed her eyes and, still clinging to my hand, allowed me to lead her to the stairs.

"Okay, here's the rail. Put your hand on it. I'm not going to let go of you," I assured her. "Just hold the rail for safety. I'm going to have my eyes closed, too. Ready? Stay close. Here we go."

My right hand on the railing, my left hand bent awkwardly behind me, I shuffled forward and felt my way onto the first step. I stepped down and felt Marilyn move into position behind me.

Step, step. Down the stairs, one shuffling movement at a time. I kept my eyes squeezed shut, letting my feet guide me. I went slowly, though after a few steps Marilyn began to fall behind.

"Come on, you've got to keep up."

"I'm trying! You're going too fast."

I'm barely moving, I thought, but did not say. I bit my tongue and took another step. From behind me, I heard Marilyn's muffled footsteps hitting the carpeted stairs. Once, twice. Three times. My left hand, still gripped tightly in her fist, began to get pulled slowly backward.

"Marilyn?"

"Slow down," she begged me. "You're getting too far ahead. Stop moving!"

Fully stationary, I risked opening my eyes. I saw what I already knew had to be true: just as it had with Irving, the staircase was beginning to lengthen.

"Marilyn," I said, my voice catching in my throat. Her eyes popped open, widening in fear as she realized what was happening.

"Help me!"

Her palm started to slide through my grasp, and I did the only thing I could do. I pulled as hard as I could, yanking her off of the stairs and sending her tumbling onto me.

We fell down the last four stairs together, crashing into the wall of the landing hard enough to crack the plaster. I saw stars and tasted blood. Shaking my head, I struggled to a standing position and found that I was now looking at the entryway, its gleaming wooden floors a shining beacon of hope.

Marilyn was still sobbing on the ground, her arms wrapped around my leg. I'd like to believe that I wouldn't have bolted for the door and left her there in any case, but I certainly wasn't going to with the death grip she had on me.

"Marilyn. Marilyn, we made it. We're here. We can get out."

She looked up, fearful and disbelieving.

"Come on," I coaxed, lifting her to her feet once more. "Look, there's the door. We can go."

"But Irving—!"

"I know. I know. We'll come back for him," I lied. There was no chance I was ever setting foot in that house again. "We can get help. We've just got to go."

I half-dragged her to the door. I was certain that it was going to be another trick, that the hallway would begin to stretch, or the outside door would open to more stairs, but I had no idea what else to do. When I opened the front door and it actually led to the outside, I burst into tears.

Eyes streaming, I raced down the brick steps. Marilyn kept pace with me, both of us running as fast as we could until we collapsed against our cars, chests heaving. Her hair was wild, her knees were skinned, her blouse was torn. I was certain I looked no better. I could feel a painful wetness on the back of my head where I'd banged it into the wall, but my hair seemed to be keeping most of the blood in place. And if that was what it took to get out of that nightmare, I counted it a small price to pay.

We stared at each other for several minutes. My heart rate gradually slowed. My mind attempted to tell me that I couldn't have seen what I thought I had. It was a bright, sunny, suburban day. Houses didn't unfold into impossible geometries. Not in a nice neighborhood like this.

If Irving had been there with us, I might have even convinced myself it was some sort of hallucination. But he wasn't. The house had him.

"We have to go back in," Marilyn said, but her voice lacked conviction.

I shook my head, eliciting a stab of pain. "No way. Sorry, no way."

"But Irving's in there!"

"We'll get him. We'll get help. We can, I don't know, tie a rope to the outside. Or make a human chain or something. Something. But we can't go back in there like this."

"I can't just leave him!"

"We'll come—" My response was interrupted by a loud slam! from the house. Our heads both jerked up to see the front door standing wide open. Irving stood in the doorframe, gripping the edges like his life depended on it. He gave a cry that was half a yell of triumph and half a sob, and then he fell bonelessly down the brick steps to the pathway below.

Marilyn and I raced over. Irving was in bad shape, and not just from the fall. His clothes were tattered and filthy. His hands were bloody and blistered. His hair was ragged, and although he had been clean-shaven when we stepped into the house, he now had what appeared to be several days' growth of beard.

"Irving! Irv? Irv!" Marilyn cradled his head in her arms, but Irving did not move. I checked his pulse and was relieved to find it present. I let Marilyn attempt to wake him up for another minute, and then I took out my cell and called 911.

I lied to the dispatchers. I said he'd had some sort of attack, that I thought maybe it was blood sugar related. I said his wife was here and would hopefully be calmed down enough when they arrived to give them better information. I gave them the address and told them we would meet them at the street. They said not to move him, and I told them that was where he had collapsed. Then I hung up the phone so I could drag him to the curb. The open door of the house gaped mockingly behind me, challenging me to come back inside. It scared me to look into it, but it scared me more to have my back to it, so I simply got as far away as I could and waited for the EMTs.

The ambulance took the Hubers away, leaving me alone. With no idea what else to do, I got into my car and drove back to the office. It wasn't even really a conscious decision. I was in shock and running on autopilot.

I wandered into the office looking like I'd been mugged in the parking lot. I stumbled to my desk, ignoring my coworkers' questions, and fell into my chair. I stared at my reflection in the blank monitor as their chatter passed over my head.

After a few minutes, a hand fell onto my shoulder. I looked up to see my coworker, Maryann.

"What happened?"

"He just—I just—he, um. There was an attack. He had an attack, I mean."

Keeping her voice low, her eyes darting around to see who was listening, she asked, "Was it a house?"

"What?"

"A house. Did something go… wrong… in the house?"

I stared at her dumbly. She pressed on.

"Monsters. Bent space. Distortions of reality?"

I nodded.

"Okay. Here."

She passed me a business card, one from our agency. The name on it was GREY MICHAEL. It wasn't anyone I knew.

"Gre—" I started. Maryann frantically shushed me.

"Do not say his name until you're ready to talk to him! Go get cleaned up first. Take a moment. Don't stumble into this."

"Who is this?"

She glanced furtively around again. "He's… a coworker. He specializes in… difficult houses. He can help you here."

I looked around the office. It wasn't that large of a space. "Okay, but… who is he?"

"When you're ready, go out into the hallway. His office is right there."

"I've never seen it."

"You will once you say his name."

Maryann moved off into the office, spreading a cover story about a client fainting and dragging me with him down some steps. I turned the card over in my hands a few times, then tucked it into my pocket and went to wash up.

I wasn't wholly successful at getting all of the blood out of my hair, but by the time I was done I looked fairly presentable and felt a whole lot more awake. My brain was working overtime trying to convince me that I'd imagined the whole thing, that I'd fallen and hit my head and made the rest of it up. But there was still a 911 call in my "recent calls" log, and I knew that if I called the local hospitals, I'd be able to find out where the Hubers had been admitted pretty easily.

I planted my hands on the bathroom counter and stared at myself in the mirror, trying to decide if I was looking into the eyes of a crazy person. In the end, I shrugged and turned away without an answer.

"All right," I said to myself. "Let's go find Grey Michael."

His office, as Maryann had said, was right there. The name was on a plaque on the door. It was impossible to miss, yet I'd somehow walked past it every day. I knocked lightly on the door.

"Come in," called a mild voice. I opened the door and met Grey Michael.

He was normal. Aggressively normal. If I told you to picture a generic white male, you'd be thinking of him. His smile was pleasant and professional, a perfect stock-image look. He gestured to a chair in front of his desk.

"Come in. Close the door, have a seat. So, you have a problem?"

I followed his instructions. "How do you know I have a problem?"

"You have my card," he said, as if that explained everything. "Tell me what happened."

I started to speak, but he quickly held up one thin finger. "Not what you think happened. Not what must have happened, because what you remember can't possibly be true. Tell me what happened, in order, without apology or prevarication."

Something in his voice made his words less of an instruction and more of an unassailable command. I opened my mouth and let the words fall out.

When I had finished, Grey Michael nodded his head. "Simple enough."

"Simple?"

"Yes. This is small, a fledgling. One trick, very little power. Shall we go?"

"Go where?" I was totally lost in this conversation.

"To the house. To remove it."

I started to refuse, but Grey Michael stood up from his desk and brushed invisible dust from his suit. "Drive. It will give you something to do."

Without thinking, my keys were in my hand, and I was heading for the door. We were out of the parking lot before I even realized he was riding in my passenger seat.

"I can't go back in there," I told him.

"You won't have to. Only one step, so that you can declare your request for assistance."

"What?"

"You need to say the following phrase, as exactly as you can: *I, as the duly appointed representative tasked with the preservation of this home and its contents, hereby invite Grey Michael inside.*" Only he didn't say "Grey Michael." His lips said "Grey Michael." The sound said "Grey Michael." But what I felt was something dark and broken, words of tortured malice.

We passed the rest of the drive in silence. Grey Michael seemed content to watch the scenery, while I was simply trying to calm my panicked brain.

When we pulled up outside, the front door was closed.

"I left that open," I told Grey Michael.

"It's not important," he said, getting out of the car. "This will all be over soon."

My courage failed me as I approached the front door. If it had still been open, I think I could have stepped inside. But to grasp the handle and open it myself was beyond me.

"I can't. I can't do this."

"Hm," said Grey Michael. "Are you saying that you've wasted my time?"

I took an immediate step backward from the look he gave me, banging my back against the house's front door. "No! No."

"Then open the door and invite me inside."

I opened it without hesitation. My fear of the house hadn't lessened, but I'd found something I feared more. I took a single step inside.

"That's far enough," said Grey Michael. "Now. Invite me."

I cleared my throat. "I, as the duly appointed representative tasked with the preservation of this home and its contents, hereby invite Grey Michael inside."

His name twisted like burned rope in my throat. It felt like nails on bone, carving secret messages on my skeleton, words that would never leave me.

"Thank you," he said, stepping past me into the house. "Now. Please remain on the porch and hold this door closed. Do not open it for anything. It could be very dangerous for you if you do."

He closed the door in my face. I took hold of the handle and exerted a gentle pull. I wondered how long I was going to have to stand like this, and what I would say to anyone who asked what I was doing.

Those thoughts were driven from my mind when the screaming started. I jumped, nearly losing my grip on the door handle, but fear of Grey Michael kept me in place.

The screams seemed to come from the house itself, as if the bricks and boards were crying out. They ranged up and down in pitch, sounding sometimes human but always terrified.

Then the scratching started, desperate clawing against the door. I felt tugging against the handle, and I leaned my weight back, heedless of the steps behind me. Not for anything, Grey Michael had said, and I would not open it for anything.

My blood ran cold as voices began pleading with me. Children, old folks, family members. They begged and cried to get out. I stood fast. They slowly died away.

"Thank you," said Grey Michael from behind me. I spun around to find him standing at the bottom of the steps, not a hair out of place. "You can release the door now. The house has been cleansed."

"What do we do now?"

"By preference, you take me back to the office. You have a house to sell, after all. And I have other work to do."

We were silent again on the drive back. At one point, he yawned. I glanced over and caught a glimpse into his mouth. It opened up like a cave. Distant lights glittered inside.

He saw me watching and raised an eyebrow. I said nothing.

We shook hands back at the office. "I'll be seeing you around," Grey Michael said. I've been trying not to think too hard about what that might mean.

In the meantime… anyone looking to buy a house? I can guarantee with absolute certainty that it is not haunted. Grey Michael made sure of that.

SUBURBIA

This is a story about fireworks and lampposts and guns. This is a story about those who see what they expect to see, and those who don't. This is a story about suburbia.

I moved out to the 'burbs a couple of years ago, before the interest rates went nuts. Got a house in a nice, quiet neighborhood with some nice, quiet neighbors. There were parts about it I didn't love. I found it kind of weird how much all of the houses and yards looked alike. I hated that I had to drive to get anywhere. And I definitely wasn't excited about having an HOA.

The realtor told me I was going to have to suck that up. "All of these places are under homeowners' associations," she told me. "And those that aren't are forming them. Everyone hates the idea until they've got that one problematic neighbor, and then it's worth all of the little annoyances just so that you can have some legal clout when telling them to knock it off."

So I signed, and honestly, it's a fantastic house. I'm at the corner of the street, so I've got a nice large lot. There are sidewalks—well-maintained sidewalks! Not the cracked and angled nonsense I knew—and streetlights that actually come on at night. It's a bigger house than I need for now, but I'm still young and with any luck I won't be alone here forever. And yeah, there are by-laws about how long my grass can be and what color I can paint my house, but in the end I just don't care that much.

About that "one problematic neighbor," though. My realtor didn't mention him by name, but there's no way she wasn't thinking of Morgan Quickley. He's directly across the street from me, in the one house that doesn't blur together with all of the others. He's got dark siding and exposed brick, while every other house is a fairly uniform cream color. There's ivy that creeps its way up the brick sometimes. The grass in the yard isn't the same green as everyone else's.

There's nothing wrong with the house. It's just different.

Morgan's different, too. That's putting it mildly. See, when the realtor didn't warn me about him while I was buying the house, she also didn't mention that he'd been here before the HOA was formed, and he'd refused to join when it did. That's why he was able to stand out. There wasn't a thing anyone in the neighborhood could do to stop him.

I found out about Morgan not long after moving in. I'd only been in the house for three days, and my moving pod had just arrived. I'd spent a long day unloading it and was finally relaxing on my couch—actual furniture! In my actual house!—when suddenly I heard gunfire from outside, sounding like it was right across the street.

Survival kicked in and I hit the ground. I looked around fast to see if I needed to get away from any windows, maybe crawl for the kitchen. Then I heard another string of pops and a long whine and realized it was just fireworks.

I stuck my head out of the front door to see Morgan sitting in a lawn chair, a Roman candle at his feet. He was waving at a scowling neighbor I hadn't met yet.

"Quickley! Knock it off with those or I'll call the cops!" shouted the angry man from his porch.

"Just welcoming in the new neighbor, Sean," Morgan called back.

"It's a school night!" Sean stormed back inside. Morgan saw me looking and turned his grin in my direction.

"Evening! Welcome to the neighborhood."

"An enthusiastic greeting, for sure. Do you always welcome people this way?"

"Oh, I welcome everything this way," he said. "You'll hear about me. Come on over! I've got a spare chair."

I pulled on my shoes and walked across the street. As I crossed under the streetlight outside of his house, it went out. I looked up at it reproachfully.

"Don't mind it, it does that," Morgan said. "Come on, have a seat. You drinking?"

He offered me a beer, which I supposed meant that I was.

Morgan and I got along shockingly well. There had to be sixty years separating us, but he was just a genuine guy, and I didn't get that vibe from anyone else in the neighborhood. I liked them all well enough, but I had the distinct impression that they'd spread a rumor behind my back at the same time they were assuring me that no matter what everyone was saying, THEY certainly didn't feel that way about me.

Morgan was about as subtle as his fireworks. If he had a problem with you, he'd tell you. You could fix it or not; that was your choice. He'd done his part by informing you. The rest was on you.

It worked both ways, too. You could say anything to Morgan and he'd take it under consideration. If you were polite, he'd see what he could do to at least meet you in the middle.

The problem came when people tried to play hardball. Morgan, as it turned out, was a world champion in calling people's bluff and getting people's goat. When he felt someone deserved it, he would be petty in ways that were absolutely remarkable.

He told me a story about early on, when they were forming the HOA and putting in sidewalks and generally dressing up the neighborhood. The folks spearheading the initiative were pressuring him to join and weren't taking no for an answer particularly well.

"Don't you want the benefits?" the man in charge had asked.

("Can't remember his name," Morgan told me, though his memory was plenty sharp on most other things, so I suspected this was just one more instance of pettiness.)

"Can't see any I'd need," Morgan told him.

"Well, what about the sidewalk maintenance?" The man gestured to the freshly poured sidewalk running in front of Morgan's house.

"Not my problem."

"Well, it's on your property, so it is your problem. The county can fine you if they're not properly maintained and cleared and so on."

"All right. Take 'em back out."

"What?"

"You heard me. Take 'em out. If it's gonna be a pain, I don't want 'em."

"It's an easement. The county's allowed to—"

"But the county didn't, did they? You did. And I was fine with that if you were going to maintain them. But you can't come put something in on my property and then tell me you're going to charge me if I don't keep it looking nice. Take 'em back out, or I will."

"You can't do that!"

A lengthy and bitter court case later, it turned out that Morgan could, in fact, do that. Partway through, his HOA neighbor offered him a written agreement for the HOA to provide maintenance at no cost to Morgan, but it was too late for that. Morgan made them pay to tear out the brand-new sidewalks, refill and reseed his lawn. For years, the sidewalks came right up to his property line, stopped, and picked up on the other side. There was a worn footpath through the grass where folks kept walking, but the county couldn't charge him to keep that clear of dirt and leaves and snow, so it was just fine by Morgan.

Years later, when other folks got tired of looking at Morgan's muddy footpath, they approached him and asked him politely if the HOA could please put in—and maintain—a sidewalk in front of his property. The man he'd had the original feud with had moved out, so Morgan said yes.

The fireworks were a similar case. He'd set some off for July 4th one year, and the man I'd seen yelling at him the other night, Sean, had come storming out of his house and snatched the lighter out of Morgan's hand, telling him that he couldn't do that around here. Morgan simply waited for Sean to leave, took out another lighter, and set off another round of fireworks.

The police arrived shortly thereafter, but it turned out that all of Morgan's fireworks were legal and there was nothing in the law preventing him from what he was doing. The police asked him if he would mind please stopping, to keep the peace in the neighborhood, and Morgan said (his face broke into a big smile when he told me this part):

"Why would I want to keep the peace with a thief?"

Sean, who'd been angrily pacing over on his lawn, blew up at this and demanded to know what Morgan meant by this slander.

"This man," Morgan said to the police, ignoring Sean, "came onto my property earlier and stole a lighter out of my hand. As long as you're here keeping the peace, I'd like my property back."

Sean blustered and got red in the face, but in the end he was forced to go back into his house and retrieve Morgan's lighter, as well as endure a speech from the police about the importance of respecting personal property and boundaries.

Needless to say, there was no love lost between him and Morgan these days. He watched Morgan like a hawk for any actual infraction of the law, just waiting for him to slip up. And Morgan, for his part, celebrated every occasion and no occasion at all by setting off fireworks in his front yard.

That was the story he told me at first, anyway, before we knew each other. We came to be pretty good friends, like I said. One evening, about a year after I'd moved in, we were sitting on his front porch and talking.

"You see that woman?" Morgan asked, nodding toward the sidewalk where a woman had just crossed under his streetlamp.

"Yeah, what about her?"

"Does she live around here?"

"I don't know, maybe?"

"Not maybe, yes or no. Does she live in the neighborhood? Have you seen her before?"

I tried to come up with a definite answer and failed. Honestly, I could barely describe the woman I'd just seen, except in the most generic terms. Average height, shoulder-length hair, business-casual clothes. Maybe glasses? I wasn't even sure about that.

"I have no idea," I told him.

Morgan sighed. "She doesn't," he said. "Not exactly, anyway. And yes, you've seen her before. She walked by last night."

"I guess I wasn't paying attention."

"You've got to start."

"Why?" I was genuinely lost. We had been chatting about movies a minute ago, and now I was suddenly in the hot seat.

"I'll give you a shortcut," said Morgan, ignoring that question. He pointed to his streetlight. "You see that lamp? Anything odd about it?"

"Looks like it always does." It was shining brightly, illuminating the empty sidewalk below it like it always did. It was the world's most useless streetlamp, because it cut out every single time anyone walked under it. It only shone when there was nothing to see.

"Walk over there," said Morgan.

"Why, so you can watch it turn out on me?"

"Oh, so you know it'll turn out when you walk over there. Then we're getting somewhere. So, here's the question: if it turns out whenever anyone walks under it, why is it on right now?"

I puzzled over his question for a moment before it hit me. The woman who had just walked under it—the light hadn't turned out on her. I'd never seen it do that before.

None of this was adding up, though. I said as much to Morgan: "You're gonna need to catch me up here. How does a streetlight finally doing its job tell you that a lady doesn't live in the neighborhood?"

"Stay here," said Morgan. "I'm going to get another beer."

He came back out with beers for us both and a couple of bottle rockets tucked under his arm.

"What are we celebrating?"

"Peculiar People Day," said Morgan. He put the fireworks into our old beers and handed me the lighter. "When I get up, I need you to light those fireworks. Now, what was it we were talking about?"

I knew what that sort of redirection meant. When Morgan had settled his mind on a subject, he was absolutely immovable. I wasn't sure why he was so unwilling to talk about something that he'd brought up, but I did know that he wasn't going to say anything more about it.

We talked for maybe another half hour until Morgan suddenly stood up.

"Now," he said, walking toward the street.

For a second, I forgot what he meant. Then I fumbled for the lighter and lit the bottle rockets. They sizzled at my feet for a moment, then went screaming into the air.

The woman from before was walking back up the sidewalk. Morgan was moving on a course to intercept her. She turned her head and gave him a quizzical look.

The fireworks exploded overhead. Morgan drew a gun and shot the woman in the chest.

I leapt from my seat, racing across the lawn, only to stutter to a walk halfway there. There was no woman, no body on the sidewalk. There was nothing but a tremendous mass of roaches, all writhing in panic as they fled from the light.

I stammered out incoherent questions as I drew closer.

"Don't ask me. Go see for yourself," Morgan said, hiding the gun in his jacket.

Sean was yelling something out his window about respect. Morgan gave him a friendly wave.

I processed none of that. My eyes were on the bugs, almost all of which had now disappeared into the grass. They were each about a half-inch long, with obsidian black carapaces that blended in well to both asphalt and dirt. There had been thousands of them only seconds ago, and now I could see no more than a handful.

I stepped too close to the streetlamp. The light went out. I could no longer see the remaining roaches.

Morgan watched me stare at the ground for a long time. He waited until I turned back to him to speak.

"Okay," he said. "Back to the porch and I'll tell you what I know. Fresh beers first, though. You kicked ours over on the way out here."

He gave me the bad news first: he didn't have the deeper answers. What they were, where they came from, what they wanted? All of that was a mystery. Talking to them was no good. They didn't speak. They looked like they were just about to, they even gave the impression that maybe they just had, but they couldn't actually make words.

What they could do, and do very well, was hide in people's expectations. People see what they expect to see, and work very hard not to see anything that will upset their views on reality. The bugs took advantage of that.

They could assemble themselves into things that were almost human. They could walk among us, watch us, learn from us. And Morgan had found out only through the most unlikely of accidents: his broken streetlight.

The bugs could fool us, but they couldn't fool something as dumb as whatever was broken in that lamp. Whether it was the weight of our tread, or the rhythm of our motion, or even something bioelectrical in our bodies, the bugs didn't have whatever it was that screwed with the lamp's circuit. It would turn off for absolutely any person walking under it—but it stayed on for the bugs.

"I saw a man under the light, and I thought it was odd that it hadn't turned off. I was looking up to see if someone had changed the bulb, and I don't know if the bugs were looking as well, or assumed I would get out of their way, or what—but we collided. Instead of the usual solid thump of running into someone, his arm just dissolved. I watched his whole body fall apart into those shiny black cockroaches, but it wasn't until I felt a tickle on my arm hairs that I realized they were all over me."

Morgan gave a shudder as he remembered, unconsciously rubbing at his arm. "Disgusting. Anyway, I put two and two together, and the next time I saw that light stay on when someone went under it, I took a swing at them. Sure enough, my fist went right on through, and I was covered in scurrying roaches again. Didn't take me a third time to figure out to get a gun so I didn't have to touch them anymore.

"After that, I kind of made it my mission to keep an eye on them. I've tried to see where they're coming from, but wherever it is, they split back into individual bits before they get there. Same thing with wherever they're going. It's been ticking me off for years that I can't sort out their game, but at least I can mess it up from time to time."

He looked across the street and gave a grin. "And if I get to irritate Sean while I'm at it, so much the better. In my opinion, he's not much better than the bugs."

The funny thing is that Morgan never realized how close to the truth he was with that last statement. Like I said, that whole conversation happened a year or so back. I spent the next few months watching the streetlamp with Morgan, starting the fireworks to cover his gunshots, occasionally disrupting a few bug collectives myself.

Then one day, I went over to his house and he wasn't there. His car was there, and so was all of his stuff, but Morgan was missing. The police poked around for a bit and said they'd look into it, but it was clear they had nothing to go on.

I didn't tell them my theory: that Morgan was right, that the bugs had been watching us even as we were watching them. That they'd gotten tired of Morgan interfering with whatever they were up to, and had decided to interfere with him, too.

I started watching people outside of the streetlamp, seeing who was happy that Morgan was gone. It was all the ones you'd expect, the ones who like that every house looks the same, that all of the grass is cut to the same length, that everything is as uniform as possible. And I started to think to myself: what if the streetlight doesn't show us all of the bugs? It can get some, yes, the weaker ones, the ones who are still building up their full human personas. But what if they can get better? What sort of person would those look like?

Probably not Sean, as much as I hate to say it. As full of bluster and bravado as he is, he stands out as an individual, and that isn't their style.

But the vice-president of the HOA, a man so bland that, although I've spoken to him a dozen times, I have never held onto his name? They could form that sort of man. A man dedicated to making sure that everyone matches, everyone conforms, everyone joins in.

He might still be a person. I've been watching him for months, and I'm not sure yet. There are a lot just like him here, which is exactly the problem and the point.

I'll be going to his house tonight to see what he hides behind his identical front door. I have a feeling that in his basement, I'm going to find something that stands out—at least until he can get everyone to be just like him.

I can't wait any longer. They took Morgan already. They have to be watching me too.

Wish me luck. I'm going to stand out.

LICKETY-SPLIT

It started out as a perfectly normal camping trip. It was me, Rosie and Jonas, just like usual. The three of us have been friends since high school, and although there are often other people in our orbits, it's always the three of us together at its core. The three musketeers, the three amigos, three against the world. We've seen each other at our best and at our worst. At this point, I don't think there's anything that could split us up. And yeah, things got a little bit more complicated when Rosie and Jonas started dating, but they made sure I never felt like a third wheel. For the most part, I don't even worry about it. Everything feels just like it always did, even if the two of them do have their hands on each other more than they used to.

All that said, I figured they could probably use a little alone time while we were out in the woods. It was great that we were still doing things together, but I didn't need to be in their space the entire weekend. Besides, I'd gotten a mushroom identification app that was supposed to help you find edible fungi in the woods, and I wanted a chance to try it out. The idea of being able to go out into nature and just find things to eat—you know, without poisoning myself in the process—really appealed to me.

So, Saturday morning, I ditched my friends to let them hike to the falls while I headed into the forest to see if I could find wild mushrooms to cook with dinner. We didn't make any real plans about when we'd be back or anything. We all had our phones, and we'd been camping plenty of times before. It's not like we were going to get lost, not with GPS pinpointing us to the nearest five feet.

I switched on the snail-trail functionality on the map to track my path, just in case I did somehow get turned around, then swapped over to the mushroom app and set about my fungal quest. It had just rained a couple of days before, so I had a pretty easy time of it. I'd brought a gallon-sized Ziploc bag with me to store the mushrooms I found, and in what seemed like no time I'd filled that up and was ready to head back with my bounty.

When I looked around, though, I couldn't make out which way I'd come. I wasn't too concerned at first. I'd been pretty focused on the bases of trees and the ground in front of me. It wasn't all that surprising that I'd missed identifying landmarks located higher up.

I popped open the map tracker, expecting it to show me the path I'd taken. Something was wrong with it, though. It should have been showing me a single squiggly line through the woods, marking my steps. Instead, it had a diagram like a tree. There was one path at the beginning, but after a while it began to branch off into multiple directions. Those branches also split, and instead of a single terminal dot showing my location, there were ten or more blinking on the screen.

Zooming in and out didn't help. Checking the settings didn't do anything. I restarted the program, and then the whole phone, but to no avail. The map was adamant that my path had taken me to multiple endpoints, and I was currently in all of them.

Fine. That was a weird glitch, but not all that important. I pulled up the pin I'd dropped earlier with the campsite's coordinates and told the app to navigate to it. It displayed "Calculating…" along with a spinning circle for a while before generating an error message: "No route found."

I rolled my eyes. Obviously there was no route; I'd just been wandering through the woods. All I needed was a direction, not a road or a hiking trail. I pushed aside the directions, swiped over until I was looking at the campsite on the map, then zoomed out until I could see the tangle of trails representing my potential current locations. I figured that even if I picked the wrong one to start from, at least I'd be heading in the correct direction, and I could reorient myself as I got closer to the tents.

Unfortunately, the GPS wasn't on board with this plan. As I walked forward, phone held out in front of me, the map spun and twirled as if I were making rapid turns. I was sure I was walking straight forward, though. I know they say that people in the woods end up going in circles without realizing it, but that's over a large amount of distance. According to my phone, I was going in circles every couple of feet.

The snail-trails were getting even weirder. There were at least twice as many as there had been before, covering the map in strange constellations. Most of them were wandering around in tight little knots as I walked, mirroring the information the compass was giving me even though I could see it wasn't true. A few of them were traveling in straight lines, but heading away from where we'd camped. And two of them were stock-still and refusing to move at all.

At this point, I was starting to get uncomfortable. I didn't have a paper map or a physical compass with me. Who needs those when a phone can do it all better and more conveniently? I hadn't brought any sort of backup plan in case my phone failed, though. It honestly hadn't occurred to me that it might. This was starting to seem like a pretty large oversight.

Still, the phone hadn't actually failed. It was only the map that was behaving badly. I sent a quick text to Jonas and Rosie to let them know something was up.

Bit lost at the moment
You two back at camp?
The reply came back quickly.
Still no
Probably a couple hours
No worries, I wrote back. At least they weren't going to be concerned about me for a while yet. I had time to fix this.

I turned the phone off and tucked it away in my pocket. It was possible that I was going to need to use it as a flashlight later, and I didn't want to kill the battery tracking nonsense paths. I started walking forward, keeping as straight a line as I could manage, heading back the way I thought I'd come. I figured I could check the map again in half an hour or so, see if it was giving better results, or at least if I could figure out a way home based on my new location.

Just stay cool, I reminded myself. *Keep calm and you'll be out of here in no time.*

It was good advice. It might even have worked if I'd been able to follow it. Something in the woods had me on edge, though. The trees seemed to be crowding in, the light fading faster than was normal. I kept having to untangle the straps of my day pack from intrusive branches that had somehow become snagged. Things rustled in the leaves above me, vanishing before I looked.

I became certain that something was following me, something just past the edge of my vision or hearing. If I turned my head fast enough, I could almost see it, a quick glimpse of something freezing in place behind a tree. I went back to look a couple of times, but there was never anything there—and when I turned forward again, the woods ahead no longer looked familiar.

The rustling grew more frequent. The feeling of being stalked intensified. I felt like whatever it was was gaining on me. I began to walk faster, but it kept pace. Fear began to set in, a bone-deep terror that spread outward until it filled my whole body. I went faster, breaking into a light jog, which rapidly became a full-out run.

The panic tightened its grip as I sprinted through the forest. Every branch whipping across my face felt like a thin hand reaching out to grab me. Every thorn scratching against my legs was a claw scrabbling for purchase. I could feel my pursuer's hot breath on the back of my neck, feel the footsteps thudding against the ground. I knew that I was only seconds away from the ripping pain of teeth tearing through the muscles of my neck.

I was too terrified to slow down, but I chanced a quick look back over my shoulder. For an instant, I thought I saw something, but my eyes had time to register no more than a vague shape before I fell, tumbling through the air. My head smacked against something solid, and I passed out.

I came to a short while later. I didn't know exactly how long I'd been out, but the sun was still shining brightly overhead. In fact, it seemed brighter than it had been before; the unnatural gloom that had been settling in over the forest had faded. The sense of panic had passed as well. Things felt normal again.

I took stock of my situation. I was in a shallow pit; the cavity left by the root ball of a fallen tree. My head was bleeding where I'd bashed it into the dirt wall and my neck and shoulder ached, but nothing seemed to be broken.

On my body, anyway. I took my phone out to check the time and found that it was smashed beyond repair. I'd landed on it with my full weight. The screen was a maze of cracks, and things rattled inside when I shook it. It wasn't going to be of any more use today.

I brushed myself off and clambered out of the pit, trying to get my bearings. I still had no real idea where I was, but I knew that the camp was generally to the west, and I could see which way the sun was trending. I took a few steps in that direction, then stopped.

Tracking's not a skill I've ever learned, but it didn't take a skilled outdoorsman to see that something big had shoved its way through the forest. Grasses were trampled, small branches broken, leaves torn off of trees and stamped underfoot. It looked like it had been going in the same direction that I had been. I could see similar signs of passage on the far side of the pit, where I'd been running before I fell in, but what had caused them over here?

The panic I'd felt, the certainty that something deadly was chasing me, brushed me again with a light, exploratory tendril. I shook it off, refusing to give in. But I took a different track through the forest.

The sun sank lower in the sky, both confirming that I was heading west and raising my level of anxiety about getting back before dark. I'd found nothing that looked familiar, no streams or paths that I'd seen that morning. I knew I'd be okay if I had to spend the night in the woods. I had a bottle of water in my pack, and the mushrooms I'd picked could be eaten raw. It wasn't supposed to get cold enough at night to be an issue. But compared to sitting around the fire eating s'mores with friends, snacking on raw mushrooms alone in the dark seemed like a pretty distant second.

Dusk set in. I'd resigned myself to not getting back to camp that night, but I was now feeling guilty about Jonas and Rosie. I knew I was all right, but all they knew was that I'd said I was lost, and now I wasn't answering my phone. They were probably out searching for me right now. I'd ruined their camping trip as well as mine, all because my phone had glitched and I'd had some weird panic attack in the forest.

And then, just as the last bit of light was fading and I was starting to look for somewhere to shelter for the night, I came across a hiking trail. I had no idea which one it was or where it went, but it was a clear sign of human civilization, and it meant that I was no longer totally lost. I'm pretty sure I cheered aloud when I first saw it. There was practically a bounce in my step as I picked a direction and started walking. Wherever it took me, I was bound to run into people eventually. I was close to putting this whole misadventure behind me.

Hiking trail or not, walking through the woods after sunset isn't easy. Even going slowly, I tripped and nearly fell a half-dozen times. Every time I caught myself it jolted my body, making my various cuts and bruises throb. I was footsore, hungry, tired and ready to give up when I came to the trailhead and a small roadside parking lot.

To my delight, I recognized the area. I was less than half a mile away from my campsite. I hurried along the road, spurred along by the smooth surface and the promise of nearly being back. Jonas and Rosie probably wouldn't be at the campsite, since they'd probably be out looking for me, but maybe they'd left some sort of way to contact them. There had to be rangers or police involved in this, right? There had to be regular protocols for lost hikers.

As I approached our camp, I saw that there was a fire going. I could hear voices; they seemed amused and relaxed, not worried and concerned. I started to feel offended. Were Jonas and Rosie just chilling out by the fire? Had they not even wondered where I was? I could have been badly hurt. If I'd broken my leg falling into that hole, I could never have made it back. And they hadn't even considered coming to look?

I drew closer. There were three people around the fire, not just two. I could see Jonas and Rosie's faces, but the third person had their back to me. Were they just socializing with some new person instead of looking for me? What was this, some sort of friend exchange? Well, we lost one, but here's a new one, so no problem!

I was about to call out to them when the stranger by the fire laughed, tilting his head back. My words died in my throat. It wasn't a stranger at all. It was me.

I clutched a tree for support and protection, peering out from behind its trunk as my mind whirled. I stared at my duplicate. In profile, at least, he looked just like me. His hair was cut the same. He was even wearing the same shirt I had on.

He launched into some lengthy monologue. I couldn't make out all of the words, but I could hear the tone and cadence well enough. His voice didn't sound like mine, but it was familiar. After a second, it clicked. He sounded the way I did on videos. He sounded like me outside of my own head.

My thoughts flashed back to whatever had been chasing me in the woods, and the path that had led away from where I'd fallen. I'd started to go that way myself. It could have led straight here.

The idea was insane, but it fit what I was seeing. Something had stalked me in the forest. It had chased me, planning to kill me and take my place—but when I knocked myself out, it thought the job was done and just moved on in my guise.

It probably wasn't alone. That was why it had come back to camp, why it was putting Rosie and Jonas at their ease. It was going to wait for them to go to sleep, then bring others in to replace them.

I had to warn my friends. I took a step away from the safety of my tree, then stopped. How could I convince them I was me? The thing that had taken my shape was doing an impression good enough to fool my two oldest friends for an entire evening. It knew how I moved, how I talked, everything. There was no guarantee that they'd know which one was me. I could probably get them to safety, but at the cost of being left behind. I'd already been pursued by this thing once today. I wasn't interested in going through that again.

Before I could come up with a plan, the thing in my chair stood up. I shrank back behind the tree as its shadow seemed to reach for me, stretching out in the firelight. The creature turned away from the fire, saying something, and began to walk into the woods. For a moment I thought it had seen me, but it headed off in a different direction, giving no indication that it was aware of my presence.

I slipped off after it, doing my best to remain silent. It was probably going to fetch the others, to tell them to be ready. I had to act now, before it got reinforcements. If I could ambush it now, when it was alone, I'd have a much better chance of stopping it.

To my surprise, it stopped a few dozen feet into the woods. It seemed to be staring at a tree. I had no idea what it was doing, but its back was to me, and it seemed preoccupied, so I seized my chance. I rushed forward, slamming my elbow into the back of its head and bouncing its face off of the tree in front of it. Before it had a chance to recover or cry out, I wrapped my other arm around its neck, kicked it in the back of the knees and leaned in, choking it.

The bark dug into my forearm as the creature flailed, trying to get free. Wild hands clawed over its shoulders, seeking purchase on my face, but I tucked my head against its back and tightened my grip.

"Who are you?" it choked out. Even in its distress, its voice was still a perfect mimicry of mine.

"I'm who you're pretending to be," I hissed in its ear. "You thought I was dead in the woods, huh? Thought you could kill me, then kill my friends?"

It scratched futilely at my arm. Its struggles were growing weaker.

"Why—" it gasped, but could not manage any more words. Its arms fell to its sides, and I felt it grow heavy in my arms as it slumped unconscious. I could still feel its pulse beating against my arm, though, so I bore down harder, refusing to relinquish my grip until its heart beat no more.

When I let go at last, it fell forward against the tree, bouncing off to land face-up on the ground. The face staring up at me in the moonlight still looked eerily like my own. I'd hoped it would change back after it was dead, show me what it really looked like, but no such luck.

"You good out there?" Jonas called from the fire, his tone light.

"Yeah," I called back, staring at my own dead body. "All good here."

I piled up some leaves, covering the body. It was a shoddy job of camouflage, but it might work for the night. I could come back out to take care of it later. For now, I had to get back before Jonas and Rosie came looking for me.

"Took you long enough," Rosie teased as I stepped into the firelight. "We thought maybe you'd fallen in a hole after all."

Seeing my confused expression, she continued. "The hole? The one you said you nearly fell in earlier, when you were running through the forest?"

"Ah, that hole." I forced a laugh. "Yeah, no. No more holes for me today."

"Why did you take your backpack with you to go take a leak?" Jonas asked.

Of course, the duplicate hadn't had my backpack. I should have left it in the woods, gotten it later. I shrugged and tried to play it off. "Hey, you never know. What if I'd found some good mushrooms?"

They both laughed. I set my day pack down and tried to relax. I was safe now. I'd made it back. I'd saved my friends. Once they went to bed, I could figure out what to do with the body. They'd never have to know how close they came to being replaced.

When the fire burned low and Rosie and Jonas turned in, I went to my tent as well to pretend to sleep. Inside, I was surprised to find another copy of my day pack. I opened it up. The contents were identical to my own, even down to the individual mushrooms in the plastic bag. It shouldn't have surprised me. After all, the duplicate had been wearing the same clothes as me, too. Yet somehow this seemed stranger.

I stayed awake listening to the sounds of the woods at night until I was sure Rosie and Jonas were asleep. I crept out of my tent and made my way back to the body in the woods. It was cold and stiff, but still stubbornly refusing to look like anything other than me. I took it by the ankles and dragged it away.

I found a small ravine not too far away, with soft, muddy ground at the bottom and overhanging dirt shelves. I dumped the body over the side and kicked at the edge until chunks broke off. The resulting dirt slide covered the corpse well, and the branches and leaves I carried over completed the job. No one would find this unless they were specifically looking.

As I retraced my steps back to camp, I spotted something reflective lying on the ground. I picked it up to discover that it was a cell phone.

I took the smashed phone out of my pocket and studied the two side by side. Except for the damage mine had suffered in the fall, they were identical. Same model, same case, everything. I pressed the power button on the one I'd found, and a chill ran down my spine as it lit up to reveal my lock screen. Reluctantly, I pressed my finger up to the sensor. I wasn't sure if I was relieved or unnerved when it unlocked.

I made my way back to the tent and slid inside, zipping the flap shut behind me. I undressed and crawled into my sleeping bag, but sleep had no interest in me. I lay awake, staring at the domed ceiling of the tent. My version of the cell phone was broken. It made sense. I'd fallen on it. It wasn't worth a second thought. And yet—wasn't that an awfully convenient accident to happen to the one thing that had to connect to an external network through a unique identifier, and couldn't be easily replicated?

I would know if I weren't me. I'm sure of it.

But I wonder if the copy at the bottom of the ravine thought the same thing.

THE DEEF

We called it The Deef. It was supposed to be a joke.

We had a game, the group of us. It didn't really have a name. It was just the cryptid game. It was simple: every time we got together, one of us had to share a monster story. That was basically it. We'd started it back in college, and just sort of never stopped.

There were more rules than that, of course. It had to be original. No more than one story introduced per get-together. Whoever had the best monster was winning.

All of these rules were unspoken, but we all understood them. They'd evolved over the years to create the friendly rivalry of the cryptid game. It kept us in touch, gave us something to talk about when we saw each other. And it was always fun to hear someone else reference your monster, either in a new story or just in standard conversation.

I made up a bunch over the years, most of them ridiculous. The Cord Goblin, an obnoxious electrical creature that can travel through wires, and which ties unattended cords into knots. The Skulk, a gelatinous creature the color of seawater which lurks in the ocean and generates that unpleasant pulse you sometimes feel when you realize you have no idea what's below you. Halitus, a bent shadow which breathes into your mouth at night.

I was rarely winning the game. But every time I went swimming in deep water, I thought about the Skulk, and I know the others did, too. That was all I wanted out of the game: to give my friends the "man, what if…?" moment.

The others took different approaches. Jennifer just went with whatever news article she'd happened across at the time, spinning it into something unearthly. Alex, too, was all over the map, with no clear thread between any of her creatures.

Rebecca, on the other hand, always started her stories the same way: "Deep in the unexplored jungles…." She was big on lost tribes and creatures forgotten by time. Less likely for anyone to think about on a daily basis than mine, but more likely to actually be real. Well, more possible, anyway. "Likely" is a bit of a stretch.

Emmanuel liked insects. Psionic beetles that lived in the roof beams of houses, putting out stressful emanations and feeding on the resultant fights and negative emotions from the families below. Gnats that laid eggs in tear ducts so that the maggots could wriggle their way into the sinus cavity, hiding safely and feeding off of the mucus until they grew into their adult form. His were usually good for a serious shudder, more so if you had a particularly vivid imagination. They weren't out of the realm of possibility, either. Bugs and parasites have some weird life cycles, and some terrifying adaptations.

And Connor—Connor liked predators. Big things, scary things, things that moved among humans, hunting them. His creations were responsible for the lost pets, the missing children, the runaways. Like Rebecca's, his stories always started the same way: "Och, so picture this thing!" He had a rich Scottish accent which somehow gave his monsters more vibrancy, more life. They were the least likely of our stories, because they were the sort of monsters that someone would had to have noticed by now—but when you were alone in the darkness, logic like that didn't matter. That's where Connor's stories would always come back to haunt you.

If he had a failing, it was that his cryptids never had a name. They were always just "this thing," which left it up to the rest of us to name. We would invariably come up with the most ridiculous name we could think of, undercutting the story. He told us one about an underground hive of man-sized wasps, networked across miles. They would steal cavers and solitary hikers, dragging them down to serve as food and hosts for the larva. Connor was waxing eloquent about the hive structure when Rebecca suggested that we could call them Beests, and we all broke up laughing. Even Connor was a good sport about it.

The Deef was another one of his, a fairly recent one. It was something like a giant boar—*och, picture this thing*—only with the grace and speed of a tiger. It stood five feet high at the shoulder, and its mouth could unhinge like a snake in order to scoop up its prey and capture it in a gnashing cavern of knives. It once lived in forested areas, but as civilization expanded, it found richer hunting grounds in cities.

It evaded detection, Connor told us, through its speed and sleekness of motion. Despite its size, it could slide undetected into alleys, behind cars, in any of a thousand overlooked urban hiding places. It slept during the day and hunted at night, when its dark coat provided camouflage in the darkness.

The most terrifying thing about it, though, was that it absorbed sound. Things grew quieter when it was nearby, dropping to utter silence in its immediate presence. You might never see it coming, but you would know it was there right before it took you, because you would feel like you'd gone completely deaf.

"Deef?" I had asked, mimicking Connor's brogue. Then Rebecca exclaimed, "The Deef!" Connor rolled his eyes at us and said, smiling, "Fine, the Deef, you reprobates. Call it whate'er name you like. You won't be calling it anything when it comes for you."

Absurd name or not, though, the Deef was one of his best ones. It stuck with me strongly. I could picture its thick, bristly fur, see its bloody snout with the expandable lower jaw. I could even visualize the way its flanks would heave as it ran, streaking silently down city sidewalks in pursuit of prey that had no reason to look behind, no idea that anything was there at all. The Deef kept me looking over my shoulder for weeks after Connor introduced it.

It wasn't just me, either. Emmanuel confessed that he'd started using his flashlight on the walk from his car to his apartment building, in case the Deef was concealing itself in one of the shadows.

"I don't really think it's there, obviously," he told us. "But then again, it doesn't cost me anything to turn on my phone's flashlight."

And that was exactly it. Obviously it wasn't real. But at night, alone in the dark—what if? That was the fun of the cryptid game.

Except that the other night, I was texting with Alex while she was walking home from the corner store.

Quiet night out here, she texted me. *The city's so different at night.*

Yeah, I sent back. *Whole different animal once everyone goes to sleep.*

It's even quieter than usual tonight.

Deef quiet? I asked.

Haha, yeah. Buncha shadows, too. Could definitely be a Deef around.

Haha, well good luck. Been nice knowing you.

That was a few days ago. Emmanuel called me yesterday morning to ask when I'd last talked to Alex. I checked my phone and saw that was the last conversation we'd had.

"Yeah, no one's heard from her since then," he said, sounding worried. "I'm going out looking for her after work today. Come help me? We'll go from her apartment to the bodega, see if we can find anything."

"What are we looking for?"

"I don't know, anything! She's missing!"

I assured him I'd come help. After work, we met up by her apartment and started walking. I still had no idea what I was looking for. The streets looked like streets. There was trash, graffiti, paint, dirt—the usual. Emmanuel and I did a slow walk to the store, scanning every alley as we went. By the time we reached the store, the sun had dropped behind the buildings.

"Now what?" I asked Emmanuel.

"Check again on the way back, I guess. See if we missed any-thing."

I thought about pointing out that if we hadn't seen anything earlier, we certainly weren't going to now that it was darker. But he had a desperate look on his face, so I shut up and we started the walk back.

Halfway there, we still hadn't seen any sign. Emmanuel start-ed shouting into alleys. "Alex!"

"What are you doing?"

"Maybe she's hurt. I don't know! Alex!"

"Shut up!" someone yelled from an apartment above us, and I ushered Emmanuel on.

At the next alley, though, he called out for her again. "Alex!" There was no answer, obviously. Even he knew there wouldn't be. It was written on his face.

This went on for a few blocks. With only two more blocks to go, Emmanuel's shouts were starting to sound hopeless. "Alex," he called out, but he was barely even bothering to raise his voice now.

"Maybe we can—" I began but stopped dead. I could barely hear my own voice. Emmanuel and I turned toward each other, the same realization hitting both of us.

"Emmanuel, what's—"

I saw it then, looming out of the alley behind him like a striking snake. It came from nowhere, seeming to rise out of the bricks themselves, standing nearly as tall as us, its mouth already gaping open in anticipation of its meal. Its hooved feet skimmed silently across the ground as it raced towards us. I tried to call out, to warn Emmanuel to move, but not a sound emerged from my throat.

It took Emmanuel behind the knees, knocking him over to land, flailing, in its massive mouth. Powerful muscles flexed and the jagged pouch closed around him. It convulsed, crushing and grinding Emmanuel inside. I could see the bulges where his body distended its gullet.

It swallowed, and the throat tightened. Swallowed again, and it grew smaller still. A third time, and it was back to normal size. It had consumed Emmanuel in seconds. He was gone, not even a drop of blood remaining. And all of this had happened in total, horrible silence.

Its meal finished, the Deef lowered its head and looked me directly in the eyes. I saw hunger there, but after a moment of regard it melted away into the alley. I never blinked, but still I lost sight of it within seconds.

I don't remember how I got home last night. I don't know why the Deef let me go at all. But I remember the look in those eyes, and I know that I've been marked.

The sun's dropping in the sky again. I have every light on already. The door is locked. It's a huge beast. Surely it can't get in here.

The city gets quiet at night.

HOUSE HUNTING

Let me set the scene for you.

The room is dark, enclosed, underground. The floor is smooth stone, chalked with a dizzying array of strange symbols all arranged in a careful pattern. They form the idea of a cage, an idea so strong that it's almost visible.

The walls are lined with bookshelves heavy with paraphernalia. Leather-bound books, thick crucibles, strange artifacts and more. Everything is carefully placed. This is not the casual collection one might find in a standard home. It is clear that each object on these shelves holds meaning and use.

There is no dust on anything. It is all regularly used and meticulously cared for.

At one end of the room, adding flourishes to the symbols on the floor, is a man in a sober black suit. His name is Miķelis, and he is an evoker. He is the preeminent magician of his time. He is nearly good enough for what he is about to attempt.

For years Miķelis has worked to perfect his craft. Other magicians may be content with a few small tricks, abandoning their study of magic as soon as they have achieved the wealth or status they desire. For Miķelis, though, the magic is the point. He needs wealth only to fund his research, status only to gain access to the books and tools he seeks. Material possessions do not interest him. He gathers magical power for the sole purpose of being able to gain still more.

Already he is the strongest sorcerer the world has seen in centuries. Still, he thirsts for more.

Tonight, he believes, will be his greatest achievement yet. It is the result of over five years of work. Starting from only the merest fragment of a burned book, he has recreated a summoning spell not seen in thousands of years. His work has been immensely thorough, for he understands the dangers involved. The entity this spell conjures could incinerate the globe in an instant. It could alter the path of stars, unmake prophecies, reach through time itself to effect its will. It is, as a rule, barred from our universe, kept out by protections far more ancient than humanity, but this spell weakens those protections enough to allow it to reach through.

Under Miķelis's direction, it will be a potent tool, an amazing advancement in his abilities. It has been bound before, and can be again. The spell details the steps, the symbols, the sacrifices. Every incantation, Miķelis has practiced, drawing upon the knowledge of the dead to confirm his syllables. Every line he has sketched over and over, until he can draw them flawlessly, perfectly replicating what was laid out in the reconstituted book.

The scene is set. The cage is prepared. The sacrifice is bound and waiting. All is exactly as the book described.

The book, alas, had an imperceptible flaw.

Miķelis, unknowing, begins the ritual. His voice flows through the wavering notes of the forgotten language. The air thickens and sparks around him. The resonance of the words pours into the chalked symbols. The lines funnel the power to its proper place. The entire space begins to glow with a color unknown to humanity, unknown to reality. It is the shape of the world separating. It is the vision of a reality beyond our own.

This color pours through the gap like syrup, puddling and filling the cage of imagination. It is not what Miķelis has summoned. It is merely a space in which the being he calls upon can exist.

The words of the spell cascade forth from the evoker, almost coming of their own volition now. The symbols on the floor dance with light, flashing out a demanding pattern, a call that must be answered. And within the space, within the blister of anti-reality, something calls back.

Miķelis speaks its true name. He fixes it into place, compelling it to heed his command. As long as his sacrifice is accepted, it must acquiesce to his desire.

The thing within the cage inhales deeply, a charybdian inrush of air. The life is sucked from the sacrifice, and it is here that the book has led Miķelis astray. The symbol that was inked in the book had a single, vital extra line. This changed the meaning from sacrifice, singular and directed—to sacrifices. Open-ended. Unbounded.

Miķelis drops even as the intended sacrifice also goes limp. He is dead before he ever has the opportunity to understand his error. Still the thing in the cage breathes in, drawing forth all that the sacrifices have to give. It takes their lives, their memories, their potential. It takes their hope and their love and their regret. It sucks out every last bit they have to offer before discarding their husks. The bodies crumble apart, too brittle to sustain their own weight.

Finally, anchored and aware, the being takes in its surroundings. It smiles as it comprehends the fate of the one that called it. It presses forward, testing the boundaries of its prison, but aside from the one fatal flaw, the spell was perfect. Nothing from its reality can cross the walls constructed here. And until the being is dismissed, it cannot return to its own plane. With the caster dead, it is trapped eternally, unable to go forward or back.

Yet a loophole exists. The being banishes the material of its reality back through the tear, stands naked and exposed in the painful mundanity of our world. Nothing of its nature could pass through the walls before it, but it is powerful enough even to recreate its own self. It imagines itself slow, weak, bound by restrictions and natural laws. It strips away its magnificence, its terrible beauty, its awe-inducing splendor, and remakes itself in the image of the impossibly limited beings of this realm.

So reduced, it steps lightly through the walls of imagination. They are no longer any impediment, for it is no longer what it was. There is the tiniest of sparks within it yet, a piece small enough to slip through the laws of reality, but for all intents and purposes its true self has been shorn completely away.

Leaving only me.

I entered this world fully formed, with complete knowledge of what I had once been and no way to access my previous power. I had access only to the magic wielded by the evoker who had summoned me, an amount so paltry that he could barely even bend local space. The spark in my belly burned, demanded that I find and consume more power so that I might again be what I once was.

Miķelis had thought himself driven by the search for power, but his need was merely academic. I literally hungered for it.

Like a slow-moving blaze, I devoured his library. Gemstones crunched between my teeth. Artifacts snapped in my hands, reduced to pieces small enough to swallow. I inhaled greedily as I broke them, catching the wisps of magic that escaped. They were nothing, like sucking on candy wrappers to get the flavor. I pressed on, hoping for something of value in this collection.

I tore pages from their bindings and stuffed them into my mouth, ripping and chewing through thick vellum and brittle parchment with equal ease. Busy fingers tore leather bindings into jerky-like strips, and I swallowed those too. Millennia of knowledge were lost from the world, and still I felt no better. These dabblings did not begin to address my deep-seated need, though they were the best humanity had to offer.

If magic was a lake, then humans were the bugs crawling across the top, unable to break the surface tension. Unaware that other things swam in its depths, things that would gladly rise up and swallow them whole—and that those things, in turn, were food for the true predators.

I was the fisherman, trying to subsist on the food that the bugs found filling. It could never work. I needed fish.

I knew spells to call them up—Miķelis had been a smarter bug than most, able at least to peer into the lake—but I needed a sacrifice. Or, to continue the metaphor: bait.

That was easy enough to obtain. I uttered a short transportation spell to step from the basement to a nearby city street. A young couple walking by caught my eye. I called out to them.

"Excuse me!"

They turned. Their eyes widened.

"Do you need help?" asked the man.

"Yes, I'm in need of a sacrifice. Would you come with me?"

"A—what? Why are you naked?"

I waved my hand, glamouring myself to appear neatly clad. "Absurd. You must have been mistaken. Will you come with me, please?"

His jaw hung slightly open as his mind concluded that what he had seen made no sense, and therefore discarded it. "A sacrifice? I don't—"

I twisted his mind, modifying his desires. He continued without missing a beat. "—see why not! Let's go."

The woman with him squeaked in shock. "You can't—"

I removed him from her memories. As a kindness, I took him entirely away. She would never remember him, no matter what others told her, and so she would never mourn him. I am merciful when it suits me. She blinked at us briefly, uncertain what she had been saying or why, then turned and walked away.

Clasping my sacrifice by the shoulder, I spoke the word of returning. The street around us vanished, replaced by the empty shelves of the underground room.

"If you'll just kneel right there, please," I told the man I'd taken. He did as I directed, eagerly waiting in his place as I altered key components of the chalked circle to bring up what I wanted. I did not need anything big. Reduced as I was, I did not even want anything big. What I needed was something small, easily handled, easily consumed.

I let the words of evocation roll off of my tongue. They clotted together in the runes of the circle, thickening the lines until the entire shape glowed. My sacrifice died with a smile on his face, excited to be doing his part even as the spell ate him alive.

The creature I summoned was a sprite of this plane, a minor entity with no real power. It far outstripped the simple magics of the humans, though, and I fell upon it greedily as it arrived. With tongue and tail and talons, I tore it to pieces and crammed them into my gullet. It shrieked as I ripped it apart, but the fear only added seasoning to the snack.

In moments, the deed was done. I licked my lips, enjoying the lingering taste. My summoning had been fresh, rich and delicious compared to the sad scraps of the library, but it did more to sharpen my appetite than to sate it.

I began to speak the transportation spell again, but a wave of weariness washed over me. To my dismay, I realized I had overexerted myself. I was so used to having infinite potential that, although I knew that was not the case in my lessened form, I had not thought to account for it. I was, of course, aware of the concept of limitations. They had simply never applied to me before.

I made my way back upstairs to Miķelis's living space. I prepared food for myself, then laid down to sleep in his bed. I dreamed a nightmare of shackles and bondage, of vital necessities dangling in sight but out of reach.

I woke in a cold sweat. The goosebumps on my skin stood in stark contrast to the insistent fire burning inside of me. It demanded that I find more power, that I restore myself to my full and awful glory. It gripped me like an addiction. I had no choice but to obey.

I needed a better technique. In such a frail body, I would never be able to summon entities of enough strength to satisfy my need. I would spend nearly all of my time sleeping to recover, and waking to find myself ever more ravenous. It would form a loop from which I would never escape.

Fortunately, Miķelis's memories held the answer. He knew of a place where a creature ran wild, a house possessed by a spirit. It was perfect. I would not have to expend any energy summoning it. It was already here; all I would have to do was corral it.

I nearly began the transportation spell before I remembered that I was attempting to conserve energy. It was possible that Miķelis had exaggerated the abilities of this creature in his memory. It would not do to spend as much power on travel as I gained from consumption.

Instead, I called up a cab and waited—waited!—for it to arrive. I do not think I had ever waited for anything in my eternal life before. It was not, I found, an entirely unpleasant experience. I was able to reflect, to consider, to plan instead of simply reacting. Planning had never been in my nature, but then again, I left my nature behind when I entered this reality. It was time to develop a new self.

The cab driver dropped me off next to the dingy "FOR SALE" sign next to the house. Smaller signs hung below the name of the brokerage, extolling the reduced price and the motivated sellers. Despite these, it looked like the house had been on the market for quite some time.

"Realtor meeting you here?" the cabbie asked as I exited. "You want me to wait until he gets here?"

"No, I'll be fine," I said. I paid the man using actual money, neither trick nor forgery. I found the experience refreshing, play-acting at being human. I was in good spirits. Even from the street, I could feel the malevolence of the house. Something dark squatted within, something with the power I needed. The hunger inside me growled. It sensed the meal soon to come.

The front door should have been locked, but it swung open as soon as I touched the knob. I could feel the house's anticipation. It wanted visitors. It was calling me in, practically dragging me across the threshold.

I smiled. It was nice to be invited. I stepped inside.

The front room was spacious, well-lit and pleasantly appointed. The canary-yellow walls put me in mind of a bright, hopeful sunrise. It was warm and comforting. I pretended not to notice that the door I had entered through had disappeared.

I continued into the house, entering a wood-floored dining room. This too seemed nice at first glance, but as I glanced around, I began to spot subtle indicators that all was not well. There were scratches on the floor that looked as if something had clawed its way out of the vent—or as if someone had been dragged against their will into it. There was a scorch mark in the corner that had not been fully scrubbed away, showing that something had burned there. Looking at it, I felt as if I could hear distant weeping.

I moved on to the kitchen. The wallpaper here was a busy pattern that did not quite manage to hide the spots of mold. The grout in between the tiles on the floor was cracked and blackened. The clock on the wall ticked in sync with my heartbeat. The room seemed to breathe as I did, growing imperceptibly larger and smaller. I felt anxiety settle over me like a net.

A person might have thought the feeling their own and begun to panic, feeding it. I, on the other hand, seized the psychic strands and yanked. I felt a sharp surprise from the far end, then a skittering sensation as the emotion tried to squirm through my fingers. I clenched my hands and wrapped the invisible threads around my fists, refusing to relinquish my grasp.

The thing occupying the house was not bright. It had its little tricks, but when they failed to work it had nothing to do but try them again. It doubled down on the decay, hoping to frighten me into letting go.

The wallpaper peeled around me. The cabinets warped and sagged open. Ants and maggots drooled from the openings, spilling onto the counters in confused disarray. The clock's tick sped up, dragging my heartbeat along with it. The tiles cracked under my feet, tumbling away to reveal treacherous holes into the basement below.

I laughed and hauled on the strings I had caught once more. They pulled free with a visceral rip, like flaying skin from a deer. The thing in the house screamed. I felt its pain and dread wash over me. I reveled in it.

I thrust my hands into the peeling wallpaper, bypassing the actuality of the house to seize the infestation within. I grabbed a double fistful of something slimy and pustulant and drew it forth. A thick bubble rose from the wall, fighting me every inch of the way. I plunged my face into it and bit down. It was ripe and juicy on my tongue, and its fear was delicious.

The bubble popped, leaving me holding a thick, fleshy strip torn from the mind of the creature. The kitchen snapped back to normal. I could sense the thing fleeing, abandoning the house it had possessed to a superior force.

Unfortunately for it, I had not come for half-measures. I raced it to the front room, where the door had reappeared, and snatched that portal away again. The invisible thing slammed into the wall, its egress denied. Snarling and trapped, it turned back on me.

The floor buckled and broke under my feet. The yellow walls raged like a forest fire, waves of heat billowing forth. The air turned to a choking miasma and filled with the sounds of screams.

I gathered it all in, absorbing it as fast as it came. Everything it threw at me only fed me, making me stronger even as it was ripped apart. Periodically it turned to flee, but I chased it relentlessly, tearing windows and doors out of its grasp. Each new wave of its attacks was weaker, more desperate. Each one left it with less and less of itself remaining.

Finally, it was nothing but a mewling thing in the corner of the attic. I towered over it, enjoying its abject surrender and utter terror. I picked it up, cradled it in the palm of my hand, and popped it into my mouth. The final bite tasted like triumph.

I ran my tongue sensually over my lips, enjoying the new feeling of strength within myself. I was not remotely satiated, not anywhere close to what I had once been. But I was more than I was an hour before, and I was riding high on the thrill of the chase.

I sauntered outside, leaving behind me an unblemished, untainted, utterly normal suburban house. As I pondered where to go next, my eye fell on the weathered real estate sign. A delightful idea popped into my mind.

I spoke a few words and found myself outside of the headquarters of the agency selling the once-possessed house. I gave a pleasant wave as I passed the receptionist and entered the office of Oliver Daniels, the agent whose name had been on the sign.

"Can I help you?" he asked, looking up from a pile of paperwork.

"I have excellent news," I informed him. "That house you've been unable to sell? You'll find it is now free of issues."

His brow furrowed. "Sorry, are you a seller? Which house are you talking about?"

"You know which house. The one that was haunted."

His face blanched. "There's no such thing."

"Not anymore, no. Not for that house. I have resolved the issue. Would you like to come look?"

He turned whiter still. I wondered briefly if he was about to pass out. "No! No, if you say so, it's… you're sure it's safe now?"

"Completely," I assured him. "I was very thorough."

He breathed out a long sigh. A bit of color returned to his face, though his eyes were still wide. "I was in there, you know. For days. I don't know how I got out. I was just on the porch one day, the open door behind me. I had my freedom! I could see my car. And yet I turned to walk back inside. A neighbor saw me, ran over to get me before I could go back in. If it hadn't been for them, I would have.

"I tried to take the sign down, but somehow it kept getting put up again. I even burned it one time, but it was there in the yard just a day later. Every once in a while a new client will ask about the house, and every time I can feel it calling me back.

"This… this is the first time in months I've been able to think about the house without feeling an urge to go there. You really did it, didn't you? You really took care of it?"

"I really did."

Tears welled up in his eyes. "Thank you. Oh my God, thank you so much. Anything I can do for you, ever, let me know."

I smiled. I took a business card from his desk and ran the nail of one finger over it. I handed it to him. "This is my card."

"Grey Michael," he read, the name I had put in place of his own. He blinked at the card. "You work here?"

"Just down the hall. The next time you find a problem like this, just come knock."

"I… I'll do that."

"And do let others know as well. I do like to keep busy."

I left his office and moved a short way down the hall. At a convenient spot of blank wall, I pressed an extra space into the building, a room that did not properly fit within its dimensions. I opened the solid wooden door to reveal an office with an imposing desk, a comfortable chair, several tall bookcases and a large picture window.

I smiled as I closed the door behind me, feeling it vanish from the wall of the real estate agency. It would be there when it was needed. For now, it was time to get settled in my new domain. I had plans to make.

That was quite some time ago. These days, rather an array of business cards bear my name, and a startling number of overlooked doors open into my office. I sit in my chair, practice my smile, and listen as voices whisper my name.

"Grey Michael."

It's nice to be needed. And really, the work is its own reward.

THE OPALESQUE

I don't know exactly how this story started. It was already in motion well before I became aware of it. My involvement in it began with Christian and Philip: Christian, who was always late, and Philip, who was always early.

Those two were part of our same friend group, but as you might expect they often passed like ships in the night. It was even a joke that they were the same person, like Clark Kent and Superman, and that's why you never saw them in the same room together. Obviously they weren't, and in fact we routinely hung out with both of them at the same time, but if either of them brought that up we'd just accuse one or the other of being a paid actor hired to throw us off the scent.

So, the night of the dinner party, the night of the attacks, it wasn't any surprise to anyone that we were several hours in and Christian wasn't there yet. Nor was it any particular surprise when Philip announced that he had an early morning ahead of him and was heading home. He was always the first one to tap out of any social gathering. It was really convenient, honestly. He clearly felt no social stigma about declaring that he'd had enough, and it freed the rest of us up to leave whenever without being the one who bailed out early.

Phil said his goodbyes, and then it was just the five of us: me, Hamish and Charlene, and Silvio and Abram. No one there was the kind to make me feel like a fifth wheel, but I definitely knew that I was the only one there not coupled up. I was just thinking that maybe I should call it an early night and follow Phil out the door when Christian showed up.

He entered with his usual gusto, banging open the door and loudly declaring, "Now it's a party! Friends, you won't believe what I've found!"

"Is it a watch?" Silvio asked pointedly. "We finished the dinner party over an hour ago."

"Ah, you only finished the dinner part. Now we're at the party bit! Anyway, we both know you didn't set a place for me."

It was true, Silvio and Abram had not. We would have made room for Christian at the table if he'd been there on time, of course, and certainly he would have gotten food, but there really hadn't been many leftovers as it was. We all knew he was never going to be there to eat it.

"As an apology for my tardiness and an attempt to win my way back into your good graces, I have brought wine," Christian said, producing two bottles from a bag slung over his shoulder. "And another gift which I discovered on the way here, but which I will only unveil once I have had a chance to properly set the scene."

Silvio accepted the bottles with a nod of thanks and carried them over to the bar. "I assume you'd like the first glass from your gift?" he asked as he uncorked the first bottle.

"Well, I'd hate for you to think it might be poisoned!" laughed Christian. "I'm merely demonstrating that I wouldn't give you anything I wouldn't drink myself."

Silvio passed a glass over to Christian. He sniffed it, sampled it and declared it good. "Fit for my hosts!" he boomed. "And as you can see, no unexplained rashes or foaming at the mouth."

"The two classic signs of poisoning," said Charlene.

"Well, I've never been poisoned, so I'm only guessing. The point is: drink up, friends!"

Silvio poured glasses for us all and handed them around.

"Only six?" asked Christian. "None for good Philip?"

Silvio cocked an eyebrow at him. "Is this your way of saying that you'd like a glass for each of your personalities? You still only have one mouth."

"We're different people!" Christian protested. "As you'll see shortly when he gets back from the bathroom, or wherever he is."

"Uh huh," said Hamish. He made air quotes with his fingers. "'Phil' left just before you got here. As if you didn't know, totally-different-person-than-Phil."

Christian looked confused. "Okay, no, but seriously. He's really not here?"

"You know you two run on different schedules," Charlene said.

"Right, yeah, but his car's still outside."

This revelation was met with confounded silence from all of us.

"Huh," Charlene said after a moment. "Maybe he was just getting ready to leave as you pulled up, and you just didn't see him in the car?"

Abram got up from the couch and crossed to the front window. He peered out, cupping his hands around his eyes to block out the light from the living room.

"No, Christian's right," he reported. "His car's still there."

We all got up to look, as if we might see something different. Sure enough, Phil's car sat in the yard with everyone else's, still and silent. We could see no sign of movement inside.

"I'm going to go make sure he's all right," said Abram, putting on his shoes. The rest of us followed suit, curious to see what was going on. Armed with our cell phone flashlights and our glasses of wine, we traipsed out into the night to see what our friend was doing.

I don't know what I expected. To see him changing a tire, maybe, or taking a nap in the backseat. Certainly he had to be somewhere in the vicinity of the car. Where else would he go? We were easily twenty miles outside of town. The house was surrounded by acres of woods. The nearest neighbor was at least a mile down the road.

And yet the car was empty and still locked. I peered inside just in case, but saw nothing more than a coffee cup in the cupholder and a sweatshirt folded up on the passenger seat. There was nowhere for Philip to hide inside the car, even if he'd had any reason for wanting to do so.

"Maybe he got an Uber?" Abram asked uncertainly. "We all drank some at dinner. Maybe he didn't want to drive."

It seemed unlikely. None of us had seen him call for a rideshare, and surely if he had he would have waited inside the house with us and left when the driver arrived. Still, no other option made any sense at all, so I slowly began to talk myself around to believing it.

Then Hamish said, "What's this on the ground?"

We all gathered around to look. He was near the trunk of Phil's car. His flashlight was focused on a patch of grass three or four feet across. The grass seemed oddly shiny and dark at the same time, like oil had spilled on it.

Hamish crouched and swiped a finger carefully across a blade of grass. A long, sticky strand stretched between his hand and the grass as he stood back up, snapping only after it was a foot or more in length. Hamish made a face as he inspected his finger.

"Uch, that's gross. Feels like snot."

"Disgusting, Hamish," said Charlene, but his attention was still focused on his finger. He rubbed it against his thumb, then sniffed it.

"Is that blood?" he asked.

"Blood doesn't stretch like that," Silvio said.

"Yeah, but look at this." He held his fingers out as we crowded around. Beneath the slimy coating, his thumb and forefinger shone red with what looked all the world like blood.

"But what would it be from?" Abram asked. We all shone our lights around, looking for the source of the blood and goo.

Silvio gasped. "Phil's under the car! Phil, are you all right?"

He knelt. An instant later he screamed, falling over backwards and scrambling to get away.

"Silvio! Silvio, what is it?" Abram demanded, but I had already seen what he had seen. Phil's hand was sticking out from under the car. But Phil was not under there. The hand ended halfway down the forearm in a ragged, bloody stump. The severed end glistened with a thick, gelatinous goo. The rest of Phil's body was nowhere to be seen.

The next few minutes were chaotic. There was shouting, screaming, and running. We all went for the house, which was good because it kept us together, but we were definitely in each other's way. I've never truly understood panic as I did in that moment. I knew what to do, knew that I should be calm, but that tiny, detached part of me could only watch as I fled like a frightened animal.

I got myself back under control once I was inside, and there was a wall between me and whatever had happened outside. I called the police and told them what we'd found. They assured me that the house was the safest place to be and recommended that we all stay together for safety until they got there. "Lock the doors," they said, as if we hadn't done that the instant that Abram's heels had crossed the threshold.

"Okay, the police are coming," I told everyone as I hung up. They'd obviously all been listening to my half of the conversation anyway, but I felt the need to say something. "They'll be here soon."

"How soon is soon?" asked Silvio, his voice rising. "Someone murdered Philip! They cut him up! And we never heard anything!"

Abram pulled Silvio close and held him as he shook. "It'll be okay. We've just got to sit tight. We'll be out of this soon."

"Philip won't!" Silvio sobbed. No one had any response to that. We all just listened to Silvio cry.

Hamish crossed to the fireplace and picked up a poker. He looked at us almost sheepishly. "Better than not being armed at all," he said.

Charlene cast a doubtful eye over the remaining implements, an ash shovel and a brush. "I'll just stand behind you, then."

"Are the windows locked?" Christian asked. "How about the back door?"

"I think so," Abram said. "They should be."

"I'll go check," said Christian, and left the room. We heard him moving around, followed by a sudden shout of surprise.

"Christian!" I shouted, leaping to my feet, but he was already hurrying back into the room. His eyes were wide.

"This is nuts, but I swear I just saw Phil's face at the window," he said. "What if he's not dead?"

"Someone tore his arm off," Charlene pointed out.

"Yeah, but that's survivable. Look, I don't know. All I know is as I turned toward one of the windows, I saw a face staring in at me, and I swear it was his. I shouted, the face vanished, I came back in here."

He paused. "I want to open the back door and see if he's outside."

"No way," said Silvio. "No. No way."

"He might be alive," Christian insisted. "And if he is, he needs our help. I'm not stupid enough to open the door by myself and let some serial killer in to hack everyone up. I want you all to come with me. And if you're all against it, then fine. We pretend I just imagined it and we never open the door. But I want to look. I don't want to leave him out there."

Silvio was already shaking his head again, but Abram spoke up first. "If there's even a chance, we should look. We were fine when we were out front together. We can afford a quick look out the back door. And if we can still somehow save Phil, we have to try."

"I'm not going," said Silvio.

Christian nodded. "Stay here with him," he said to Abram. "The four of us will go look. We'll be right back, either with Phil or with the knowledge that we couldn't have helped him."

Hamish, Charlene, Christian, and I made our way to the back door. We let Hamish lead since he had the only weapon, but once we entered the kitchen, the rest of us armed ourselves with knives.

"Where did you see him?" I asked.

Christian indicated one of the windows. "He was right there. I was walking this way when—"

"Look!" Hamish cut him off, pointing the poker at a different window. I swung my head in that direction just in time to see a face disappearing into the darkness. It was poorly lit, and I had only barely glimpsed it, but it might well have been Phil. There had been something wrong, though. He had seemed almost to glisten, like an oil slick. I thought about the dark slime on the grass and wondered how badly hurt he was.

"Is he okay? What's he doing?" asked Charlene.

"I don't know," said Christian. "Back me up. I'm opening the door."

We nervously took up defensive positions as Christian turned the handle. The door opened, letting in the cool night air. Outside was dark and quiet. Even the bugs seemed to have gone silent.

"Phil?" Christian called, taking a step onto the back stoop. "Phil, say something if you need help."

He paused and we all listened, but heard nothing. Christian took another step outside, raising his cell phone light high. "Phil-ip!"

"He's not there," Hamish said. "I don't know what you saw, but—"

There was a sudden skittering of feet, and then the window smashed. Something huge, jagged and opalescent smashed its way through. It stood as tall as a small horse, with legs like a praying mantis and a shell like something from the deep ocean. As it scrabbled frantically inside, two of those serrated legs dug deep into Hamish's shoulders. Hamish shouted, swinging frantically with the poker, but he was inside its grip and couldn't get a good hit.

"Help me!" he cried, but I was frozen by what I saw on the creature's shell. It was lumpy and misshapen, the shiny surface raised into smooth protrusions that looked strikingly like various animals. In the middle of them all, staring at me from less than a foot away, was a human face. It was unmistakably Phil's, sticking outward from the hard shell of the creature as if it had been shoved into a wet mold.

The creature hissed. A rank vapor rolled outward from it, stinking of rot and stinging the eyes. I fell back, coughing, and as I did so the mouth on its belly irised open. Its entire underside was one tremendous mouth, ringed with row upon row of slicing, sharp-edged teeth. It contracted its forelimbs, dragging Hamish closer, and he screamed again.

Then Christian was there, grabbing the poker away from Hamish and smashing blow upon punishing blow down onto the creature's shell. The thick surface resisted the first two hits, but on the third strike a ragged crack appeared. The creature hissed again, filling the room with that horrible stench, but Christian continued to pummel it.

Charlene, emboldened by his success, began to stab at it with her knife. Her slashes skidded off the shell, so she switched to striking at it from underneath, stabbing it in the soft grey tissue of its mouth.

I struck it one good blow in the mouth with my knife, but it jerked as I hit it and pulled the knife away from me. I nearly tried to grab it back, but the gnashing teeth dissuaded me. Instead, I seized the nearest limb and wrenched it upward, off of Hamish's shoulder. I could feel spines tearing into my palms, but I ignored the pain and shoved as hard as I could until I saw Hamish twist free.

Unwilling to lose its meal, the monster lunged forward, dragging its entire bulk into the house. It knocked me over, pinning my leg beneath it. The wet slime engulfed my shin. The teeth began to dig in. I felt myself being drawn under.

Before I could be dragged beneath it, Christian stabbed downward using the poker as a spear. The shell, now spiderwebbed with cracks from the repeated blows, shattered beneath this final assault. Whatever the poker struck beneath the protective carapace must have been vital, for the creature collapsed almost at once.

I tried to pull my leg free, but the teeth threatened to flay my skin and instead I called for help.

"Get this thing off of me!"

It was Abram and Silvio who rushed to my aid. To the aid of all of us, really. We were all bleeding, coughing, and panting from exertion. The encounter had taken less than half a minute, yet I felt as if I'd finished a triathlon. Abram and Silvio had barely had time to get to the kitchen doorway before it was all over.

They lifted the monster's body, allowing me to slide free. They brought towels, bandages and antiseptic. They wrapped my hands, Hamish's shoulder and a dozen miscellaneous injuries that Charlene and Christian had suffered. They were simple, important tasks. They gave us something to focus on. They kept us from having to think about what had happened.

Eventually, though, everything was cleaned and bandaged, and a dead monster still lay at our feet. Ichor dripped from its wounds, mixing with our blood and its horrible thick saliva to make a spreading puddle on the kitchen tiles. And the face of our dead friend still stared sightlessly up from the creature's side.

"What is it?" Abram finally asked. It's not like he thought any of us would have the answer, but someone had to say something. "How could… where did… what *is* it?"

"What do you think this means?" Charlene asked, gingerly touching the image of Philip's face.

"Exactly what we already knew," Hamish said grimly. "Philip's gone."

"You don't think maybe—" Charlene started, but Hamish cut her off.

"No. Look at all the rest of these. Squirrels, cats, that one looks like maybe a fox—these are what it's been eating. It kills them, and then somehow presses their face into its shell. Look, the smaller ones are less distinct. It's been growing as it eats, working its way up to bigger and bigger things. The impressions of the small animals have been stretched out as the shell grows. The bigger ones, the ones it's only been able to get recently, they're perfectly clear. And Philip…."

He trailed off, not needing to finish. Philip's face was as clear as if it had been sculpted. He was gone, like everything else depicted on the creature's shell.

"But why?" Silvio asked. "What does it get out of taking impressions of the things it eats?"

"Mating ritual, maybe?" I suggested. "Animals have all sorts of weird ways to attract mates. This would show how proficient of a hunter it was, so that—"

I stopped abruptly. Christian's face, normally ruddy and animated, had gone slack and turned a sickly pale green. "No, no," he muttered. "Mates. Of course."

"What?" I asked.

He looked around at the shattered window, at the wide-open room. "Everyone, quick. We need to get to a safer space."

"But it's dead—" Abram started.

"Now!" barked Christian. Abram jumped, alarmed.

"Is the living room good enough?"

"Somewhere without windows would be best. Somewhere we can all fit."

Silvio was shaking his head. "It's an open plan. There's nothing like that."

"Anywhere where we can turn the lights off and hide, then!" insisted Christian.

"What's going on?" I asked plaintively.

"I told you I found something on the way here. Come back to the living room, I'll show you."

We all followed him in a tight herd. Christian retrieved the bag that had contained the wine and reached inside. He pulled out a smooth, gleaming white pearl bigger than my fist. Oily rainbows flickered across its surface as he held it up for our inspection.

"Is that a pearl?" asked Silvio.

"I thought it was. Not a real one, obviously, but something manufactured, maybe. I found a cluster of them on the side of the road on the way here, nestled up against the trunk of a tree. I thought maybe they'd fallen off of a truck. There certainly wasn't anyone else around to claim them, so I took them.

"But we know now, don't we? They're not pearls." Christian walked over to the fireplace and set the pearl down on the bricks. Kneeling next to it, he raised the poker over his head and swung it downward, impacting the smooth sphere with a resounding crack.

The pearl smashed open. A thick grey liquid oozed out into the fireplace. Among the brittle shards, something moved. It was about the size of my cupped palm, with jagged legs and a smooth, shimmering shell still unmarked by any protrusions. It was the creature we had fought, wrought in miniature.

Christian crushed it brutally with the poker. He grabbed his bag and upended it, dumping out five more spheres. Again and again he brought the poker down, shattering the shells and destroying the tiny creatures within.

"Mates," he said in between blows. "There's no such thing as one of something. Nothing's unique. Everything that lives, breeds. We didn't find the only one. We just found the first."

"But you found its nest," I offered.

"I found *a* nest. What are the odds these are the only six eggs? And if these were laid in a clutch, the one that we killed, the full-grown one, probably had siblings, too."

He stood, his murderous work done. "Assuming that one was even full grown."

Just then, blue strobing lights washed through the room. Through the front window, we could see a police car outside.

"We need to get them in here," Christian said, striding to the front door. "They have no idea of the danger they're walk—"

As he opened the door, a creature took him in the left shoulder with a hooked forelimb. It spun him around and dragged him out backwards, dropping its bulk across his torso and driving him to the porch with a sickening snap. Christian's legs kicked twice and went still.

I heard the confused shouts of the police, followed rapidly by gunshots. The creature on the porch jerked from repeated impacts before collapsing over what was left of Christian's body. Even as its life drained away, I could see the shell slowly rising, molding itself into the beginnings of a head-sized lump.

There was a scream from outside. It was followed by more gunshots, then another scream, this one more intelligible.

"Get it off! Get it—"

Then there was nothing.

I would like to say that I made a considered plan, that I decided that the creatures outside were probably occupied, and it would be safe to make a run for it. I would like to say that I urged my friends to join me.

The truth of the matter is that something snapped in my mind, and I ran. I had seen too much that night, and all I wanted was to be somewhere where I never had to see anything like it again. Hamish and Charlene ran with me, I know. I know this because I heard Charlene screaming Hamish's name, and Hamish simply screaming, as something massive dragged him off into the night.

I do not know if Charlene made it to her car. I don't know if Abram and Silvio were safe in their house. All I know is that I got to my car and floored it out of there, spitting chunks of dirt from the yard as the tires dug for traction. I hit the road and never looked back. I didn't stop until I was all the way back home, at which point I collapsed against my steering wheel and wept.

I called, of course, once I was myself again. I tried all of their phones. I don't know what I would have said if they had answered, but it doesn't much matter, as none of them picked up.

Abram, Silvio, Charlene—I know where they are. They're all out there somewhere in the woods, their faces pressed horribly against the inside of an opalescent shell.

MALUM INTERFECTORUM

I wasn't sure what I was more surprised to discover: the ragged hole in my backyard, or the man stuck in it. The hole was a crack about eight feet long and maybe two feet thick at its widest point. It looked as if the earth had just pulled apart, separating like a wet paper towel. It had not been there yesterday. I'm certain I would have noticed.

Likewise, I would have noticed a person in my yard, especially one struggling to escape a hole. Not that he was struggling when I found him. By then he was just slumped over, looking resigned to being trapped from the waist down in a hole forever. Honestly, I was a little afraid that he was dead at first, but he lifted his head when he heard my footsteps approaching.

"Hey! Do you need help?" I called. Sort of a stupid opener. What was he going to say? *No, I like it fine in this hole, thanks*? Obviously he needed help.

"Yeah, I'm kinda stuck," he said. We were both really nailing the scintillating conversation.

"So, what happened?" I asked, drawing closer. I eyed the ground warily. I wasn't sure what had caused the crack, and I didn't want to be too close to it if it suddenly expanded.

"I was hiking around in the woods." He waved a hand vaguely in the direction of the forest that backed onto my property. "Got lost, came out here, thought I was saved. Then, bam! Ground fell out from under my feet, and I tumbled in here. Must've been a sinkhole or something.

"My leg's twisted and I can't get any leverage. I yelled for a while, but your house is a pretty good distance off that way. So, I was just conserving my energy for a bit, figuring out a new plan."

He grinned wryly. "Hadn't really come up with one, so I'm glad you came along."

He was talking a pretty good game, but I could see from the sweat on his pale skin that he wasn't doing so well. I thought about going back to the house for some sort of tool, but I wasn't sure what would work for this. A winch, maybe, but I didn't have one of those. Maybe just a length of rope? Honestly, I couldn't think of anything that would work better than just grabbing him under the arms and hauling him up.

To do that, though, I was going to have to straddle the hole in the ground. It wasn't a hard step physically. The crack was slightly less than shoulder width. But I had no idea how deep it went, or when it might spread larger again. It had opened up between one step and the next the first time. What would happen if it shifted again when I had a leg on either side?

I knew exactly what would happen. I'd fall screaming into the darkness below along with my new friend. I could picture it with perfect clarity, and I didn't care for the image at all.

I could hardly leave the guy stranded in a hole, though, and delaying wasn't going to help things along. So I took a deep breath, squared my shoulders and stepped across the crack.

"I'm gonna grab you under the shoulders," I told the stranger, bending down. "I'll lift up while you push however you—whoo, that's some stink coming up from there!"

"Oh yeah, that sulfur stink? I finally stopped smelling it. Figure my nose shut down after the first few hours. It's something else, though. Honestly, I was real worried I was suspended over your septic system or something."

"Not this far back," I assured him. "But yeah, there's sure something down there." I took shallow breaths to avoid taking in too much of the warm, stench-laden air. "C'mon, let's get you out of there. On three. One, two, three!"

I pulled as hard as I could. The stranger scrabbled at the broken edges of the dirt with his hands and twisted his hips back and forth, trying to rotate to a position of greater freedom. I was starting to see spots when suddenly, with a cry that was half pain and half relief, the man slid free of the earth's grasp.

I deposited him none-too-gently on the ground, hopping clear of the hole to make sure I didn't end up in the predicament I'd just freed him from. "Man, you were really in there? How're you doing?"

I could see the answer with my own eyes. His right leg was twisted, not fully backward or anything, but definitely further than it ought to go. He didn't seem to be moving either leg as he lay there panting. He reached his hands down to his legs and felt around, as if confirming they were still there.

"Still got feeling," he said. "Gotta say, I was a bit worried about that. They've been kinda folded up in there for a bit."

He braced himself on his elbows and rolled up to a half-kneeling position. "I think I can... oop!"

His right leg gave out as he tried to put weight on it, spilling him back onto the ground. I hurried to his side and crouched next to him, offering him support and stability.

"Come on, let's get you back on your pins, see if you can walk this off a bit."

With my help, he regained his feet. His left leg supported his weight without issue, but I felt him halfway collapse onto me as he tested his right leg again. I looked over to see him gritting his teeth, holding back the pain.

"Hey, it's all right, lean on me," I told him. "Come on, we'll get you back to the house."

With him hanging off of my shoulder, I made my way back across the yard toward my house. I could tell that he was fading as we went, because he kept putting more and more of his weight on me. That was basically fine until about halfway across the yard, when suddenly he got heavy. Not like "leaning a bit harder" heavy. Like "doubled his weight" heavy.

I stumbled, dropping to one knee. Without me to lean on, the stranger fell forward. He was pretty clearly unconscious as he fell past, but that wasn't what grabbed my attention. I was more focused on how red his skin had gotten, and the two jet black horns jutting out of his forehead. He definitely hadn't had those before. It's the kind of thing that catches the eye.

The vision, if that's what it was, only lasted for the split-second while he was toppling to the ground. As soon as he hit he let out a moan of pain, and just like that he was back to normal.

"Sorry, sorry!" I exclaimed, getting him upright again. His weight was back to normal along with the rest of him. I brushed my hand against his forehead as I was getting his arm settled around my shoulders, and I felt nothing but skin. By all appearances, he was a regular person.

I knew what I'd seen, though, impossible though it was. He'd had the visage of a demon.

The rest of the way back to the house, I kept stealing glances at him, trying to see through his disguise again. Try as I might, though, I could see nothing but the human. I could almost believe that he was a person, that I'd imagined it, but it all fit too neatly.

I'd believed his story, odd though it was. I'd accepted that he was just a lost hiker who had happened onto my property just as a surprise sinkhole that stank of sulfur opened beneath him, trapping him. It was a crazy story, but there he was in the hole, and there didn't seem to be any better explanation since demons weren't real.

But if demons *were* real… then it was really straining credulity to ask me to believe that he wasn't one who had just crawled up from Hell. And what I had seen in that fleeting moment was definitely a demon.

I still walked him into my house, though. I helped him limp up the steps of the back deck. I got him to the guestroom and sat him down on the bed. I told him to make himself comfortable, and I went to get him some water while I tried to figure out exactly what on earth I was doing.

On the face of it, inviting a demon into my house seemed like a great way to get my face ripped off. It was pretty hard to picture this guy as a threat, though. One of his legs wasn't working, and he was absolutely exhausted on top of it. The more I thought about it, the more likely it seemed that the reason his disguise had slipped was that he had passed out on the way to the house. If he couldn't even walk across the yard, what kind of threat could he really pose?

Anyway, demons weren't the only thing in Hell. Souls got cast down there on the regular, according to the church crowd. You were supposed to get wings and a halo when you went to Heaven; maybe everyone who went to Hell got horns. It was possible that this was a soul who'd found some way to sneak out.

For that matter, this could all be some kind of divine test. Honestly, the whole thing was starting to open up theological questions that I wasn't all that keen on thinking about. It had been a lot of years since I'd been to church. Now that I had a demon in my guestroom, that was starting to feel like a questionable decision.

The water glass overflowed, jerking me back to reality. I shut off the faucet and wondered briefly if I could bless the water. Probably you needed a priest for that, but then again, anyone could say grace, so maybe not?

I decided that giving a demon a glass of holy water to drink was uncharitable in any case, so I just brought it in as it was. He accepted it with thanks and drank greedily, emptying the entire glass in one go.

"Need more?" I asked.

"No, but can you do me a favor? I don't think anything's broken in my leg, but it's definitely twisted. I think maybe my knee's dislocated. Can you help me straighten it out?"

I looked at his leg, which was still at a slightly odd angle. "I don't know what I'm doing, but I can grip and twist just fine, I guess. Can't imagine it's gonna feel good, though."

"It'll feel better than leaving it." He propped his leg up on the bed and gripped his thigh. "Okay, grab it there by the shin. Twist it to my right when I say go. Ready? Go!"

I twisted his leg, and three noises sounded almost simultaneously. The first, by the barest of margins, was his scream. The second was a pop, a thick noise of tendons releasing stress. The third was a heavy groaning from the bed as if it had suddenly taken on an extra load.

My eyes snapped up to the stranger's face. Sure enough, he was slumped over, having fainted from the pain. His skin was again the mottled red of live embers, and his hair flopped over two dull horns each the length of the first joint of my thumb.

After a moment, he groaned, and his eyes fluttered briefly. As they did, his disguise reasserted itself. The horns vanished along with his fiery coloration, and the bed creaked again, relaxing as his full demonic weight was lifted. I averted my eyes back to his leg and pretended that my attention had been there the entire time.

"Wow," he said. "Okay, that sucked. But I can bend it now."

He suited action to word, wincing as he did so. "Well, a little bit, anyway."

"Probably ought to have a doctor look at that," I told him.

He waved his hand dismissively. "Nah, I should be able to walk it off. The bad bit's done now."

"Give it the evening to rest at least. You have anyone waiting for you?"

"No." He shook his head ruefully. "Wouldn't have been hiking alone if I did."

"Well, you can stay here tonight, and we'll figure out getting you back to your car tomorrow if your leg's better."

"Oh, yeah, that's way on the other side of the woods. I'll have to figure out where I parked it. It was a little gravel lot on the side of the highway, not much more than a wide spot by the trailhead."

"Got the address in your phone or anything?"

"Phone was in my backpack. I managed to knock that into the hole while I was trying to get free."

I nodded as if this made sense. "Well, we'll figure it out."

There was an awkward silence for a moment. I made my excuses and left him alone, retreating to the safety of my basement game room to gather my thoughts.

I knocked pool balls around the table as I tried to figure out what his plan was. Escape from Hell, sure. Rural nowhere wasn't much of a place to invade, though, and obviously things hadn't gone quite according to plan. He'd been pretty solidly stuck when I found him. Maybe something had tried to close the exit on him to prevent him from getting out?

If so, that favored the theory that he was a damned soul escaping and not a demon invading. That didn't necessarily mean he was any better, or I was any safer. Humans do some horrible stuff. It felt better if he was human, though. It made his disguise more honest, and I felt I could understand his motivations better. If I were in Hell and found a way out, I'd take it, too. And I probably wouldn't tell the truth to whoever found me, because I wouldn't want to get locked up in the nuthouse immediately after escaping from Hell.

Of course, there was always still the outside chance that he was actually a hiker and that I was having some sort of hallucination. I was certain that this wasn't the case, but crazy people always think they're sane, so I couldn't fully discount it.

A thought occurred to me: if there actually was a backpack in the hole, it would show that he had been telling the truth. It would be easy enough to check on. Bring out a flashlight, check the bottom of the hole, see if there was a backpack there. If there was one, I was crazy, and he was just a hiker with absurdly bad luck.

I laughed as I considered it. Imagine getting totally lost in the woods, then finding your way out only to have the ground crack open under you. Then being rescued... by a crazy person who thought you were a demon. That kind of luck could give you whiplash.

Above me, I heard the bed groan and the floor creak as if a heavy weight had just settled. I frowned for a second, then realized that my visitor had likely just fallen asleep and settled back into his demonic form. Hellish form, I corrected myself. Not a demon. Probably.

I ascended the stairs as quietly as I could, then sneaked down the hallway. I eased open the door to the guest room and peeked inside. My guest was asleep with his back to the door and the comforter pulled over himself, but the mattress was sagging under his weight and one red, clawed foot was sticking out from beneath the covers.

I closed the door with barely a click. After liberating a flashlight from the hall closet, I made my way out of the house, listening the whole time for that telltale creak to let me know that he was awake again. It never came, though, and once I was outside I began to breathe easily again.

The hole looked no different from how I had left it just a short while before. I got down on my stomach and crawled the last half-dozen feet or so, just in case anything else was inclined to give way. Nothing did, however, and shortly I found myself peering into a deep black chasm. The sulfurous smell hit me again, and I leaned away to take a deep breath before moving back to see what was inside.

The flashlight illuminated the rocky walls and some occasional small ledges, but no clear bottom. The crack seemed to grow wider as it descended, as if I were looking down through the top of a great empty pyramid. It was not a particularly comfortable sensation.

I shone the light around, but saw no backpack or even any place where one might have come to rest. I wanted to be thorough, though. Obviously, the lack of a backpack didn't necessarily mean that my guest was lying, but the presence of one would definitely exonerate him. So, I wanted to be sure that I had checked as carefully as possible.

I stuck my arm into the hole, searching the walls for a snagged pack or even just a scrap of fabric. I found nothing but torn earth.

After a moment, I concluded that there was no backpack to be seen and pulled my arm back. That was when something brushed against my hand.

There's no sugarcoating it. I screamed. It was high-pitched and embarrassing.

I yanked my hand back, banging the knuckles on the rocky wall hard enough to jar my fingers open. The flashlight tumbled from my grip. It spiraled away into the pit, flashing end over end until the light was too distant to see. As far as I could tell, it never reached a bottom.

I skittered backward and sat there on my knees for a minute, holding my bruised hand and staring at the pit. After a minute had passed and nothing had risen up to attack me, I moved slowly forward again and risked a look inside.

There, tucked up into a small crevice beneath the lip of the hole and almost impossible to see, was a leather pack. A cord dangled from the side. It was this that had touched my arm.

So, he is just a hiker then, I thought, pulling the pack out of the hole to examine it. Doubts immediately began to creep back in. It was far too heavy, and didn't look much like a hiking backpack. It was just a folded-over roll made of some pale leather and tied shut with a braided cord of the same material.

I untied the pack and let the leather flop open. Inside were several pieces of gleaming bronze armor, but I barely saw them. I was staring raptly at the sword.

It was beautiful and terrifying. Its blade was translucent and almost glowing, like the tail of a comet. It was feather-light when I picked it up. I knew it had to be razor-sharp. Nothing this perfect could ever fail at such a basic aspect of its being.

Two words were carved into the hilt: *malum interfectorum*. I knew that this meant Doomslayer, just as I knew that this was the sword's name and its purpose for being. To hold it was to know these things. It ached to be wielded. It longed to be put to use.

I could not imagine such a stunning weapon being trapped in Hell. It had to have been stolen from the angels, to have languished there until the man I had found—the demon, the soul, whatever— had stolen it once more. Perhaps it had even led him out. A blade such as this would always know the way free from such confines.

I was startled from my reverie by a voice from behind.

"So," said my visitor. "You have found my armor."

I turned and beheld him in his demonic visage. The idea that he might have been a trapped soul fled. I had previously caught only glimpses of his form, and had lied to myself that there was humanity beneath it. The thing that stood before me had nothing in common with a man. It was sharp, ageless and cruel.

Still, it had rescued this sword from the pits of Hell. It must have something within it that could be moved by truth and beauty.

"Step away from my possessions," it said, "and I will not play with you before I kill you."

I took an uncertain step back. The sword seemed to pull against my motion, resisting retreat.

"Why did you come here?" I asked.

"To destroy," the demon said matter-of-factly. "To spread despair, blight and ruin. To mix among you and make you think less of each other, to cause you to resent your lives and those around you. To make you suffer as I have suffered."

"You escaped from Hell only to create it again?"

It set its mouth into a grim line. "I can never escape. I was sent, as were so many others. Legions of us disguised as mortals to fool the unwary, to add bitterness and hatred and overcrowding. I am only one among millions, a soldier with a mission to undertake.

"Now, hand over the Malum that I may begin."

"But this sword," I pressed, desperate to understand. "It could never work for you. Surely you could tell that. Why did you steal it?"

"Steal it?" The demon grinned. "It was made for me when I was an angel."

It saw the horrified expression on my face. Its smile widened. "We have been together for millennia, the Malum and I. Everything I have done, it has seen. It was there when I fell. It did not care. A sword knows only blood."

I shook my head, denying the obvious falsehood of its words. Seeing me distracted, the demon charged. It was frighteningly fast, closing the distance between us in an eye blink.

The sword in my hand was faster. It flashed upward as if it were responding to my thoughts. I thrust wildly outward, and the Malum slid gracefully into the demon's chest, slicing apart boiled-leather skin to cut through vital parts within.

The demon sagged at my feet, impaled almost to the hilt. Its clawed hands reached up weakly, scraping at my forearms before falling away. Its body teetered and collapsed, sliding free of the sword. It hit the ground at the edge of the pit, slid backward, and tumbled away into the darkness.

Orange ichor dripped briefly from the Malum's blade. Moments later, it was free of the filth and, once again, clean and bright. It rejected the demon's blood as completely as I knew it must have rejected the demon itself.

I regarded the sword, marveling at its purity. The demon had been lying, of course. One such as he could never have wielded a blade such as this. It would have twisted in his grip, refused to do his work. It was made to slay things like him, not to serve them.

An idea began to grow in my head. Millions, the demon had said. Millions like him, sent here to divide and destroy us. All blending in.

With the Malum Interfectorum, I could stop them. I could find and kill those who had come to ruin our world. Once they were dead, surely all would be able to see them for the demons they had always been. And even if not, I knew I had the power of rightness on my side. The Malum would let me do no wrong.

I picked up the demon's armor and began to put it on. It fit like it had been made for me.

I strode back to the house, feeling invincible in my enemy's armor. Tomorrow, I will begin my quest. Tomorrow I will start to cleanse the world.

THE DINNER PARTY

It wasn't like I was snooping. I was just out for an evening walk, and my neighbor Raul had his curtains wide open. There was light, there was movement, and I looked. Anyone would have. I wasn't sticking my nose where it didn't belong.

Raul was having a dinner party. There were three people I didn't recognize seated around the table with him. Judging by the smiles and animated gestures, everyone was having a good time—except for Raul. He was gazing blankly ahead, totally disengaged from the party around him. I gave a little wave because I thought he'd seen me, but when he didn't respond, I realized that he was just staring at his own reflection in the window.

I'll be honest, I kind of stared at him, too. He looked awful. He had bags under his eyes that I could see all the way from the street. His face was slack, like he was in a daze. And he'd lost a lot of weight since the last time I'd seen him. Not in the "hey, your diet's working really well" kind of way. It was more of a "we've had to strictly ration our supplies to make it through this long winter" look.

I wondered if he was going through something that I'd missed hearing about. It had been a few months since we'd talked. Everything had been fine at that point; he and Diane had just gotten back from a big RV trip, and their daughter Maura was visiting from college on break. He'd seemed happy and healthy then. Something must have gone wrong.

Speaking of Diane and Maura, I noticed that neither one of them was at the table. I craned my neck around, trying to see if they were somewhere else in the room, but it was just Raul and his three guests. It struck me as odd until I noticed that although the table was set, there was no food on it. So obviously they were just in the kitchen, getting things ready.

Something still felt off, though. I found myself waiting, watching for Diane or her daughter to emerge, but neither one ever did. The guests didn't seem to mind the delay. Their conversation was as spirited as ever, despite Raul's noninvolvement. The chatter passed back and forth over his head, but he just stared sightlessly outward, his gaze passing through me without him even knowing I was there.

I almost went to knock on the door. I knew things weren't right there. But I convinced myself that I was wrong, that everything was fine, that it would be weird to interrupt the party for no reason. Raul and Diane had guests over. They didn't need me barging in. And what would I say?

"Hey, I was staring in your window, and I saw that dinner wasn't ready. Are you okay?"

I didn't want to sound like an idiot. I turned away from the window and headed back down the street to my house, where I made my own food and pretended I was going to stop thinking about Raul's dinner party.

It kept bothering me, though. When I woke up the next morning, I was still thinking about his face. He'd looked absolutely wretched. And his wife hadn't been there. Were those two points coincidental? Or connected?

All morning I kept constructing scenarios to explain it. Like: he and Diane had both fallen ill, and he was freshly released from the hospital, but she was still there. The people I'd seen were family members there to nurse him back to health.

Or maybe just Diane had gotten sick, and he was losing sleep worrying over her. The visitors could be her family who'd come to be close to her, which might explain why he'd looked like an outsider during their dinner camaraderie.

Then again, there might not be any illness at all. Maybe Diane had left him, and those guys were old college buddies in town to cheer him up, to help recover from the shambles of what had been his life. Didn't seem to be working, but that didn't mean that they weren't trying.

I tossed around all of these ideas and more, hypothesizing situations from the mundane to the absurd. They were all possible. I just didn't have enough information to say for sure.

One thing was certain, though: whatever was going on, Raul wasn't well. So if I brought him food, I'd be doing a good thing, right? And if, while I was over there, I happened to ask what was going on, that was just basic neighborly conversation. I could say that I saw him when he was out the other day. I didn't have to admit that I'd been looking in through his window at night. Not that there was anything wrong with what I'd done! It just sounded a little creepy without all of the context. Easier just to sidestep it with a white lie.

The early afternoon found me crossing the street with a bag of tortilla chips in one hand and a plastic container of my specialty homemade bean dip in the other. I didn't make this for just anyone. This was guaranteed to smooth over any weirdness over how I'd known he was sick. No one was going to ask any questions if it meant I might not leave them the bean dip.

I knocked on the door and waited, mulling over what I should say to Raul. *Saw you weren't looking well, brought you some food*? It had the advantage of simplicity. *I heard something was up; can I help*? Shifted the blame off of me for looking in his window, but it opened up the possibility of Raul asking who'd been talking about him, and I didn't have a good scapegoat handy.

I was considering acting surprised: *Hey, I made too much bean dip, so I thought I'd see if you wanted—whoa, you don't look so good*, when the door opened. It wasn't Raul standing there, though. It was his guests from last night, all three of them.

"Hello!" the one in front greeted me jovially. He had a broad grin and an air of haphazard dishevelment. He seemed mildly astonished to find himself answering the door, as if he had expected to be somewhere else. His thick black hair sat on top of his head in an untidy mess, looking as if it had been dropped there from a height. The other two hovered in the background, looking on with interest.

Up close, the idea that they were family seemed much more likely. They all shared the same hair, the same thin build, and the same slightly disconnected manic expression. They didn't look much like either Raul or Diane, though, so I wasn't sure whose family they might be.

I realized after a beat that I had been staring instead of answering. "Uh, hi!" I began. All of my carefully considered words had abandoned me. "Um, sorry. I was expecting Raul."

"Ah! He cannot come to the door. Extremely sorry. He would be, too, no doubt. What do you have there?" He cocked his head to the side as he regarded the container of dip.

"Oh, well, I thought Raul might be—that is, I was making dip, and I thought he… would want some. I made too much, anyway," I managed, remembering my story. I held out the container. "Here! This is for him."

"A food offering, is it?" The man at the door took the plastic dish from me. His fingers were thin and cold, like the branches of a tree in winter. "For Raul?"

"Well, for all of you, really. I mean, it's not like he's just going to eat it in front of you."

"No, to be sure. It is a rude host who does not offer food he has to his guests, indeed." His brothers had drawn closer and were peering over his shoulders at the dip. "And so this is for us?"

"Yeah, for sure." All three of them were looking at me. Their gazes were somehow expectant. The silence stretched out. I began to feel awkward, and spoke to fill the gap. "There's not a lot, I guess, but if you like it I can always make more."

"Mm, mhm. This is merely symbolic?" The one who had answered the door looked at me, seeking agreement.

"I mean, yeah, sure." I fidgeted, uncomfortable in the face of their ongoing smiles. I was beginning to feel that there was a joke being told at my expense. I attempted to steer the conversation back to easier ground. "Hey, so, is Diane here? Or Maura?"

"No, they are out." The grins continued.

"But they're okay, though?"

"They had a bit of a downturn, but both have stabilized now. They will have no future issues."

"Okay, good, that's good. And Raul?"

"Has a bit farther to go, just a bit. But we expect him to stabilize tonight as well, or tomorrow morning at the latest."

"Cool, great. Good to hear. So, are you guys family here to take care of them, or what?"

He considered my words, then nodded enthusiastically. "We are a family, yes. And we are here to take care of them."

"Okay. Awesome. Tell Raul I said hi, yeah? And I hope he feels better soon."

"We will, yes. Thank you for your offering."

"Yeah, absolutely. It was nothing."

"It was so much more than that!" Still their grins persisted. If anything, they were wider than they had been at the start of the conversation. It was getting downright creepy. I decided to bail.

"Listen, I gotta run. Good to meet you, and tell Raul I hope he's feeling better soon. Enjoy the bean dip."

"Yes, this was a fortuitous meeting. We will enjoy the food you offer soon."

"Okay, great. Well, bye." I gave a gesture that was halfway between a wave and a salute, then turned away, feeling stupid without quite being sure why. Just as I heard the door close behind me, I realized that I still had the bag of chips in my hand.

I almost took it back home. Raul's family was strange, and I didn't really want to prolong my interaction with them. But what kind of maniac would bring someone bean dip and no chips to eat it with? Besides, they'd seen me with the chips. I didn't want to give the weirdos any room to think that I was the weird one. It felt like losing a game I didn't know I'd been playing.

I took a deep breath, walked back up the steps, and knocked on the door. It was opened promptly this time. All three men were in positions so similar that I wasn't sure that any of them had moved. The container of dip was gone, though, so they must have gone somewhere to put it down, at least.

"Hello!" said the lead one again, just as jolly as before. "You are back."

"Yeah, sorry, I forgot to give you the chips to go with the dip."

"Aha!" he said, taking the bag from me. He turned it over, examining the packaging. "A bounty."

I couldn't tell if his comment was sarcastic or not. His face was still all smiles, and his tone was totally unreadable. I felt a little defensive. "I just didn't know if you had chips around or not."

"No, none," he assured me. "There is surprisingly little food in the house, I fear."

"Well, hey, like I said, I've got plenty of bean dip if you don't have time to get to the store."

"Twice offered! Our thanks indeed. You are splendid."

I was pretty sure no one had ever called me splendid before. "Uh, thanks. Well, like I said, I've gotta go. Thanks for taking care of Raul and his family."

"It is our pleasure."

This time, I successfully made my escape. I hurried back to my house, absurdly afraid that if I loitered outside for too long they would call me back. I wasn't even really clear on what had been so uncomfortable about the conversation, except for everything. The one who'd talked had been perfectly nice. The two in the back hadn't said or done anything wrong, other than smile too much. Yet my heart was racing like I'd just had a near-death experience, and my skin felt strangely numb.

Raul's family was more than weird. Something about them was flat-out wrong.

I skipped my walk that night. I didn't want to run into one of them outside, or accidentally catch their eye through the window somehow. I stayed inside, watched TV and ate bean dip until I was too stuffed to remember the creepy feel of his fingers on my hands. It took a lot to get there, but I was determined.

All was well until the evening of the next day. I was just starting to think about dinner when there was a knock at the door. I opened it without thinking, assuming it was a package or something, but then froze when I saw it was the three brothers. The same one, the spokesman, was in front again.

"Hello!" he began. I had the unsettling feeling that if I were to play this greeting back over the other times we had met, it would match up exactly. There was no variance in his timing, pitch or cadence whatsoever.

"Hey. Uh—how was the bean dip?"

"Regrettably, spoiled." He held out the container.

"What?" I accepted the dip, legitimately taken aback. "I just made it fresh. It couldn't possibly have—uch!" I made the mistake of opening the lid. A thick, rancid smell oozed over my hands. I nearly dropped the container in my haste to seal it again. The stench lingered, a physical presence strong enough to supersede my aversion to the visitors.

"Man! I don't know what happened there. I've got plenty more, if you want."

"All spoiled as well, likely."

"Nah, I can see why you'd think that, but I just had some this morning. Hang on, I'll grab you some."

I stepped into the kitchen and opened the refrigerator. A wave of foul odor rolled out, slapping me in the face. I staggered back a step. My eyes teared up as I dry-heaved. This was more than just the dip. The entire contents of the fridge had spoiled. More than that; I could see mold growing thickly over every food surface, filling containers and nudging its way out to spill onto the shelves.

"Unfortunate! It is as I have said." The foremost of the brothers was behind me, looking over my shoulder into the refrigerator.

"How did this even happen? It was fine this morning! And the refrigerator is still cold." I shut the door, gagging again as the movement forced a new wash of stench. I turned it into a cough, embarrassed to be showing such weakness in front of a stranger. Then it struck me. "Also, hey! What are you doing in my house?"

"We have come for dinner." He smiled pleasantly, as if this were the most obvious thing in the world.

"Look, I know I said you could have more bean dip, but I think you can see that that's not on offer right now. I don't know what went wrong, but I definitely can't make food out of anything in there."

"Unimportant," he said, waving a hand magnanimously. "You have other food."

I raised an eyebrow. "Yeah, so?"

"You have offered."

"Dude. I offered you bean dip."

"It was symbolic, you said."

"No, it was literal bean dip. It was in a plastic container. I'm sorry it went bad, but I don't owe you anything."

"You made a food offering. For all of us, you said."

"Okay, look. You're getting creepy. I want you out of my house."

"We will leave when you have fed us."

I took an involuntary step back as his two brothers stepped out from behind him. They were thinner and smaller than he was, but not by much. It seemed impossible that they had been hiding behind him. Yet there they were, all three of them staring me down in my kitchen. All three still bore those manic smiles, as if this were some sort of a game.

"Enough!" I let anger disguise my rising panic. None of the intruders made any attempt to stop me as I pushed past them and headed back to the front door. "You're all getting out of my house right n—yahh!"

My declaration devolved into a startled cry as I yanked the front door open. There on the front step was the first of the brothers, standing as calmly as if he had just knocked on the door and been waiting for me to open it. I jerked my head to look behind me. Only his two brothers stood in the kitchen.

"We move where we will when we are disregarded," he told me. He placed his unnaturally long fingers gently against my chest, pushing me backward as he re-entered my house. "You will not be quit of us until you have discharged your obligation."

"Fine!" I snarled, attempting to regain my composure. "You want food? Here!"

I stormed back into the kitchen and tore open the pantry door. I could immediately tell something was wrong; it smelled earthy and rank like an uncovered grave. The light flickered on and confirmed what I already knew. Everything in the pantry had rotted away. The cereal boxes sagged, their cardboard soggy and warped. The cans bulged ominously. The potatoes were seething with grubs while the dried beans crawled with flies.

"Tsk," said the visitor, directly behind me once more. "Your food."

"Whatever you're doing, stop it!" I kicked the door shut, but by now the whole kitchen stank. "Look, I'll feed you. What do you want? I'll go get it."

He shook his head. "You will not leave."

"Then what do you want me to do? I can't feed you if you've ruined all of my food!"

"Not quite all."

I stared at him, uncomprehending. "What, am I supposed to dig through that mess to find something that's still edible?"

"None of that is edible, nor what was in the icebox. Yet there remains another food source in the house."

"Ohh," I said, feigning comprehension. "Yeah, okay. Let me go get it."

All three of them watched me as I left the kitchen and headed down the hall, eyes wide and curious. My phone was charging in the bedroom. It would only take a moment to call the police. I just needed a second of freedom.

I did not bother closing the door. I thought it might arouse suspicion. I simply picked up the phone and, keeping my eyes on the door, began to dial.

I had gotten only as far as 9-1 when the phone was torn from my hand with superhuman strength and speed. The charging cable was dragged across my hand with enough force to rip the skin. I whipped around to find the brothers crowded behind me. My phone was crushed in the hand of the lead one, the jagged edges of the plastic and glass sticking into his palm, but he did not even seem to notice. His eyes, and the eyes of his brothers, were fixed firmly on my hand. His tongue peeked between his lips to lick the lines of his rigid smile.

I glanced down at my hand, confused, and saw that I was bleeding. I looked back to the brothers, to their fixated stares, and finally realized what sort of food it was they were looking to eat.

"No way," I said, covering the cut with my other hand. The motion snapped them out of their trance, and their eyes drifted back to my face.

"You should not call—" the leader began, but I cut him off.

"You're insane! I'm supposed to let you drink my blood?"

"And more. You offered us food."

"I didn't offer you my flesh!"

"You did, though you knew it not. Now confirm your offering. Invite us to feast, and we will leave."

"And what happens to me?"

"You will not survive."

"Wow, that's a heck of an enticement. You really know how to make a sales pitch. No way. Come and kill me if you can. I'll fight you."

"We will not fight you." Still he smiled, the expression tingeing all of his words with mockery. "It will be an offering, or we will have nothing."

"Then why on earth would I give myself up to you?"

"If you do not, we will watch you starve even as you would starve us. And when you are dead, we will find another. And another, and another, until we have our offering.

"You could prevent the suffering of others. You could save yourself from a slow death. All you need to do is fulfill your promise. You have already offered. Simply provide."

They stared at me for what felt like an eternity. I could feel their hunger radiating off of them. I shook my head. "Never."

"Then we will wait together until you change your mind."

That was nine days ago. I have had nothing but water since then. I tried to give even that up, to hasten the end, but it was too painful, and I caved. I've regretted that each day since, as the hunger digs in deeper and tortures me in new and painful ways.

My body aches all of the time. My stomach is in a constant cramp. I feel weak, confused, and feverish. My skin is starting to flake off, and my hair is falling out. All I want to do is sleep, but the brothers are constantly surrounding me, talking to me, smiling at me. Always smiling.

"Fulfill your offer," they cajole me. "Release us and we will release you."

They sit me at the empty table for meals, taking up seats around me as if we were all waiting to be served. They talk about what I would taste like, laughing about what parts they would eat first. They set out plates and remind me that I have but to say the word and they will fill those plates with meat.

"You can even have a bite, if you like," one tells me. I think it is still the leader talking, but neither my eyesight nor my memory can be trusted anymore. "You don't have to die hungry. We can give you the final taste of food."

I consider it more and more each day. But somewhere deep inside, I still have hope. During our empty meals, while they banter and laugh, I stare out the window into the neighborhood, hoping to catch someone's eye. I see people passing by regularly, but so far, no one has noticed me watching them.

There's still a chance, though. There's still time. I was too late for Raul, but someone may not be too late to save me.

TOAST WANTED

This is the story of how a novelty toaster ruined my life.

First of all, I want to clarify that I'm not the kind of guy who buys a novelty toaster. I got it at a white elephant gift exchange a couple of years back. You know, one of the swaps where everyone brings a gift and then you pick blindly and see what you get? Well, what I got was a toaster that burned the image of Jesus into the toast. People seeing Jesus in their breakfast was big for a while, I guess. I kind of remember when that was a thing.

Anyway, this toaster made it so you could have a miracle every meal. At least, that's what it said on the box. I kind of hoped someone would steal the gift so I'd get another chance at drawing, but no one did, so I took it home, put it on a shelf in the garage and forgot about it.

Then sometime in the middle of last year, my regular toaster quit working. I put in a couple of slices for breakfast, pushed the lever, and realized ten minutes later that the toast had never popped up. For a minute I panicked, sure that it was on fire and I somehow hadn't noticed it, but as it turned out the toaster contained two slices of perfectly cool, untoasted bread.

Ordinarily I wouldn't even have cared, but I had someone over and I was kind of trying to make a big thing out of breakfast. You know how it is. I'd made bacon and scrambled eggs, and toast is just part of that. You can't make a plate with eggs, bacon, and some floppy uncooked bread. And the eggs and bacon were already done, so I was committed to the meal at this point.

I'd started preheating the oven, figuring I could probably manage to toast the bread in there if I was careful, when I suddenly remembered the novelty toaster out in the garage. It only took a minute or so of rooting around before I came up with my prize. Breakfast was saved!

The toaster performed as advertised: it took bread and made it into toast. I popped the first couple of slices out, noted that they did in fact have a face lightly burned into one side, then promptly cut them into triangles for better presentation on the plate. That was about as much attention as I was inclined to pay to the toast, but my overnight companion was apparently a more curious sort.

"What's with the bread?" she asked, holding up one of the triangles and turning it back and forth, trying to make sense of the markings.

"Goofy toaster thing," I told her. "Puts the face of Jesus on your toast. I didn't buy it. I got it as a gift a while ago. I only got it out today because my regular toaster died. I'm not weirdly into Jesus."

I was rambling, but that was all right because she wasn't listening. She'd picked up the other triangle and was holding the two pieces together, looking at the full picture.

"Doesn't look much like Jesus," she said.

"Well, it's heating elements on bread. You're only going to get so good a picture."

"Sure, but doesn't Jesus usually have a beard?"

I looked. It was actually a surprisingly clear picture. There was some nice shading which I found very impressive given the medium. My date was right, though. It didn't look anything like Jesus. It was a slightly heavyset guy, a little bit jowly, probably late fifties. He had glasses and a scowl on his face. He didn't look holy at all.

"Huh," was my intelligent contribution. I held up my own pieces of toast, which showed what appeared to be the same man in profile. This had to be a joke from someone at the factory. Someone had swapped out the plates, or whatever was inside. "Well. Maybe it's Jesus in his later years."

"Jesus didn't have any later years," my date pointed out.

"I know how to solve this problem." I took a large bite of the toast. "There! Now it's not a picture of anybody."

It's funny. I genuinely can't remember her name or what she looked like, but I remember that face burned into the toast. It had kind of stuck in my mind even before I knew it was important. It really was an excellent likeness of someone who was definitely not Jesus, and that seemed like a weird sort of screwup to have happened in the manufacturing process. If it hadn't looked like any-thing, I could have understood that, but to look distinctly like a different person?

So, the toast was still on my mind when I went out for groceries that day. I wasn't actively thinking about it or anything, but it was still there. Enough so that when I spotted a heavyset guy down at the end of the aisle, my first thought was, "He looks kind of like the guy from my toast."

We were heading opposite ways down the aisle, getting closer to each other, and as he drew near, I started to get weirded out. He didn't just look kind of like the guy from my toast. He looked exactly like him. Same glasses, same slightly sagging cheeks, same haircut. I told myself that I was imagining it, that it was just a strange coincidence, but I couldn't stop staring. The more I looked, the more certain I was. I'd seen this man in my toast this morning.

"You need something?" He'd caught me staring.

"No, sorry, you just remind me of someone."

"Yeah? Who?"

Jesus, I thought, but the man didn't look like he had much of a sense of humor. I just shook my head and said, "Just someone I used to know. You're the wrong age, though. Sorry."

We pushed our carts past each other and went our separate ways. I refrained from looking back over my shoulder for fear that he'd catch me staring again. But when I got home, I put another slice of bread into the toaster. The image that came out was definitely the man I'd seen in the grocery store.

I told myself that it was just a weird coincidence. The toaster had a weird flaw, the guy had a generic kind of face. That was all it was. But it was still bugging me when I got up the next morning, so I made toast again. I had a vague idea that I could reverse-image search the picture, maybe find some sort of facial recognition program to compare it to online photos or something. I don't really know how this stuff works. I just know it's out there.

In any case, it turned out to be irrelevant. When the toast popped up, I snagged it out of the toaster and was confronted with a picture of a totally different person. This one was a man with a hipster beard in maybe his mid-twenties. No glasses, no scowl. No chance that it was the same image as yesterday.

The profile view showed some odd markings below his ear, maybe birthmarks. It was clearly an image of a specific person. There was no way I could dismiss this as a defect.

I put in another piece of toast and got the same image back, as identical as variations in the surface of the bread would allow. I peered inside the toaster, trying to see the piece that made the image, but all I could see was flat, featureless metal. It was like it was creating these pictures out of nothing at all.

I thought about opening it up, but there was a label on it warning of a risk of severe electric shock, and I had no idea what I'd even be looking for anyway. Some sort of plate with shifting pins? That might explain how it was able to do two different pictures, but not how it made a picture of a man I saw later in the day.

That part really was just happenstance, I told myself as I ate my toast. It's just got some sort of pre-programmed set of options, and one of them happens to be a generic older white guy. I probably saw dozens of guys like that every day. Really, there were lower odds that a toasted image *wouldn't* look like one of them, when you thought about it.

In fact, that explained the whole thing. I looked around online and found that you could buy selfie toasters where you could put in whatever image you wanted. This must have been one of those models that had somehow gotten into the wrong box. They probably made them all in the same factory. Once I could figure out how to change the settings, I'd stop getting the factory presets on my toast.

I was able to keep telling myself this right up until I took my dog Odin out to the dog park. He was having a good time roughhousing with the other dogs, but at one point it started to turn a little too serious. I stepped in to grab his collar just as the owner of the other dog came to pull his away. I was looking down at Odin at first, so he didn't really register at first; all I saw was the hand on the collar and a pair of skinny jeans.

"Thanks," I said as I looked up. "Sorry about—"

I froze as I found myself looking directly at the man who'd been on this morning's toast. Same facial features, same beard. The marks behind his ear that I hadn't been able to make out in the toast were a series of small tattooed stars. It was perfectly clear now that I was looking at him in person. The image had definitely been him, not just someone like him. It was too perfect to be a coincidence.

"No problem," he said, not seeming to notice my alarm. "C'mon, Bruno. If you're gonna be a bully, you can't play."

He gave me a half-wave as he towed his dog away. I stared after him, trying to figure out what this meant. Something insane was going on. My toaster was predicting the future. Or I'd just gone totally crazy. Of the two, the second option seemed a lot more likely. People went crazy every day, after all. Toasters very rarely became prophets.

Odin twisted in my grip, anxious to get back to running around with the other dogs. I let him go and watched with envy. He was carefree, blissfully unaware of magic toasters and whatever strange messages they were trying to send.

"Enjoy it while you can," I told him on the car ride home. "When I get sent to the loony bin, you're gonna end up at the pound. Then you'll understand why this matters."

***

I became obsessed with the toaster. I had to know what it meant, what it was trying to tell me. I made toast every morning and studied the two pictures, looking for anything that connected them to the previous ones. I took photos so that I could compare multiple days of images side by side. I took notes, made measurements, searched for answers.

I could find no links. The people were random each day. All races, all genders, all ages. They were most often in the range of 25-50 years old, but there were more than a few whose wrinkles stood out prominently in the char, and at least a couple of children who couldn't have been any older than eight. The ratio was about 60:40 men to women, but there was no clear pattern for when one or the other would appear. Sometimes I'd go a week with nothing but women in my toast.

The only thing they all had in common was that I saw them at some point during my day. It was usually just a passing glance, but as my obsession grew, I began to scan crowds as I walked through them, determined to catch my target unawares. I reasoned that if I could follow them, maybe overhear them, I might find out what connected them all.

This, too, was of no use. I did begin to spot many of them before they saw me, and even successfully followed a few unobtrusively. They all simply seemed to be going about their lives, though, no different than anyone else I had passed. Why, then, did the toaster care about these specific people?

I found out almost by accident. Actually, completely by accident, for certain meanings of the word. I was out walking Odin one day, doing my now-standard paranoid scan of my surroundings. I noticed I'd caught the attention of a young family walking on the other side of the street and gave them a cheery wave, trying to act like I was normal.

Their child, a small boy, spotted Odin. His eyes lit up. "Doggy!" he yelled. Before his parents could stop him, he took off at a run, directly across the street and into the path of an oncoming car.

I don't recall hearing the child scream. I do remember the twin screams of the parents as the car sent their son spinning away, tossed through the air like a bag of garbage. I remember the screeching tires as the car skidded to a halt, and then again as the driver saw what he'd hit and fled the scene. I saw the driver's face as he looked back, pale and shocked. Even frozen in horror as it was, I recognized the man from that morning's toast.

The boy, unbelievably, was all right. More or less, anyway. One leg was badly broken, and an entire side of his face was bleeding from being scraped across the pavement, but he was lucid and crying, which under the circumstances seemed like a very good thing. The parents took their son to the hospital while I waited for the police.

"Any chance you saw the plate?" the policeman asked me, after I'd given him my story.

"No, but I can describe the driver." I gave a thorough description based on what I'd seen in the toast.

The policeman looked skeptical. "Yeah? You saw all that in the instant he turned back?"

"I had a very clear view of him," I insisted. "It's sort of burned in."

They let me talk to a sketch artist, who ended up making a very good likeness of the man. They even put it up on the evening news, though I think none of the police expected anything to come of it.

It worked, though. According to the news the next night, the man turned himself in after seeing his face on the news. He begged for clemency, saying that he wasn't a bad person; he'd just panicked in the moment.

That got me thinking. What if what linked the people wasn't a common goal or plan, but a concept? Not something they were on the outside, but something they were on the inside?

The next day, my toast had a picture of a bearded man with facial tattoos. The two pictures looked more like mugshots than ever. On a whim, I went to the website for the local jail and started clicking through the recent bookings. It only took a few minutes before I was presented with a mugshot that looked almost identical to the picture in my toast: Richard Bowman, booked on a swath of charges ranging from drug possession all the way up to murder in the first degree.

My plan had been to go out to the jail to see him, but then I thought: what if I didn't? What would happen if I disproved one of the toaster's predictions? Now that I knew where it thought I would be, I could just not go there. I had free will, after all.

Then I thought of all the ways I could meet a violent criminal that didn't involve walls separating us, and decided that this wasn't the time to test causality theories on my psychic toaster. I hopped in my car and drove off to the jail.

On the way there, I tried to figure out how to ask to talk to Bowman. They probably knew who his family was, and they definitely knew his lawyer. I probably needed credentials to pose as a reporter. I thought about just saying "I saw him in my break-fast," but decided that this was not really a situation that called for the truth.

In the end, I didn't have to say anything. As I was parking out-side the jail, I saw several guards overseeing a half-dozen men being loaded into a small bus. One of them turned and met my gaze. Even with the distance and fences between us, I recognized Richard Bowman.

With Bowman being transported, I could easily imagine all sorts of scenarios where he and I had met under less separated circumstances. I congratulated myself on my decision not to test the toaster's abilities.

I was at last beginning to form a theory about whose picture the toaster created. It was showing me people who had done—or would do—bad things. Over the next few weeks, I tested this theory, and slowly refined it to be more precise. Each day, the toaster showed me the worst person I would see that day.

Some people, like the man from the hit-and-run, had just made one very bad decision. Others, if I made a point of going where I knew they would be, would show up day after day. Often they seemed to be perfectly normal citizens. No one but me knew what they were actually like. I fantasized about digging up their secrets private-investigator-style and turning them over to the police. Everyone would be amazed at my prowess. "We had no idea," they would say. "However did you figure it out?"

I would tell them about my investigative techniques. I would not tell them about my toaster.

The morning toast had turned from a worrying aberration into an exciting puzzle. I researched the people it showed me, hunting for hints about what might have been in their past. I watched the news to see if anything they had done that day featured. It was a game, and it was fun. Until the day my mother came to visit.

It all started innocuously enough. She called to say that she'd be in town for a week for work, and I invited her to stay at my house.

"If it's not an imposition," she said.

"No, of course! It'll be great to see you for a week."

"I'll bring your stickers," she promised.

I laughed. Growing up, Mom had always traveled for work. She was gone about a week every month, and for as long as I could remember, she'd always brought me back a small sticker from wherever she'd gone. I had a huge wall map of the United States that was covered in these stickers. She and I would put them on the map together over the city she'd been in, and she would write the date on it.

The map was folded up in a box somewhere, but I still had it. Mom was continuing to travel for work, and whenever I saw her she'd give me the envelope full of stickers she'd been saving for me. I hadn't gotten around to putting a lot of them on in the last few years, but I always meant to, and I still enjoyed getting the stickers.

Mom rolled in early on Saturday morning. She'd always preferred to drive through the night, so I knew to expect her early. Still, she got there before I was fully functional, so I let her in and told her to get set up in the guest room while I showered and generally made myself presentable.

I emerged from the bathroom to the smell of breakfast cooking. Mom waved at me from the table as I entered the kitchen. "I made breakfast, I hope you don't mind. There's plenty for you. By the way, I love your toaster!"

I let out a small laugh. "Yeah, it's—"

"Where did you get the pictures of me?"

My blood ran cold. My mother was holding up a piece of toast which unmistakably bore her image. She was smiling as if it meant nothing. And why would it mean anything to her? But to me, it was horrifying.

"You okay?" Mom asked, noticing my sudden freeze.

"Yeah, I'm fine!" I forced a smile. "I just—yeah, breakfast sounds great. I'll—how was your drive?"

We made small talk as we ate. I pretended everything was fine, but I heard almost nothing she said. My mind was racing. This couldn't possibly be right. My mother was a wonderful woman. She was no saint, but there was no way she was the worst person I was going to see today. Unless maybe we didn't go out? That would make sense. If I just stayed in all day and didn't see anyone other than her, then by default she'd have to be the worst person I saw. That was probably all it was.

"I used up the last of your milk in my coffee," my mother said. "And I notice that your fridge is a little low on veggies. You're eating well, I hope?"

"Yes, Mom, I'm fine. I just usually go grocery shopping on Saturdays, so I'm low on stuff."

"Well, don't let me break up your routine! I'm sure I can entertain myself while you're out."

"I can go later."

"Don't be ridiculous. Go, do. Pretend I'm not even here."

Reluctantly, I left the house to go to the store. I tallied the people I passed, every person who met my eyes clanging another condemnation against my mother. She was worse than that man, worse than that woman, worse than that whole family. By the time I got home from the store, I'd crossed paths with hundreds of people.

I wondered if she'd hit something on her way here, like the man I'd seen before. Some*one*, I didn't want to say to myself. But her car looked fine, and she seemed completely unrattled. Still, something bad must have happened. Maybe she stole something from me while I was at the store? I turned it over in my mind all day, watching her for clues. I saw nothing out of the ordinary.

The next day, I was up before my mother. I wanted to hide the toaster before she saw someone else's face on the toast and asked questions about who it was. I'd thought about telling her my theory, but I obviously couldn't now.

Before I put the toaster away, though, I popped in a piece of bread and set it to toast. I wanted to know who to be looking for later on.

A few minutes later, the toast popped up. For the second day in a row, it was a picture of my mother.

I left the toaster on the counter. Mom wouldn't have any suspicions. She would think it just made sense to have the same picture day after day. Anyone would. Anyone but me.

My thoughts whirled. Was my mother hiding some dark secret from me? She didn't seem any different. How long had she been doing it?

I googled her hometown crime statistics, missing pets, missing people. Nothing looked out of the ordinary. I started to breathe more easily. Whatever it was, it wasn't as severe as I'd feared.

Then my mother came in for breakfast. She had an envelope in her hand. "I've got your stickers! Do you still keep them on the map? Where is it?"

"It's out in the garage," I told her. "It's put away right now."

"Well, un-put it away. We've got stickers to put on."

I rummaged around in the garage and returned with the map. We spread it across the table. Mom clucked her tongue as she looked at my pile of unattached stickers.

"You're so far behind! Well, I have my own record of where I've been. We'll get this fixed up."

So saying, she picked up one of the stickers and affixed it to the town where it belonged, adding the date she'd been there.

An idea that had been tugging at my sleeve for attention suddenly grabbed me by the wrist and pulled. Her hometown wasn't the place to look for unusual activities. The travel map was. All of the locations marked with the dates she'd visited. That was what I needed to search.

I waited until she went to bed that night, then took my laptop into the kitchen and set it on the map. I picked a city at random—Denver—then pulled up a missing persons website. I told myself that I'd start with the worst thing possible to get it out of the way first, then move on to more reasonable ideas.

There were two people who had gone missing from Denver around the date of Mom's travel.

I told myself that it was fine, that Denver was a big city. I just needed to pick somewhere smaller. Ogden caught my eye, down in Utah. I put it into the database.

Another missing person.

On and on I went, frantically typing in city after city. I breathed a sigh of relief every time I found no match, but there were far too few of those. More than half, maybe even more than two-thirds of the ones I checked had people who had gone missing while she was there.

This was everything I'd been looking for in all of my research on the strangers I'd seen in my toast. This was the huge case, the break no one else was ever going to get. Her pattern didn't exist if you didn't know where she'd been over the years. I knew. The map laid it all out. It would link together hundreds of cold cases.

And all I had to do was turn my own mother in to the police.

She was a murderer, a serial killer. The most prolific one I'd ever heard of. The evidence was all there in front of me. And even if I tried to explain it away, the toast made it clear that I was lying to myself.

I laid awake all night agonizing over this. The next morning, my mother commented on it.

"You look rough. You should get more sleep before work on Mondays. Here, I made breakfast."

She passed me toast. It had her face on it.

All week I fought with myself. I told myself that I'd misunderstood something, made some illogical leap. Meanwhile, I kept finding news articles of bodies found in shallow graves, matched to missing persons whose dates and locations coincided with my mother's travels. And every day, no matter where I went or how many people I saw, the toast bore my mother's face.

Friday night, the local news had a report about a teen who had been missing since last week.

"Poor kid," my mother remarked. "I hope they find him."

I thought of the news articles of the people they had found, the bodies buried on the roadside. I searched her face for any hint of compassion or remorse and saw nothing. She was utterly unconcerned.

She left late that night. I knew what I had to do. I had to call the police. If I didn't, there was every reason to believe that she would find a new target on the way home, a new victim to leave under shallow sands for the animals to dig up. She had to be stopped, and I was the only one who could do it. I was the only one who knew.

I turned the phone over and over in my hands. I stared at the screen. I dialed no numbers.

Eventually, I went to bed.

The next morning, the toast showed me my picture. It's been the same every day since. I know what I need to do to stop it. I know what has to be done.

Instead, I just tell people that it's a selfie toaster. It's easier that way.

PAST OWNERS

GHOST HUNTERS WANTED. NO EXPERIENCE NEEDED.

That was what sucked me into all this, that stupid ad. They even used the Ghostbusters logo. Totally illegal, sure, but it's a Face-book ad and who cares, right? The familiar logo caught my eye, the text made me laugh, and I thought, "Sure, why not?" And I clicked their stupid ad.

"Past Owners," that was the name of their show. Well, "show." It was going to be a YouTube channel. You know the shtick: going into haunted properties, talking up the murderous history, getting excited every time there's a squeak or a draft. Keanna was convinced that she had a new angle, though, nothing to do with ghosts at all. Her hook was SEO and targeted marketing. She was fresh out of some ad school and full of ideas about how to reach untapped markets and build a following.

Her idea was this: even people who don't care about haunted houses in general care about haunted houses in their town, right? People like hearing about themselves, and their hometown is enough a part of themselves to scratch that itch. Keanna was sure that through keywords and location-specific ads, we could pitch each episode of our show to locals, people who weren't already burned out on the whole ghost-hunting thing.

I was skeptical, but she was offering a regular paycheck and it sounded like fun, if nothing else. The "no experience needed" in the ad was because she'd already lined up her camera guy and tech folks. All she needed was a gofer to do—well, everything else.

I had one big question for Keanna before I joined up. "Do I need to believe in ghosts for this?"

She laughed. "Definitely not. Only Emmerich does and—nothing against him, but we don't need two Emmerichs around here, that's for sure."

So, I signed on as van driver, cord-carrier, coffee-getter and general stuff-doer. The team was small: Keanna, Merete, two guys named Jeff, and Emmerich. Everyone seemed genuinely pleased to have me on the team, and I was happy to meet all of them. Especially Merete, who was smoking hot. She was the one who was going to be in front of the camera, so it made sense. Plus, she had this accent—man. Definitely convinced me that Keanna was going to be able to sell this show, that's all I'm saying.

The Jeffs were in charge of the cameras. Everyone called them Stand Jeff and Sit Jeff to tell them apart. Stand Jeff was the guy who worked the standard camera, the kind you carry around to film people with. Sit Jeff dealt with all of the remote cameras. His whole deal was run from a control center, keeping tabs on a dozen different screens at once. Different skill sets, both camera-based, both named Jeff.

I asked Stand Jeff if we could call one of them by their middle name or something, and he looked disgusted.

"Yeah. You could. Except that his middle name *is* Jeff."

"Wait, he's named Jeff Jeff?"

"No, he's named Mark. He goes by Jeff just to tick me off. He won't even respond to Mark now. If you don't call him Jeff, he just pretends that he didn't hear you."

"Well, do you have a middle name?"

Stand Jeff looked offended. "Screw that! I'm not letting him steal my name. I was Jeff first."

And then there was Emmerich. Everyone else was mid-twenties, I'd say. Maybe thirty for Stand Jeff. But Emmerich had to be fifty, and a hard-worn fifty at that. He was a happy guy, always smiling, but he looked like he'd spent his entire life outdoors and only found out about sunscreen last week. His skin was weathered and wrinkled like a broken-in baseball glove. His hair was close-cropped and bristly. He looked kind of like Malcolm McDowell, only if he were a walnut.

Emmerich was responsible for all of the weird tech. EMF meters, infrared stuff, Geiger counter, defibrillator, regausser—don't quote me on the names of any of these, he lost me like six words in—whatever weird stuff might pick up a ghost, Emmerich had it and knew how to use it. Between his hard-sided cases and Sit

Jeff's banks of computers, the twelve-passenger van barely had room for the six of us to sit.

"You think this stuff can really pick up a ghost?" I asked him.

"Another skeptic, I see."

"I mean, yeah. People die all the time, everywhere. I really think I would've seen a ghost by now if they existed."

"Perhaps you have. Not all hauntings are equal, you know. Haven't you ever felt someone watching you when you were alone? Or suddenly had your mood shift for no reason?"

"Those are your ghosts? They're gonna make for some pretty lousy TV. 'We were walking around in the dark, when this man suddenly became creeped out! Ooooooh!'"

Emmerich was unfazed by my mockery. "Some ghosts are minor. Some are major. If we're lucky, we'll find something in between. If we're not, my equipment is good enough to pick up even the minor ones."

"So, the show might just be you pointing to a meter and explaining that this spike was a phantasm?"

He shook his head vehemently. "Trust me, we see a phantasm, you won't need any explanation from me. Like I said, not all hauntings are equal. Your standard phantom, that's just a lost scrap of a person. You might not even know it's there without serious equipment like mine. Temperature changes, tingling sensations—that's about as far as a phantom can go.

"A phantasm, now, that's a full-fledged evil location. It's a space-bending, time-dilating, hallucinatory murder waiting to happen. Phantasms are sentient and sadistic. They will lure you in, chew you up and swallow you whole. You spot a phantasm, you drop everything and run. If you still can."

Emmerich was staring me dead in the eyes. I opened my mouth to make a joke, but nothing came.

"Check," I said instead. "Gotcha. Noted."

I didn't get it, of course. But then again, Emmerich still came along, so maybe even he didn't really get it then.

***

It was our very first location. Keanna had found this amazing place outside of town, a full-on mansion called the MacDermott house. It had some kind of intense past, a hundred and fifty years old since Old Man MacDermott murdered his whole family and stuffed himself up the chimney, ghost haunted the attic and stared out the window forever, I don't know. I wasn't listening. I mean, I was listening, but Marete was reading and so actually I was just listening to her accent and imagining other words. I kept the van on the right side of the road and got us to the MacDermott house without incident, so whatever. I think I did fine.

The setup went like setups do. Emmerich and Sit Jeff and I hauled heavy stuff into various locations around the house and ran cables as inconspicuously as we could. Stand Jeff got a bunch of shots of the outside of the house, and then filmed Marete talking about the history of the place. Keanna helped Sit Jeff get everything up and running, supervised Stand Jeff's camerawork for a bit, and then probably took a nap or something. I don't know what producers do. She wasn't helping me haul equipment, that's all I know.

Once everything was set up, we all ditched and went out to a nearby pizza joint to get dinner. Keanna wanted to wait until sunset to get started, so we ate dinner and cracked jokes until dusk, then headed back to the house.

Sit Jeff parked himself behind his display of monitors and declared that everything was rolling and ready to go. Stand Jeff and Marete took a thermometer and an EMF meter and wandered off to film in various rooms. Emmerich had me grab some of the more esoteric machines and follow him off to take soundings or something. Keanna was off on her own, I thought at the time. Looking back, it was probably already too late to save her.

Emmerich and I were down in the basement when my walkie crackled to life.

"—ere are you guys?"

"Basement. Camera… four?" I flashed my light up at the wireless camera we'd fixed to the wall earlier, reading the tag. "Yeah, four."

"No w—" The walkie cut in and out erratically, fizzing with static. "—hing there but—"

I waved my light at the camera again. "See the bright light? That's us."

Nothing but static came from the walkie, so I took a picture of the camera and texted it to Sit Jeff.

Moments later, my phone buzzed with a response. It was a photo of the camera banks, centered on the monitor labeled CAM-

ERA 4. It showed an empty basement room, the same one we were in.

I glanced over at Emmerich's machines, which were completely silent. Emmerich was tapping on the walls. Both of us were completely visible to the camera.

Ha ha, I wrote back. *Earlier picture. Very funny. Text me if anything's really going on.*

On the walkie, I said, "Basement's looking quiet. Stand Jeff, Marete? Anything up where you are?"

"Come up," said a voice on the walkie. It didn't sound like either of the Jeffs, and it definitely didn't sound like Keanna or Marete.

"Jeff? That you?"

"Come up."

I looked over at Emmerich, who shrugged. "Nothing down here," he said.

We were almost out of the basement when Emmerich paused.

"How many stairs were there on the way down?" he said.

"I don't know. Like, ten? Twelve?"

"There are thirteen now."

"Okay, so it was thirteen. What, is that an unlucky number of stairs?"

"I don't think there were thirteen on the way down."

"Man, if there are thirteen stairs on the way up, there were thirteen on the way down. That's how stairs work."

"There weren't thirteen," he said mulishly, shaking his head. I sighed and pushed past him.

The ground floor was quiet. I thought about shouting, but something held me back. Instead, I reached for the walkie again.

"What room are you guys in?"

"Come up."

"Upstairs, then? We're back on the ground floor."

"Up."

"Thanks, man. Helpful." I turned to Emmerich. "Up, then."

He looked concerned. "I want to swap out some of the equipment."

Back in the main room, the chair in front of the bank of monitors sat empty. Emmerich and I exchanged glances.

"Sit Jeff?" I said into the walkie. "Where'd you go, man?"

"I'm with the others. Come up."

"All right," I said uncertainly, eyeing the monitors. I couldn't see anyone on any of the screens. "Emmerich's just grabbing some stuff."

"Come up and join us."

"Okay, yeah. We'll be right up."

I flinched as Emmerich pressed a small box into my hand.

"What—" I started to say, but he pressed two fingers to my lips. For the first time since I'd met him, he wasn't smiling. He tapped the box in my hand, which had a post-it note on it.

TURN THIS TO MAX, it said. The box had a single dial, like a car radio knob. It had two rubber antennae sticking out of the top, and its back was a single speaker.

I gave him a questioning look. "If you need to," he told me. "Not before."

"I don't thi—"

Emmerich put his fingers to my mouth again. With his other hand, he pointed down the unlit front hallway.

In the gloom, at first I couldn't see what he was pointing at. Then, with a shock, I realized:

The front door was gone.

The large wooden door, with its half-circle of leaded glass above and rectangular windowpanes down either side, was no longer there. Instead, the hallway terminated in a small alcove with a chair, lamp and end table. It would have looked like quite a cozy reading nook had I not known that it should have been the way we entered the house.

"Emmer—" I tried, but he pressed his hand against me harder, mashing my lips into my teeth.

The walkie crackled to life again. "Come up."

"Let's go up," Emmerich said. He held up a box identical to the one he'd handed me and looked at it meaningfully, then back at me. "They're waiting for us."

Together, we walked up the house's narrow staircase. I counted the steps this time. There were thirteen.

The stairs let out into a dark hallway lined with doors. Every one was closed. An aura of menace hung in the air, an almost palpable sensation. I could feel it settling into my lungs with each breath.

I tried the first door. It was locked. Emmerich tried the one across the hallway, with the same result.

I glanced back downstairs. The steps stretched away into blackness, far beyond the reach of my light.

"Up," said the walkie.

At the end of the hallway, a set of folding stairs led up to a gaping hole in the ceiling. I cast a pleading glance at Emmerich. He gripped his little plastic box and walked toward the stairs. With dread in my heart, I followed.

The attic was dusty, black and silent. Our lights barely seemed to pierce the air, illuminating mere feet in front of us. A splintery wooden floor stretched out beneath overhanging beams. Boxes and discarded furniture were strewn erratically about.

"Oh, good," said a voice. It came from the walkie, but also from above, behind and all around us. "You've come to join us."

The walls heaved, then, spitting out a darkness with tangible form. I dove for the stairs, fully willing to crash headlong down them, but instead skidded off of bare wooden planks. Laughter echoed as I scrambled to my feet, searching desperately for an exit that was no longer there.

Behind me, heavy footsteps thumped across the floor, and static crackled. "Wha—no! No!" shouted a facsimile of Sit Jeff's voice, and I whipped around but saw nothing. Instead, a hand caressed the side of my cheek and I heard Marete's soft voice in my ear. "We've been waiting for you."

A rough hand grabbed my other shoulder then, spinning me away. "Up! Move!" shouted Emmerich, pulling me to my feet. He dragged me across the attic, our footsteps drowned out by the cacophony of voices calling out from around us. Phantom hands grasped at my arms and clawed at my face, but Emmerich's presence was more solidly real than any of them.

"Was there an attic window?"

"What? I don't know! Maybe?"

"Think!" Emmerich towed me in a circle, the attic closing in around us. When we had first come up here, it had stretched out in every direction. Now, we were tripping over boxes with each step, and I could see all four walls with a sweep of the light. "When we pulled up, did you see a window? A dormer on the house? A circular pane at the top? It doesn't have to open, it just has to be there. Think!"

The walls were closer now, no more than two steps away. They were closing in, forming a coffin. "There's no window!"

There were no windows. There were no doors. There was no escape.

"Not *is*. Was! *Was* there a window?"

"I don't—" And then a scrap of memory caught my attention, a piece of the house's history that Marete had been reading in the car. The ghost had been seen in the attic window. I was sure of it, sure she'd said it. "Yes! Yes, toward the street, an attic window!"

"Then run!" And with that, Emmerich shoved me away from him, dropping his flashlight to twist the dial on his little plastic box to the max. As feedback squealed forth at an ear-shatteringly painful volume, the walls around us wavered, and for just one instant I could see moonlight streaming through a window.

I charged for it, twisting the dial on my own box high. A tortured electronic scream shrieked forth, holding back the walls as I dove bodily into the window, smashing through it into the wide open night, twenty-five feet above the ground.

I don't know how I survived the fall. The ground was soft enough, and I landed just right, I suppose. If you count three cracked ribs, a broken ankle and a broken elbow just right, anyway.

I do. I didn't even feel the grinding bones until I was back in the van, jamming the keys into the ignition and slamming my broken ankle onto the accelerator to get away. And even then I didn't stop until MacDermott house was miles behind me and my body was screaming at me to stop and rest.

That was almost a month ago. I don't know what happened to the others, not exactly. I saw Emmerich at the end, as I tumbled out into the air. He looked stretched, broken, his limbs bent into unpleasant angles and his skin pulled taut until it was starting to tear in places. But it was the look on his face that is seared into my mind, a look of horror and hopelessness and horrible comprehension, all blended into one. It was the look of a man who knows in terrifying detail everything that is about to happen, and understands that knowing will not make it hurt any less. I wonder if he knew he was saving me at the cost of himself—or if he thought that the window was the other direction, and was attempting to offer me to the house as he flung himself to safety.

I don't sleep much anymore. Minutes at a time, maybe half an hour if I'm lucky. Or unlucky, perhaps. Because every time I sleep, I'm back in the MacDermott house. Voices taunt me, bubbling up from the darkness. Hands grasp at my body, pulling me back.

Hallways stretch away as I run down them, lifting doors out of my reach. And always, always the whisper:

Did you really think I'd ever let you go?

I think I made it out in time. I remember the glass cutting my skin, the impact with the ground. I can feel the hard casts on my arm and leg, bite my finger for the pain, pick away a scab to see myself bleed. I'm sure that I'm here.

But then again, that's exactly the sort of hope the house would want me to have.

DAVID KNOWS A SHORTCUT

There were three things everyone could tell you about David. The first, the one everyone noticed immediately, was that he was handsome. Like, Hollywood handsome. He had a roguish charm, too, a disarming smile that lit up his face and made everything all right. Men, women, it didn't matter. Everyone liked David. He was impossible to stay mad at.

The second thing was that he was obsessed with his watch. He couldn't go ten minutes without checking the time. To his credit, it was a nice watch; I don't know anything about watches, but I could tell that it was sleek and well-made. Judging by the reactions of folks who did know and care about watches, though, I got the feeling that it was more than just something you'd pick up at the mall.

David wasn't ever ostentatious about his watch. He wasn't wearing it to show off. He just looked at it a lot. Folks commented on it sometimes, asking him if there was somewhere he had to be, that sort of thing. David always just shrugged and said he had no internal clock, and he liked to know what time it was. Then he'd grin, and everyone would grin along with him. David's grin made you feel like you were in on a joke with him, something secret from everyone else. Charisma, like I said.

The third thing everyone knew about David was that he knew a shortcut. Didn't matter where he was or where he was going. He knew a shortcut. Going to the movies? David would meet you at the theater; he knew a shortcut. Friend's housewarming party? See you there; he knew a shortcut. Interstate road trip to the middle of nowhere? David knew a shortcut.

The damnable thing was that he was always right, too. No matter where we were going, David would be there first, leaning on his car waiting for us or already inside. He was never a jerk about it. He'd even explain the shortcuts if you asked. It's just that they never seemed to work out for anyone but him. Sure, they'd shave off a minute or so if you were lucky, if you caught the traffic lights right and didn't get stuck at a left turn. But for David, they worked every single time.

David, of course, just shrugged it off. "Just lucky, I guess," he'd say, and grin. That grin should have been classified as a superpower. He could get away with anything with that.

No one was ever allowed along with David on his shortcuts. He had a million excuses. He was low on gas and couldn't afford the extra weight.. He'd spilled something rancid on his passenger seats. His A/C was out. The radio was stuck on talk radio at maximum volume. Local vandals had superglued his doors shut, and he'd only gotten the driver's door open so far.

Most of the excuses weren't particularly believable, but we all just figured that David liked to drive alone. It was a little idiosyncratic, but he was a good guy, and no one cared that much most of the time.

Sometimes, it grated a bit. He wouldn't ever give anyone a ride to parties, saying that he liked to leave on his own schedule. He'd never pick anyone up from the airport. One time, my car wouldn't start when I had a job interview. I called him and begged for a ride, or even just to borrow his car, but he refused. Said two tires had been slashed and he had to get them replaced, but I knew it was just the same old refusal. I called a cab, showed up late and didn't get the job.

Next time I saw David, I was ready to chew him out, but I noticed that he had two new tires on his car.

"Scoping out my new Bridgestones?" David asked with a smile, as if knowing he'd caught me checking on his excuse. And I grinned along because I'd been caught. As if I'd done something wrong.

Overall, though, David was a great guy, one of those friends that you can just always talk to. He was equally there for casual bar chatter or serious life conversations, and he always knew when to crack jokes, when to offer advice and when to just listen.

And so, when I got the call that my mother had been in an accident and was on her way to the hospital, it was David I called.

"David! David, please, you've got to come get me," I begged him when he answered the phone. "I've got to get to the hospital. Please, it's my mother."

"Whoa, what happened?"

"Car accident. She was in town, visiting. She was borrowing my car. Please, David, I don't think she's going to make it. I know you can get me there in time, you always know a shortcut, David, please!" I was babbling. I didn't care. I had to get there. The policeman on the phone had said that the paramedics were doing everything they could for her, which did not sound positive at all.

"Listen, I—"

"David, you've got to!"

"Listen." David's voice cracked out of the phone like a whip, shocking me into silence. "I'm on my way to you. You need to answer me this. Is this the most important thing in your life?"

"David, it's my mother!"

"Don't Lifetime me here. This isn't about your mother. It's about you. After she dies, she won't know whether you were there or not. Is it that important to you that you be there? Is it the most important thing in your life? Answer me truthfully. You can't take this back."

I paused, choking back the instinct to just blurt out another affirmative without thinking. "It—yes. It is."

"I'm outside."

I tore open the door and he was there, impossible though that was. I didn't ask questions. I just jumped into the passenger seat of his car and gave him the name of the hospital. David backed out of the driveway and sped off down the street.

"Thank you, David, so much. I can't ever—"

"Shut up," David said, his eyes locked on the road. "There are things I need to tell you, and we're not going to have a lot of time. I need you to listen like your life depends on it, because it does."

He took a left into another neighborhood, then a right down a residential street. A cul-de-sac loomed ahead of us. The garage of one of the houses was open, its interior dark. David gave the car more gas.

"Keep your eyes straight ahead," David said. "Do not look at me. You're about to see a lot of terrible things. Looking at me will be worse."

He accelerated, the car scraping briefly as it bumped over the lip into the driveway. We flew into the garage, its shadow swallowing us. I slammed my eyes shut as I braced for impact, scrabbling frantically for any support I could find.

The crash never came. I eased my eyes open to find that we were speeding down a road of unmarked asphalt. The sky around us was grey and uninviting, the world wrapped in a dismal fog that obscured vision after a few dozen feet.

"Where—" I began, turning to look at David.

"Eyes ahead!" David snarled. His voice seemed to come from all around me, and I could feel warm breath lapping over my shoulders as he talked. I flinched and snapped my face back toward the windshield.

"You will get there in time," he said. His words wrapped around me, as if I were hearing them from inside of his mouth. "And the price you pay is that you will never truly leave here."

Outside, ragged figures lined the road, twisted humanoid shapes with too many eyes and not enough bones. We sped past them, but more and more were clustering as we drove. They began to spill onto the road, forcing David to swerve to avoid the touch of their outstretched hands, to dodge collisions with their lumpen bodies.

"Who are they?" I asked.

"You need to buy a watch," David said, ignoring me. "A mechanical watch, not something dependent on electricity and internet. Something that cannot fail while even the most basic rules of physics hold true. Hone your internal clock. Keep your watch precisely wound. When it begins to slip, it is time to leave. You can stay ahead of them if you never relax."

The road arced away from the ground at an impossible angle. It twisted upward, but it also somehow turned inside out as it went, or possibly reversed. I can't explain it. It hurt my eyes to look at it. When I closed them, it left afterimages on my mind, dancing spots of corrosion burned into my thoughts.

I felt the car lurch through the twist. I heard David hiss, felt the sibilance on my entire body like a tongue. I kept my eyes shut and tried not to think of what I had seen.

The car steadied. David resumed speaking as if nothing had happened. "This is the last time I'll see you. Two in one place brings them sooner, and in greater force. It's unsafe."

Although his voice was all around me, it was becoming difficult to hear him. A faint, shrill piping was growing in my awareness. Quiet though it was, it was somehow managing to drown him out. I pictured the pipers, mad capering shapes hurling themselves through an insane dance, forms I had never seen before nor wanted to again.

I opened my eyes, and they were surrounding the car, just as I had pictured them. Their faces were warped, monstrous. Their eyes bled secrets and insanity. Their pipes were alive, moving to their own music. I felt the urge to unbuckle my seatbelt, to open the door, to join them.

The fog ahead of us darkened, tightening in around us. The pipers fell away, their dance carrying them off to unseen mysteries. I started to crane my head to follow them, but I felt David's rank breath on my neck and managed to keep my gaze forward.

The light fled from the world around us, pitching us into utter darkness. For an instant, everything was gone. I could not hear David, could not feel the car. My mind still sagged under the impossibility of the road, and I wondered what had happened to me as I had bent through it. Was I now one of the formless things abandoned by the roadside? Would I take up my place among the pipers?

And then we were careening down a cement ramp, tires shrieking in the echo chamber of the hospital parking garage. David slid to a halt just outside of the elevator.

"Go," he said. "You're in time."

I tumbled out of the car, turning back to look at him. He was normal, looking just as he always had, no sign of whatever I had felt in the car. He gave me a small wave as he leaned over to pull my door shut.

"It's been good knowing you," David said. He gave me his trademark grin. "Good luck."

The elevator ride took eons. The wait at the front desk while they located my mother was an eternity. There was a doctor there when I arrived, saying something, but I didn't hear him. I knelt at her bedside and took her hand, the tubes connected to her alien under my grasp.

"I'm here."

She saw me. She smiled. She said my name. And she died.

The machines screamed. The doctors and nurses rushed around, wheeling my mother away. I just sat there, and they let me sit.

After a while, I felt someone else enter the room. They approached slowly, as if worried about disturbing me.

"What do you need?" I asked, not looking up.

There was no answer except the shuffling of feet as they drew slowly closer.

"Do you nee—" Fear drove me to my feet as I looked up to see one of the ragged figures from the road advancing on me. My chair tumbled away behind me, crashing to the ground as I staggered away.

The thing spoke not a word as it approached. It merely reached out as it drew near, its rubbery fingers grasping plaintively for my flesh. I threw medical supplies and furniture at it, but nothing slowed its steady progress.

I tore open a door at the back of the room, but it was only a small closet. I was trapped, pinned. The creature blocked my exit.

In desperation, I crammed myself into the closet, hoping to at least buy another few moments. I could still hear its soft footsteps outside, though they were nearly drowned out by the hammering of my heart.

And then, quietly, I heard another noise. Subtle, drifting in on a faraway wind, but there: the sound of piping. There was a slight motion behind me, not of something in my space, but of space itself. I thought of the painful inversion of the road, and I smiled. I stepped deeper, down, through an indescribable path.

The walls unfolded around me. I began to run.

I knew a shortcut.

ECLIPSE BLINDNESS

Everyone knows you're not supposed to look at the sun. But we've all done it from time to time, right? Not like stared at or it anything, but just glanced up at the wrong time and gotten an eyeful. It's not a big deal. You squint, you blink away the afterimages, you move on with your life. And on cloudy days, you can kind of look for a while, and it doesn't even cause a problem.

So, a couple of years back, there was a big solar eclipse. I wasn't in the path of totality, but I still went out to look like everyone did. Thing is, I hadn't planned ahead enough to get those special eclipse glasses. I read a little bit the day before about making a pinhole camera to safely look at the eclipse, but it sounded like that was just going to be a stupid picture on paper, and if I wanted to not really see it, I could probably just look online.

I figured I'd just bring my regular sunglasses, then wait until it started getting dark and look then. That was going to be the cool bit anyway, and once most of the sun was covered up, it was bound to be basically safe to look at it. Obviously, everything online was full of dire warnings about how looking at the eclipse could make you go blind, but there's always someone online shouting about how something or other can kill or maim you. It's like when you look at a tag on a piece of furniture and it always says that like the stuffing or something is "known to the State of California to cause cancer." California seems to know that about an awful lot of things. And I'm not saying they're wrong, but the constant drumbeat of it just kind of dulls the warning, you know?

Anyway, so I looked at the eclipse, and it was pretty cool. It was hard to make out at first, what with how bright the sun is, but when I squinted a bit I could see that there was a big bite out of it that was slowly getting larger. Also, when I looked away I could see where it was shining through a tree, and all of the little dots of light in between the leaf shadows were making crescent moon shapes. Or crescent sun shapes, I suppose. Crescents, at any rate. And I guess that's what the pinhole camera would have shown, so actually it would have been neat after all. Fine, lesson learned.

I probably looked at the sun a little too long, because I had some gnarly afterimages for a little bit there. They were those blue-black spots like you get after a bright camera flash, only they stuck around for half an hour or so. I was honestly beginning to get a little worried that I really had done something stupid before they started to fade. I was looking up "eclipse blindness" online and freaking myself out when I noticed that the spots were gone from my right eye, and my left eye cleared up soon after that.

Mostly cleared up, anyway. I was still getting this odd sort of blurriness in one bit, like you'd see in old photographs where someone moved before it was done developing. Just a real faint overlay of something else over the actual picture. I figured it was just another aftereffect that would fade in a little bit, and I didn't worry about it too much until I went to bed that night.

When I closed my eyes, though, I got a bit spooked. That was when I realized I could still see those overlay images through my left eye, even though it was closed. It wasn't all of my eye, actually, just a fat crescent, same as the shape of the sun shining through those leaves. But in that crescent of my vision, I could see things that didn't match up with the world around me, even with my eyes shut. In fact, I could see them better without anything else behind them to hide their shapes.

Through that torn bit of vision in my left eye, I could see a room that didn't match the one I was in. My bedroom was maybe eight by ten feet, carpeted, with light grey walls that I'd never gotten around to hanging any art up on. The ghostly room I could see was much bigger, the size of a hotel lobby. I couldn't make out any colors, but there was a lot of glass and shiny metal. It looked fancy, wherever it was.

When I turned my head, my view of the other room shifted just as if it was actually there. Even looking from side to side without moving, my head changed my view exactly as it should. I spun around, trying to take it all in, and that's when I noticed that there were people there, too.

My eyes popped open in surprise, which made the images harder to see, but did not make them go away. I could still see wisps of movement as the people passed through my field of vision. Cautiously, I closed my eyes again.

No one seemed aware of me. I was as much of a ghost to them as they were to me. More so, because at least I could register their presence. They had no idea I was there at all.

I saw one figure heading for a distant exit and decided to follow him. I wondered what would happen if I left the building. Would there be a world outside, or would this weird vision reveal itself to be just a hallucination? If it was there, I figured I could find a street sign or something to tell me what I was seeing, and that might help clarify if it was real.

I made it about three steps before I walked face first into my own wall. It was a genuine shock when I hit it. I had been focusing on the ghost world so intently that I had legitimately forgotten that my eyes were closed and I was in a different space.

For a moment, I was tempted to go outside and try to find someone to follow in a larger space. Then I had an image of myself wandering blindly across neighbors' yards and into the street and decided that perhaps I should go to bed instead. There was a good chance that this would be gone in the morning, and if not, I could deal with it better after a full night's sleep.

I laid on my bed and closed my eyes, which left me staring at the ghostly metal ceiling far above me until I fell asleep.

In the morning, the visions were still there. There seemed to be more people than before. It made sense if it was morning there, too. I did my best to ignore them as I got ready for the day, but my bathroom was still in the middle of that same large room, and it was very distracting to have people walking through me as I showered. I tried to keep my left eye open as much as possible, but that just led to me getting shampoo in it. Eventually I gave up and accepted that I was going to have to shower with immaterial beings from now on.

Later that day, I walked out to the center of a big field and closed my eyes. On the walk out there, I was able to tell that I was somewhere busy by the speed at which wisps had been zipping through my vision, but I hadn't expected to find myself in the middle of a street with a car bearing silently down on me.

I yelled and threw myself to the ground out of sheer instinct, but the only thing that happened was I got grass in my mouth. The car went through me like everything else from that world, as did the others behind it. I wasn't there to them.

Once I calmed down, I closed my eyes again and made my way to the street corner. Although I was in the middle of what looked like a major city, there were no traffic lights or crosswalks. The corner had only a tall oblong pyramid rotating slowly in place. The pedestrians waited or stepped into the intersection based on no logic that I could see. The cars never hit them, though, so clearly the system worked.

The pyramoids, as I came to call them, were my first clear indication that this was a completely different world. Like I said, it's been a couple of years since the eclipse. I've had a lot of time to look around this place now. They run a lot of things off of various forms of the pyramoids, everything from lights to farming to traffic control. They're some form of neural interface.

I have an idea that everyone in this world I can see is psychic, or at least psychically linked. People seem to know where everyone else is and will be. I've never seen a traffic accident. I've never even seen two people run into each other. I don't know if this is because of the pyramoids, or if they built those as an extension of this ability, or what. Everyone and everything is linked, though.

I've been hoping for years to figure out a way to break into this connection, to get them to notice me. I'd love to be able to talk to them, to exchange information. I haven't told anyone else about my eclipse vision because I know how crazy it sounds, but if I could bring back real information from another world, they'd have to believe me. I've tried all sorts of things to be seen or heard or felt, but nothing works. I'm just not there for them.

Until last week. I was out at the grocery store and a man at the end of the aisle caught my eye. I couldn't figure out why at first; he looked just like anyone else. I looked around to see if there was something else near him that I'd spotted instead, and that's when I realized that I could only see him with the damaged crescent of my left eye.

He didn't look like the ghost world, though. He looked just like anyone else, in full color and opacity. I stared at him, trying to figure out how this could be—and he turned and stared back.

I fell back a step, shocked to be observed. He raised an eyebrow and quirked a smile at my reaction. He said something, some short sentence or word, but I couldn't hear him any more than anything else from that world. He tipped an imaginary hat at me and walked out of my field of vision.

I haven't seen him since. What I have seen in the other world is panic. People are running, fleeing, carrying children and backpacks and armloads of possessions. Cars are streaming out of the city, their trunks jammed full and roped down to hold them shut. Still, everyone moves in that effortless ballet, with no accidents and not even any real traffic jams. They cooperate as well as always, but whereas before they were always doing so in peace and joy, now the overwhelming feeling is terror.

The people are gone now; the city is abandoned. Worse than that, the city itself has begun disappearing. Building by building, street by street, it's going away. In most of my usual locations, I can't see anything of the other world through my left eye anymore. It's just dark when I close my eyes now, like it is for everyone else.

For other people, they're just seeing the inside of their eyelids. For me, I know I'm staring off into a dead, empty blackness that used to be a world.

I don't know who the man I saw was. I don't know how he did what he did. But I do know that he saw me.

He saw me. He said something.

Every night, I stare into the hole that used to be a world and I wonder when that man will come for our world as well.

THE KEEPER
OF THE DEAD

I live off of state route 1714, a road too minor to even merit a name. I bought my place out there precisely because it was so unregarded, so far away from government interference. I like being able to do whatever I want with my property. I put up fences and No Trespassing signs and now I can go out there and hunt, or ride my ATV, or dig a big pit in the backyard and install a concrete bunker if I feel like it. No one's going to stop me from living my life, is my point, and a road that no one cared enough to name seemed like a good place for that.

Turns out the road did have a name, though, just not an official one. The folks around here call it the Gravel Graveyard. It's paved these days, has been for a couple of years now, but the name's stuck around.

I found out why it was called that the first time I drove down the road with my windows open. It stinks of death, of uncovered corpses baking in the sun. There's no metaphor for that smell. It just is what it is.

I hadn't really looked too much at the shoulders of the road before then. Sure, I'd seen the occasional dead animal, but I'd never thought much about it. It's a road, and squirrels are dumb. Some of them are gonna get flattened. Not worth giving any thought to it, in my opinion.

It's seven miles down SR-1714 to my driveway, though, and the road reeked of rot and decay the entire way. I was starting to worry that I'd hit something, that I was going to get out to find a dead possum in my grill, but as soon as I turned into my driveway the stench faded. I breathed deeply again, testing, but the smell was definitely gone.

I turned my truck around and headed back to the road. Soon as I got to my mailbox, I could smell the death again. I looked around and sure enough, there was a dead raccoon lying in the ditch not ten feet from my driveway. It was pretty flat, like it had been there long enough to decompose inside its skin, but it didn't look like anything had been chewing on it. I wondered if maybe it had been sick.

A hundred feet down the road was a squirrel lying next to another raccoon. I had a brief, funny but morbid image of the two of them crossing the road to see each other before *wham*! They get nailed by a semi. It didn't actually look like they'd died at the same time, though. The squirrel was old and desiccated, while the raccoon still had the bloat of new death. Again, there were no animal marks on either corpse, no sign that mice had been chewing at them or birds had been pecking pieces off. There weren't even any flies around.

I kept on my slow roll, looking for roadside casualties, and I found them practically every fifty feet on one side or the other. I saw birds, snakes and turtles in addition to the more common squirrels, raccoons and possums. There was a fox half-hidden in the weeds a couple of miles from my house, and I even saw a deer at one point.

I found that one particularly strange. Round here, deer are considered good eating. If I'd hit one, you'd better believe I'd be putting it in the back of my truck. Especially if I was going to have to get a new grill for the front, you can be sure I was going to get something out of the deal. Leaving it lying on the side of the road just seemed wasteful. It wasn't like it had gone under the wheels like the squirrels.

All of the animals had one thing in common: they'd been left there to rot in the open. Nothing had touched them since the car that killed them.

I turned around before I made it all the way back out to the main highway. I'd identified the source of the smell, sure enough. It was just that in doing so, I'd uncovered a whole new mystery.

I've been a hunter for most of my life. I'm not new to dead things. You find them in the forest all the time, half-eaten or decomposing, crawling with maggots. I've been sitting at the side of a lake cleaning a fish before and had birds come up to try to steal the guts right out of my hands.

Nature doesn't wait to make new life out of death, is my point. Everything feeds on everything else. Except not on the Gravel Graveyard, apparently.

I asked Earl about it the next time I was down at the bar in town. Surprised him a bit, I think. I admit, it was an unusual question to spring on a man after he asked what you wanted to drink.

"Earl, how come nothing gets eaten on the Gravel Graveyard?"

"How come what? You taking up roadkill cuisine?"

"Not by me, by anything. The whole road's littered with dead animals, just laying around."

"Well, windy country road, some folks maybe driving a little faster than they ought, you're gonna get that."

"The whole thing, Earl. I counted 215 dead animals before I got bored earlier this week, and that was just in the first couple of miles from my house."

"Shoot, that was *before* you got bored?"

"I'm serious, Earl. There's something up with it. There's no reason why all of those carcasses would just be sitting around like that."

"Could be that the ones that came down to eat them got hit themselves."

"Then why's it just my road? Why not all of the others around here?"

"You telling me you went driving down every backroad in this county? Shoot, you weren't kidding when you said you got bored."

"No, I didn't check out the others, but I think I would've noticed if they were covered in rotting animals. That's not how things work."

"Isn't it? You've been living here eight months, yeah? Have you noticed your road being covered in dead animals before today? 'Cause it sure has been. That's why we call it the Gravel Graveyard."

Earl had a point there. I hadn't particularly stopped to do a tally before today, so I really had no proof that my road was different than any other. However, I spotted a flaw in his argument.

"Yeah, but if it wasn't just 1714, then how come that's the only one that got named the Gravel Graveyard? If they were all like that, you all would've just called it Stink Route 1714 or something like that, and done the same for every other one like it."

"You get touchy when you drink," Earl told me, which is exactly what he said every time he was losing an argument in his bar. To my ear, it was as good as an admission that I was right, so I let the conversation drop.

After I got home that night, I got my shovel and hiked back along my driveway to the road. I figured I could at least clear that raccoon away from my mailbox, give the mailman the ability to breathe while he was delivering my letters.

As I came up toward the road, though, I stopped in my tracks. Something huge and black was folded in the ditch, crouched about where the raccoon had been. I couldn't tell what it was in the moonlight, but it was definitely moving.

I clicked my flashlight on. Whatever it was let out a raucous call, something between a croak and a cry. It unfolded huge wings, larger than my arm span, and beat them harshly against the ground as it took several ungainly steps away. Despite its enormous size, it rapidly took to the air and disappeared into the night.

My best guess was that it was some kind of vulture. I didn't think that they were nocturnal, but I was no expert on birds, so all I could say for sure was that this one appeared to be. Whatever it was, it had been eating the roadkill, so at least it was performing a useful service around here.

Except that it turned out it hadn't been. I walked up to the mailbox and saw that the raccoon was still there where it had been the other day, exactly beneath where the thing had been crouching. I figured maybe I just wasn't seeing where it had torn pieces free, so I kept walking closer.

I reached for the raccoon with my shovel to flip it over, and that croak-cough call came again from the trees. The bird hadn't gone far away, it seemed, and it didn't like me messing with its prize. I reached for the corpse again with the shovel, testing, and received another rasping cry in response, followed by a rush of air.

I ducked instinctively. An expansive wing bristling with sharp feathers rushed past my head, buoyed on the night breeze. I felt talons graze my right shoulder, snatching futilely at empty air. The bird swooped by and disappeared into the night sky, possibly wheeling around for another attack.

Moving the raccoon's body could wait until morning, I decided, which was fortunate as I was already moving at a run back down the driveway toward my house. I kept checking over my shoulder as I went, certain that I'd see huge black wings blotting out the moon, but the bird seemed to have lost interest once I moved away from its food.

That had to have been what it was doing, I told myself as I examined the small rips in the shoulder of my shirt. I'd just interrupted it before it could feed. It was obviously going to come back now that I was gone. In the morning, the raccoon's corpse would be nowhere to be seen.

The logic was inescapable. It was also wrong.

In the morning, the roadkill was still there, slightly flatter than it had been the day before but smelling no less worse. I thought about stopping to get it out of the way right then, but as I started to get out of the car, I noticed a small dot in the sky, far overhead, lazily circling.

I got back into my vehicle. I didn't have my shovel in the truck anyway. If I kicked it out into the weeds, I'd just get the stink all over my boots. It was just as well to put it off until later.

That solitary dot was still there in the sky when I came home later that day, just drifting in long circles over my road. I wondered how long it would stay. For that matter, I wondered how long it had been there. Maybe it had been like the dead animals at the side of the road. Maybe I'd looked at it a hundred times, but never really seen it.

This was all ridiculous, I knew. I was psyching myself up into some strange headspace over a stupid bird. It was just some vulture circling because of all of the dead animals. Everyone knew that SR-1714 was a bonanza for roadkill. That's why they called it the Gravel Graveyard in the first place. The vulture was there for the smell, the same thing that had caused me to start down this weird path in the first place. If I got rid of the smell, the bird would leave, too. Simple as that.

The next day, I put my shovel and my shotgun into the back of my truck and parked right at the end of my driveway. I got out, refusing to look at the sky, and grabbed the shovel from the back. I marched over to the raccoon, scooped it off of the ground, and flung it off into the woods.

Finally, I risked a glance up. There was nothing there.

Emboldened, I moved down the road a ways, leaving the truck where it was. There wasn't anything like a shoulder on this road, so any time I parked I was going to be taking up most of the space.

I'd do that when I started covering some distance, but for these first few, it was easy enough to do on foot.

I had the squirrel up on the blade of the shovel when I heard that cry again. If anything, it was more disturbing during the day. Its rusty-nails-across-tarnished—metal quality fit better with the night than with a sunny, warm morning.

The bird was swooping directly at me, beak open, claws reaching. I hadn't seen its face before, and I wished I hadn't now. It looked half-dead itself, putrid flesh oozing off of a burnt skull. Gobbets of skin hung from each cheek, sweeping backward as it stooped toward me to give the impression of grasping tentacles.

I screamed something incoherent and flung the squirrel at it, then dropped the shovel and ran for my truck. It struck me in the back as I ran, dragging deep furrows up my shoulders and sending me sprawling on the side of the road. I was still free, though, so I pushed myself back to my feet and ran on.

The bird was circling back around as I snatched my shotgun out of the back of the truck. My first shot went wild, but I couldn't possibly have missed with the second. The thing was almost on me when I fired, and I saw some of the pellets strike its rotting flesh. The shot did nothing to slow its dive as it slammed into me, claws burrowing into my chest and beak tearing at my face.

I was knocked to the ground by the force of its impact. The creature stank worse than any of the dead animals along the side of the road. I could barely breathe for the smell, and trying was utter agony with its talons in my chest. I screamed and swatted at it, trying to push it away, when it began to speak.

It was the same damaged tone as its cry, but broken up into syllables. They weren't words I recognized, nor did I waste time trying. As soon as it stopped pecking at my face, I grabbed it and threw it toward the woods.

I fled for my truck then. I did not stop to grab my shovel or my gun. I just dragged myself into the cab, gunned the engine and floored it. I didn't know where the bird was, and I didn't care. All I knew was that it wasn't on me.

Every breath burned. My shoulders, chest and face all throbbed with pain. I knew the cuts were infected. How could they not be? The creature was made of filth. I had to get to the hospital, had to get these treated.

I was looking at my phone, trying to figure out where the nearest hospital was, when another shriek tore my attention back to the road. The bird was in front of me again, somehow having passed my truck and circled around to dive straight at my windshield. I jerked the wheel, hoping to dodge around it, but my truck jounced off the edge of the road, jumped the ditch and slammed broadside into the trees.

I was flung violently around the cab, ricocheting off the airbag and colliding with the far window. I slid to the floor, dazed, before succumbing to unconsciousness.

The bird came and stood over me then. It came into the cab of my truck, cramming its mass into the narrow seats, and perched above me. It covered me with its wings, wrapping me in its stench and blocking out the light. It pressed its rotting forehead against mine and again began to speak.

I still didn't know the words, but this time I understood the meaning. It was a prayer for the dead and disregarded. It was a benediction and a condemnation, a welcoming to the ranks of those that did not matter. This bird, this being, was the only one who noticed when they fell. I had touched what was holy to it. I was now part of its fold. It would keep me from now on.

I woke up with the truck still steaming at the side of the road. I pulled myself painfully back to my feet and stumbled out of the bent door. I saw another car approaching and waved them down. The hospital would have questions about some of my injuries, I was sure, but I would tell them it was just from the accident. I didn't want to think about any of the rest of it ever again.

The car didn't stop. The driver saw me, both him and his wife. I saw their heads turn toward me and my broken truck in a moment of passing interest. That momentary regard was all I warranted, though. I was nothing to them.

The same happened for the next car, and the next. I tried standing in the road, but that earned me only a blare of the horn as they swerved around me.

Finally, defeated, I coaxed my truck into starting one more time. With the airbag pooled in my lap and tangling in my arms every time I made a turn, I navigated slowly toward the hospital. The truck shrieked and rattled, its noises reminding me of the bird's cries. I tried to focus on the hospital. They could help me there.

They could have, it's true. They even did, more or less. I was able to get a bed after hours of waiting once I was the only prospective patient there. But as I sit alone in this sterile room, my bruises and battering from the car accident mixing with the diseased wounds from the keeper's attack, I know that no one is coming to help.

I'm just another broken thing at the side of the road. Not worth giving any thought to.

I'll patch myself up as best as I can, then figure out where I go from here on my own. Wherever it is, I know the keeper won't be far behind. No one else may notice me anymore, but it will. It will be with me always.

THE FONTENOT HOUSE

New Orleans is a city alive with death. Things have a way of coming back from beyond. There's something about the city that gives everything an extra spark. That sort of force can interact with the world in strange ways.

One of those ways was the Fontenot house. It was a small, unremarkable place, just one four-room shotgun shack among many. No one owned it, as far as anyone knew. No one knew which Fontenots the house had belonged to. It was just there. And it was very haunted.

Or so the story went, anyway. As was so often the case, no one telling the story had actually seen any strange goings-on at the house themselves. They hadn't personally seen the flickering lights in the windows at night, or felt the unnatural warmth in the walls, or heard the sounds of a faraway gathering. No one knew anyone who had disappeared. But they knew someone who knew someone who had, and anyway, there was no reason to believe that it wasn't haunted. Why else would there be stories about it if it wasn't true?

There were doubters, of course. There always were. One such was René Landry. He had spent all of his seventeen years of life in New Orleans, and although he was not so bold as to disbelieve all of the stories of the city, he certainly felt that many of them were simple tales to lure tourists. He made the mistake of saying so to a group of friends one night, and was challenged to put his money where his mouth was.

The bet was simple: spend the night in the Fontenot house. René was given a GoPro camera, a mildly drunken sendoff, and a strict ultimatum not to leave before sunup. There was no prize on the line, only pride, but that was more than enough. The camera was set to take pictures every minute, easy enough to flip through afterward to get a complete picture of the night.

"Maybe you'll get a picture of a ghost!" they told him, laughing.

"The ghost of peeling wallpaper, more like." René held the camera up, gesturing for his friends to lean in for a photo. They smiled and waved as the camera snapped a picture.

"First one down," René said. "See you three hundred and fifty-nine photos from now."

"When you find out the truth, don't be too proud to run, René! We'll let you live it down. Eventually."

"Like I need your approval," he told them. "I don't see any of you going in here at all."

The old wooden door shut behind him. René clicked on his flashlight to supplement the moonlight filtering in through the grimy windows. He could hear his friends doing ghost impressions on the porch. He smiled and shook his head as he looked around to determine the best place to spend the night.

The front porch opened onto the bedroom, but the floor was thick with dust and René shuddered to think what sorts of things might be living in the decayed padding of the bed. The leather chair in the corner was no better. It had a musty odor that he could smell from across the room. It stood out even among the overarching smell of dampness that arose from the house in general. René began to think that it would have been wise to have brought a sleeping bag.

He moved on to the living room. His light illuminated a corduroy couch that must have been at least three times his age, and showed every year of it. It was a faded orange that clashed riotously with the boldly patterned green rug covering most of the floor, while also taking up arms against the mildewed mustard-yellow wallpaper. Empty curio shelves painted in various bright hues lined the walls. Even in the dim light, the room's colors were an assault.

The dining room was a stark contrast. It was dominated by a large mahogany table and matching chairs, the dark wood standing out like a three-dimensional hole against the cream-colored walls. A towering china cabinet stood against one wall, still filled with dishes.

As René tilted his head back to take in all of the cabinet, he noted with curiosity that he could no longer touch the ceiling. In the previous two rooms, he had been able to tap it with the flashlight. Now his hand swung freely, with at least a foot of free space remaining. The floor felt even, so he concluded that the ceiling must have been constructed on a slant. It was an oddity, but not when compared to a corduroy couch.

The final room was the kitchen. The cabinets stood open and bare, their doors reaching outward in mute pleas to be filled. A large iron stove squatted in one corner. A small alcove opposite it led to a tiny bathroom. A sink, toilet and rusted metal tub were all crammed into a space that looked like it was intended for a pantry.

René took a desultory look through the cupboards and rattled the drawers, but found nothing but a few pieces of discarded cutlery. Something was off about the room, but it took several minutes until he realized what it was: there was no back door.

There wasn't even a space for one. The cabinets lined the back wall entirely, with the counter running in an unbroken line beneath them. But who had ever heard of a shotgun shack without a back door? It would trap all of the heat from the kitchen inside, making for a miserable summer. Besides which, René could see the back porch through one of the kitchen windows. No one would have a porch you couldn't get to from the inside of the house. The slanted ceiling was weird, but this was just plain crazy.

René tapped his hand along the back wall below the cabinets, searching for a weak spot, a seam, anything to show where a door had once been. The wall was oddly warm under his hand, the plaster uncomfortably soft. It felt like putty under his fingertips, though it did not yield.

He leaned in, holding the flashlight close to concentrate the light. The textured pattern of the plaster crawled away from the light, wriggling away like there was something live beneath it. René jerked backward, taking several brisk steps away from the wall. The room was darker than he remembered. The windows were higher and smaller. As he watched they shrank away, closing down to a pinhole and then vanishing entirely. The only light in the room came from his flashlight, and it was somehow no longer enough to illuminate the far side of the tiny space. Darkness stretched out all around René, engulfing him and his tiny cone of light.

In panic, he turned his light to the floor, desperate to see anything. The wooden planks were still there, but instead of the regular, sensible lines, they now spread outward in complex, interlocking butterfly patterns. The patterns continued on past the edge of his light, fifty feet or more. The walls were gone. The stove was gone. René stood alone in a barren desert of wood, trembling.

He told himself that it was impossible, a hallucination. He closed his eyes, reached outward with his hand, and walked slowly toward the back wall. He took two steps, three, four, and reached nothing. He squeezed his eyes and continued walking. Five steps, ten, enough to have walked half the length of the house, and still he encountered nothing. When he opened his eyes, he was still alone in that wooden desert, intricate butterflies under his feet.

Far away, René could hear a quiet clattering. He trained the light in the direction the sound was coming from, but could see nothing. After a moment, he began walking toward the noise. He recognized that it might be a poor idea, but nothing else was coming to mind as a valid option right now.

He walked for several minutes, the clattering growing steadily louder as he approached. Other sounds became clear in the background as well, the quiet creak and groan of hinges, the whispering of wood being drawn across other wood. The sound broadened, seeming to come from everywhere in front of him. René wondered if he was heading toward some manner of forest, if what he was hearing were branches rustling. He could feel no wind, though.

A part of his brain screamed that this was crazy, that he was inside a small house, that none of this could be happening. René carefully closed that part away. If he paid too much attention to those thoughts, he knew he would start to panic. This was insane, but it was better not to think too much about it right now. Later, he could assess this. For now, simply reacting was best.

Something glimmered at the edge of the light, something moving. The clattering was everywhere now, a continuous roar. René moved cautiously forward until he could fully see what was before him, but although his light illuminated it, his mind refused to believe.

Stretching out in either direction was an ocean of cabinets and drawers. Wooden doors lifted and fell in gentle waves, clacking and clattering as they went. René continued walking, unable to comprehend what he was looking at. There was no end he could see, millions of hinges moving millions of panels, nothing but cabinetry forever.

René reached down and gently touched the lid of the cabinet in front of him. It pushed against his hand, raised by the ones pressed up against it. René could not see what caused their movement. Something out in that impossible ocean must be the source, but whatever it was lay far beyond his light.

He stared at the cabinet sea for several minutes. His brain refused to generate any coherent sense. The doors rose and fell, clattering and whispering.

The thought that finally jarred him back into action was humorously prosaic. It occurred to him that the GoPro had been taking essentially the same photo every minute that he'd been standing there. Somehow, this was what he needed to restore mobility to his limbs, to restart his mind.

Whatever the way out of here was, it wasn't across that sea, at least not on foot. René turned his back on it and traveled back the way he'd come, hoping to find something more reasonable in the other direction.

He walked for an indeterminate amount of time. The clacking of the ocean faded behind him, and for a while there was nothing but the sound of his own footsteps. The butterflies beneath him were unvaried and seemingly infinite. René began to wonder if there was any end to this at all. The dust ahead of him was undisturbed, so he knew he was not walking in circles, but beyond that he had no guidance at all.

Finally something broke the unending sameness of the paneled desert. A structure rose up before him, a towering ziggurat constructed from wooden beams. It reached high into the sky, and as René craned his neck up he realized that there was indeed a sky up there. Faint light filtered down from somewhere, too little to see by yet, but enough to give hope that he was making progress, that he would not be trapped in infinite darkness when his flashlight gave out.

As René drew even with the massive tower, he realized that it was made of doorframes stacked together, each one sized for a normal house and all of them alike. He pushed on one tentatively, ready to run in case of collapse, but it appeared firmly rooted to the ground. He reached up and pulled on the header, lifting himself off of the ground and swinging briefly before releasing.

He looked speculatively upward, fighting a strange desire to climb it. It looked fairly simple, with wide footing and solid places to grip. Maybe at the top he could see more of what was around him.

Or maybe you could fall to your death, the sane part of his mind whispered. René clamped down on it once more, still unwilling to let it resume control. But he did skirt around the ziggurat, superstitiously refraining from passing through any of its myriad doorframes.

The blackness around René relaxed into a deep gloom. He could not make out the light source, but he began to see shapes ahead of him, tall oblong stripes darker than the areas around them. They stood silent and still, unbothered by the interloper coming toward them.

When he was close enough to catch them in the beam of his flashlight, René saw that they were trees, of a sort. They were mahogany, but their trunks were smooth and polished, their bases carved with intricate scrollwork. The branches spreading out high over his head were equally detailed, and the leaves growing from the trees were thick and carved of the same dark wood as the rest of it. They were utterly motionless, and strain his ears though he might, René could detect no sound.

Darkness descended again as he entered the carved forest. The interlocking leaves blocked out the little light that had filtered down. The sound of his footsteps echoed back at him from strange angles, giving the impression that others walked with him, close by but unseen. They never drew closer, though, and whenever René stopped, the echoed footsteps stopped immediately after.

There was a strange beauty to the dark forest. René turned off his flashlight, closed his eyes and let himself walk forward by feel. The thick trunks slipped by under his hands, cool and marble-smooth. He moved gently from one tree to the next, oddly calmed by the touch of the trees.

Suddenly, there was no next tree ahead of him. He opened his eyes and was surprised to find it bright enough to see by, still clearly night but now navigable without the flashlight. He could make out the landscape ahead, rising into hills that went on for what seemed to be miles.

The forest stood behind him, a bulwark against the rising land. A few dozen feet ahead, set into the wooden floor, were a series of dark rectangles, a patterned line continuing as far as he could see.

René approached curiously. The rectangles were doorframes again, horizontal this time. Each one limned the edge of a pit that stretched down past where he could see. There were handholds carved into the walls of each pit, a rough ladder that suggested they led somewhere that was intended to be reached. René hesitated, looking at the empty, yawning doorframes, before stepping carefully along the floor between two of them and continuing on through whatever the house had become.

The wooden floor gave way to textured ground, a field of tightly woven green fabric. It brushed up against René's calves as he walked, silencing his footsteps and replacing them with a soft, continuous shushing. An enormous moon hung off to one side, trapped in the square of a titanic window set into a spotted, yellowed cliff. Its glow was what illuminated the land around him.

As René walked, orange ridges began to show beneath the stands of green fabric. They grew more frequent, gathering together and rising higher and higher, until the green was far below him and he was clambering up a steep orange hill. The incline was intense, but the ridges kept his footing secure. René tucked his flashlight into his back pocket to allow him to grip with his hands as he climbed, and he made swift progress.

At some point, he felt the flashlight slip from his pocket. He turned and made a grab for it, but it was tumbling away, bouncing and rolling back down the hill he had spent so much effort ascending. He watched it go, then looked to the crest of the hill. It was close, beckoning him, and the room was bright. He climbed onward.

The crest of the hill butted up against the yellowed cliff. It was pitted and decayed, offering plenty of options to climb. The window containing the moon was not so far above, all things considered. He could reach it if he tried.

And then what? his sanity asked. *You can't escape through the glass.*

He had not been thinking about escape. He had been thinking about sitting on the sill and basking in the moon. He had been thinking about diving from the edge and knowing that the orange hill hundreds of feet below would catch him safely, that he was not meant to be hurt in this place.

You'll die, his mind insisted, and reluctantly René agreed that he had no reason to believe that he would not. Tearing his gaze from the cliff, he looked ahead, down the far side of the hill.

The descent looked to be as steep as the way up had been. Beyond it the green fabric fields resumed briefly, before fading away into some sort of terrain made of smoothed lumps. And beyond that, far beyond, was another cliff. The moonlight barely reached it. It seemed to have an odd geometric texture, but René could not make out the details from where he was. The only way to find out, he thought, was to go forward.

His first steps down the hill were slow and cautious. The angle was perilous, the footing uncertain. He turned around and began to back down, using his hands to stabilize himself, but it was slow and arduous work. After a few minutes, he sat down to catch his breath.

The first slide was accidental, a small slip. He caught himself before he had gone more than a few feet. As he steadied himself, though, he looked at the slope ahead of him and considered the distance. Sliding would be so much easier. If he was careful, he would surely be able to control it.

He slid again, braking with his hands, going twenty feet or more. He stopped only to confirm that he could, then released his grip and allowed gravity to pull him along once more. Down he went, faster and faster. The friction heated up the seat of his pants and he laid down on his back to distribute the heat. He was afraid that if he tried to stop himself, he would sear the skin from his hands, and so he continued his pell-mell plunge down the hill.

He crashed into the fabric fibers at the bottom, rolling over and over until he came to a stop dozens of feet away, dizzy and exhilarated. He stood slowly and waited with his hands on his knees for the world to stop spinning before straightening up completely.

Ahead of him stood a single wooden doorframe. It was not connected to anything. René could easily have walked around, had he so chosen. Instead he stepped boldly through, his sights set on the distant blocky cliff.

The lumpen ground he had seen from the top of the hill was made of a smooth tan leather, soft and well-worn. It rose and fell in small hummocks and was studded with tunnels, some no bigger than his arm, some large enough to walk inside. René peered inside one and called out. The distant echoes suggested caverns below of great depth and complexity.

The cliff, his mind insisted, and René pressed onward, walking steadfastly past the tunnels.

As he reached the base, René saw at last what gave the cliff its blocky shape. It was made of doors, countless identical doors set haphazardly together, stretching upward in a cyclopean nightmare.

He rattled the closest knob, but it was firmly locked, as were the ones on either side.

One of these has to lead out, insisted his sanity. *One has to be real.* And at last René let that part of his mind out, let it gibber and roil and insist that this was wrong, that this was fake, that this was not how reality worked. He watched it with a detached sense of wonder, like watching a strange animal through the glass walls of a zoo. It was interesting, but it was not relevant. And it was certainly not him.

René reached up, seizing hold of the top of a doorframe. He stepped lightly onto a doorknob and hoisted himself up. He climbed following a pattern that was perfectly clear, although he could not possibly have explained it. One door was right, that was all. One door led out.

With certainty and direction, René moved quickly and easily up the vertical surface, stepping from knob to knob with the grace of a mountain goat. Some doors swung open, and he used them to maneuver sideways, heading toward his goal. He did not look to see where they went. He knew they were not his.

Finally he reached a door that, when it opened, revealed a moonlit porch and a city beyond. The sky was touched with grey, but the street was empty and the surrounding areas still asleep. René looked at the porch where he had been drinking with his friends only hours before. It seemed unfamiliar, alien. The idea of even setting foot on it was unpleasant.

He removed the GoPro from his forehead and hung it carefully from the doorknob, then closed the door. It latched with a sense of finality.

René dropped swiftly down the cliff, his hands and feet finding holds without conscious thought. His mind was on the windowsill high above the orange hill. If he hurried, there would still be time to sit beneath the face of the moon.

His friends returned well after dawn, laughing and joking. They were surprised not to see René waiting for them on the porch.

"Maybe the ghosts got him after all," one offered, but the laughter at that comment died out when they saw the GoPro hanging from the doorknob.

They searched the house from front porch to back, but it was empty. They called his phone and checked his house, but he was nowhere to be found. Finally, they downloaded the pictures from the GoPro, hoping it would provide some answers.

What they saw was nightmarish, impossible. The sea of cabinetry, the dour mahogany forest, the threatening leather landscape—it shook every one of them, rattling a core belief that they had not understood that they held.

They deleted the photos and never spoke of them again.

René was never found.

The Fontenot house still stands.

A TALENT FOR DESTRUCTION

I always wanted to be a painter. When my wife and I bought our house, I had an idea that I'd set up a studio in the attic and paint. It would be a nice little getaway from the rest of my life, just a chance to settle down away from all of the outside distractions and paint whatever came to mind.

It never came together. That wasn't anyone's fault, not even mine. Life just happened. Work took up a chunk of my day, the commute took another piece, and then we had kids and the rest of my free time just vanished. I still told myself that I was going to set up that studio someday. The attic was perfect for it, after all, or would be once I cleared some of the boxes out of the way. I knew I'd get to it just as soon as I had a little break.

Well, you know how that goes. Soon enough our oldest daughter was ten, and I hadn't touched a paintbrush in a dozen years or more. I didn't mind it, exactly, but I still thought about it from time to time and sort of wished that I'd find or make the time for my old hobby.

Then one day I was up in the attic putting the Christmas decorations away, and I saw that someone had cleared a big space up against the back wall, right where the light from the big round window shone. All of the boxes that had been in the area had been stacked up to the sides, their position taken by something large draped in a sheet.

Curious, I went over and pulled the sheet aside. Beneath it was a large wooden easel with a canvas propped up on it, blank and begging to be painted.

I grinned to myself. Obviously, this was a surprise my wife Zoya was setting up for me. She'd realized that I was never actually going to get around to putting my studio in place, and so she'd taken it upon herself to do it for me. It was an extremely sweet gesture, and honestly probably the only way I was actually going to get back into painting before the kids went off to college, if then. If she'd taken the time to set up the space for me, it would be rude not to use it, after all.

I didn't say anything to her when I went back downstairs. I hadn't seen any paints around, so I figured she had a presentation planned whenever she was going to give it to me. I certainly wasn't going to ruin her present by telling her that I'd seen it early. It wasn't my birthday for a while, but maybe she was thinking about doing it as a Valentine's Day present?

A couple of weeks went by, and Zoya hadn't said anything about the easel in the attic. I was up there for something else—a legitimate reason, not just to snoop to see if she'd done anything— and to my surprise, I noticed that the sheet over the easel had some paint spatters on it. I was pretty sure it had been clean and new before.

The paint was dry to the touch, which probably meant that I had just been wrong about the newness of the covering. As long as I was over there anyway, though, I lifted the sheet to peek at the easel again. I love looking at blank canvases. They're so full of potential. It was one of my favorite things about painting: the knowledge that there was always another fresh start just waiting for me.

The canvas was no longer blank. It was painted in a flurry of blues and blacks, an impressionistic style that I'd always admired but never mastered. The background was an array of medical devices and personnel, clustered and overlapping in a manner that conveyed urgency and haste. The central piece, stretching diagonally across the canvas, was a cutaway of an arm, showing a snapped ulna.

Ordinarily, I might not have been sure which bone was which. But just two days ago, my younger daughter Kara had fallen while climbing and broken the thinner of the two bones in her forearm, the ulna. The doctors had shown us the X-rays and told us that although the break looked severe, the cast would only have to stay on for a little over a month.

I didn't have copies of the X-rays, but from my recollection her break looked almost exactly like the one shown on the canvas before me.

I lowered the sheet again, puzzled. Was Zoya coming up here to paint? I wouldn't have minded if she was, though I had no idea it was something she was into. Why keep it a secret from me, though? Was she worried I'd be angry if she was better than me?

That night before dinner, I tried to ask Zoya about it.

"Hey hon, you know that little art studio in the attic?"

"Oh, are you finally going to set that up?" she asked me brightly. "That's fantastic! Let me know if we need to get rid of anything up there to clear out space. We could probably get rid of half of the junk up there and never miss it."

Her response baffled me. It was possible that she was pretending she didn't know about it to still keep it a surprise for me, but if so, why offer to help me set it up? I couldn't figure out how to ask if she really didn't know or if she was just acting like she didn't, and the conversation naturally moved on to other topics.

The next day, though, it was still bothering me. I decided to go back to the attic, bring down the painting and show it to Zoya. She could hardly deny having set up the studio in the attic once I showed her that I'd seen her work.

Only when I looked under the sheet this time, the arm painting wasn't there. There was a different canvas, showered in bloody shades of red. A thick vertical column spiked upward at one side, and at its base was the shape of a man. The red paint was thickest and darkest at his head, spreading outward in a lake to cover the rest of the canvas.

I found it deeply unsettling, not least because the figure bore at least a passing resemblance to me. I touched the paint, but it was dry. Zoya must have painted it last night after I went to sleep. The work was excellent, but I still had no idea why she was being so secretive.

I took the new painting off of the easel and replaced the sheet. As I did so, I spied the painting of the broken arm leaning up against the wall; I'd missed it behind the easel before. I picked it up as well and carried them both to the attic ladder.

The paintings blocked my vision as I took my first careful step onto the pull-down stairs. It was slightly precarious, but I'd climbed these stairs hundreds of times, and I was unconcerned.

And in fact, I was doing fine until something pushed me hard from behind.

Both paintings went flying into the depths of the attic as I threw out my arms, desperately seeking to catch myself on the lip of the attic floor, or the flimsy railings of the stair, or anything. The shove was too strong and my movements too slow, and I could only windmill helplessly as the floor rapidly rushed up to meet my head.

I woke up to Zoya shaking me and frantically calling my name.

"I'm okay," I slurred. I lifted my head, but the spike of pain that brought on caused me to instantly put it back down. There was a wet sound that confused me as I did that, like something was cushioning the hardwood floor. I raised my hand to my head and brought it away sticky. I was bleeding profusely.

"The ambulance is on its way," she told me. "Just stay there."

"There's someone in the attic," I said. I couldn't let myself be taken out of the house without warning her about that. "There's someone upstairs."

"You hit your head, baby. Just lie still. Help is coming."

I didn't want to lie still. I wanted her to listen to me. I was so tired, though, and so I closed my eyes just for a minute. The last thing I saw before I woke up in the hospital was the curtain of blood slowly making its way out from my head, carpeting the hallway.

The doctors diagnosed me with nothing worse than a mild concussion and a nasty bruise, and sent me back home. I was told not to do anything strenuous for the next week, and warned specifically against things like ladders in case there was any lingering dizziness from the concussion.

I spent my time listening intently to the noises of the house. Whoever was up there would have to creak a board or scrape against a box eventually. If I could figure out what part of the attic they were in, I'd be better equipped to challenge them once I was back on my feet.

Zoya inquired about my odd new habits, but I played them off as nothing to be concerned about. The person in the attic had already shown a propensity for violence when they'd pushed me down the stairs. Judging by the painting, they'd even been planning it. Who knew what they'd do to Zoya if they caught her up there? I couldn't let her risk herself.

After a week had passed, though, I had heard nothing definitive, and I was tired of waiting. I armed myself with a crowbar and a Maglite, pulled down the attic trap door and headed back up the stairs.

The easel still sat against the back wall, bedecked with more paint splatters than ever. The paintings I had hurled away in my fall were stacked near it, leaning against the wall. Someone had moved them.

I searched the attic from top to bottom, shoving boxes aside and jabbing my crowbar into corners. I checked the rafters and banged on the plywood panels covering the beams of the floor. I found nothing.

Finally, I turned to the easel hiding under its sheet. It was the last place I hadn't looked. I didn't see how the intruder could be hiding under it, but I also didn't see anywhere else he could be.

With a swift yank, I whipped the sheet aside. The easel tottered back and forth. The painting it held fell to the ground. There was no person there. There was nothing but three new paintings, the one that had fallen, and one propped up against each leg.

The leftmost painting showed the entrance to my attic, exactly as it was. A woman's head peered upward from the stairs. Her face was turned away, but her hair was styled like Zoya's. Her attention was on something off to the side of the painting. She did not see the dark shape with the sharp blade behind her.

The painting on the right showed the far side of my attic, boxes stacked high in shadowy pillars. They framed the large window that let most of the natural light into the room. Through it, my large oak tree was visible. Two dark shapes hung from its branches, their necks bent at unnatural angles. The details were blurred by the thick glass of the window, but they were the right size to be my children.

Heart pounding, I stood the final painting upright. It completed the triptych, showing the central portion of the attic. Unlike the others, it conveyed no direct threat. Instead, it showed only an empty easel with a bare wall behind it, not a painting to be seen.

"What are you doing in the attic?" Zoya called from below me. I heard the stairs creak as she took the first step.

"Stop!" I called out frantically. I had to keep her out. The painting's statement was clear: if she discovered the easel, or if my children did, or if I tried to get rid of the art—my family would die.

I cast about for an excuse as I rushed back to the stairs. On what pretext could I keep them all out of the attic? My mind seized on one that was close to the truth.

"I'm setting up that art studio," I told Zoya. I climbed down and shut the stairs behind me. "I don't want you to see it until I have something to show you. It needs to be a separate space."

She believed me, for why wouldn't she? Encouraged me, even. Which means that several times a week, sometimes even daily, I trudge up these stairs and make my way across to that paint-spattered sheet, dreading what disaster I will find beneath this time.

I have seen accidents both small and large, losses and failures aplenty. The worst, though, are the days when I take the sheet aside and see nothing but a blank canvas. Those are the days I have to paint my own destruction.

Zoya has not asked again to see my studio. She has been busy with the mishaps befalling our family. I would love to move, to throw it away, to burn it all down—but that threatening triptych hangs on the back wall of my attic, promising what will happen to everyone I love if I ever do.

And so, I paint, and I hope, and I dread.

EAVESDROPPER

I can hear wishes in white noise. Or at least, I could.

The first time I noticed it, I was in a gas station bathroom. I was pretty young, but old enough to not have my dad in there with me, so maybe six? It was a different time. These days you're probably not allowed to let a kid go into a gas station bathroom alone until they're old enough to vote.

Point is I was alone, and I'd just washed my hands. The bathroom had an air dryer, which was still sort of new back then. I pressed the button and it started blasting my hands, making that jet engine roar the way old ones did. Behind that noise, though, I swore I could hear someone talking.

As soon as the air dryer stopped, so did the words. I looked around, but there didn't seem to be anyone talking in the bathroom. I pressed the button again. Another long roar, and I was certain there were words hidden in it. I leaned closer to the nozzle of the dryer and listened intently. There was definitely someone talking.

"Please let this work out," they were saying. "I really need—"

The dryer cut off, and once again the words ended with it. I peered up into the nozzle and poked my fingers inside, but nothing seemed out of the ordinary. I don't know what I might have expected to find that would have explained it, anyway. I started the dryer again.

"Stay green, stay green, yes! Okay, I can still make it as long as… oh, come on, stay gre—"

It was hard to tell through the covering noise of the air dryer, but I didn't think that had been the same voice. I reached for the button again, when a louder voice behind me made me jump.

"Quit playing with the machine, kid. I need to dry my hands."

I scurried outside guiltily, ashamed to have been reprimanded by an adult. My parents were waiting by the car.

"Was wondering what happened to you," my father said. "Ready to go?"

"There was an air dryer," I began. I was going to tell him about what I'd heard, certain that he or my mother would be able to explain it to me, but he cut me off with a laugh.

"Playing with the new technology, huh? I hope you didn't keep anyone else from using it. Don't want people leaving the bathroom with dirty hands!"

"I didn't," I mumbled, thinking about the man who'd chased me away. I probably had.

I didn't want to bring up the air dryer again on the ride home, especially because my story made it clear that I'd been monopolizing it for some time. My parents probably weren't going to like the part where I'd stuck my fingers inside, either. On the whole, telling them what I'd heard was a lot more likely to get me into trouble than it was to get me answers.

That night as my mother was filling the bathtub, I could hear words in the rush of the water. I leaned in to hear better.

"Leave the faucet alone," my mother said.

"Shh. I can't hear them when you talk."

"Don't you shush me! I'm your mother. Can't hear who?"

I gestured at the water. She cocked an ear toward it and listened for a moment, then shook her head.

"It's just water, baby."

"There was someone talking! He was saying 'I promise that I'll never,' but I couldn't hear the rest because we were talking over him."

"I think you just imagined it." She turned off the water, cutting off any further chance of hearing what was said. "Okay, into the tub. And wash your ears. The potatoes you're growing in there are talking to you."

It wasn't just the noise of the water, though, and it wasn't in my head. I began to notice it more and more. The voices formed out of any sort of tumultuous sound; water and wind were the best, but I could hear them speaking behind everything from jackhammers to fire to radio static—though that one did sometimes turn out to just be other stations sometimes.

Aside from the radio, no one else ever heard the voices I did. I learned pretty quickly to stop asking, so as not to be considered weird. But when I was alone, I'd turn on a hair dryer or something similar and just listen to different voices drift in and out.

They were all hoping for things, I noticed. That was the only similarity. The voices were all ages, all genders, all sorts of emotions. A lot of them were afraid or sad, but I heard plenty that were happy and more than a few that were angry, sometimes murderously so. I listened to those with as much interest as every other.

Looking back, it might not have been the most healthy hobby. I basically grew up eavesdropping on random people's thoughts. These weren't deep, dark secrets, though. They were the sort of thing that you can read on people's faces. Real surface-level stuff. I was just reading it in white noise, and for people I never met.

I never did figure out where the voices were coming from. For a long time, I thought that maybe it was people I'd meet in my future, that these things I was hearing would someday become relevant to me. As I've grown older and none of them have ever become clear, I've moved away from that idea. I've also wondered if maybe these are past lives, snippets of things that were important to me before somehow bleeding through. It's possible, of course, but it feels like I'd be hearing from the same voices regularly if that was the case, instead of the melange of humanity I get.

The most likely idea, insofar as you can apply the word "likely" to any part of this, was that I was just getting random broadcasts from actual, current people. Some of the stuff I hear is pretty specific, with the names of people and places, but I was never able to prove that anything matched up to things in the real world.

Eventually I just stopped caring what the answer was. I liked my little window into people's thoughts. I didn't mind if I never knew who they were. I knew what they wanted, and that made us close. I figured they were probably out there somewhere. I liked looking at random people on the street and trying to decide if I'd heard them wishing before.

That all changed recently. It's now become pretty obvious that whatever I was hearing wasn't from anyone I've ever seen, or anything current. About a week ago, all of the wishes changed. Every time I listened, every voice was shouting variations on the same theme:

"I've got to get my family out of here!"
"Please let this be safe."
"I'm sorry, I'll never be bad again, just let him not see us."
"Help us! Help!"

Over and over again, in the roar of passing traffic, in the crash of the ocean, in the wind in a field. All of the things I'd spent a lifetime training myself to listen to, shrieking endlessly for help, for someone to save them. Thousands, maybe millions of voices.

There was only one that was different. I began hearing it more and more often. It sounded deadly satisfied, full and lethargic, like a cat sprawled in front of a fireplace. It only ever said one word: "Home." It was still a wish like all of the others, but it had focus behind it.

The last scream died out yesterday. I heard the other voice one final time. This time it uttered a second word: "Closer."

There are no more voices in the white noise. I listen and I listen, but there's nothing but the endless, empty rushing of air.

CRACKED

Hey, I want to talk to you about this new website, Siczine. No, I don't! Sorry. I mean, I sort of do, but only to tell you to stay away. You can find it on Google if you care.

I'm sorry, I can't control this. Do not google it.

That's the mistake I made. I was watching YouTube videos, and I saw a recent comment at the bottom of one of them:

not sure if anyone cares but last night I hacked my friends Facebook account using Siczine. Just google for it if you wanna try it yourself

It had nothing to do with the video. It was obviously spam. But as I was scrolling past, a reply posted:

Checking it out now. Looks great so far.

Probably still spam, but it looked like there was a chance it was the real deal. It was clearly working for someone. I admit, I was intrigued. It was possible, after all. I was just reading how Gab got cracked twice in two weeks due to uncaught exploits, so certainly this sort of thing happened. And too many people miss out on great opportunities because they think things are too good to be true. You never know if you don't go look!

Please don't go look. It is far, far too good to be true.

So, like I said, it was pretty clearly spam. But the thing is, I was curious. I have an ex, Ariel. She and I had a pretty bad breakup. Words were said, things were thrown, accounts were blocked. That was all about six months ago, and it's all in the past now. I'm over it, she's probably over it, we've moved on.

Only she's still got my account blocked. And I was sort of wondering what she was saying about me where I couldn't see it. We've still got a bunch of mutual friends, so if she was telling them lies about me, I ought to know about it, right? If only to defend myself.

I figured Siczine—crack your friend's FB in only 20 minutes!—was probably nothing, but on the off-chance that it really worked, what did I have to lose? Obviously, they were going to try to mine me for data, but if I loaded it up in an incognito session and gave them a dummy credit card for whatever trial they wanted me to sign up for, there wasn't much they could get. I suppose maybe they'd have Ariel's password at the end of it, but that sounded like her problem. Anyway, if it really worked, they could have had her password with or without my help, so it wasn't like I'd be making anything worse.

I checked to make sure my antivirus was up to date, then punched the name into Google. As promised, it popped up at the top of the results: "The Original SicZine Facebook Password Hacker," followed by something in Russian. I figured that was a good sign, since everyone knows that the Russians are eating our lunch when it comes to hacking. I clicked the link.

The page was an unappetizing salmon color, but I wasn't here for their design sense. The bold text at the top made it made it clear that they were just as ready to get started as I was. "Hack a Facebook account: Our interactive hacker will guide you through the process."

I liked it. Simple, straightforward. They make it so easy!

I didn't mean that last part. I had to say it. It was easy, but I'm not enthusiastic about it. It was a honeypot, one that I can't escape from.

Anyway, the first thing it wanted from me was a captcha to prove that I was human. It was the standard pixelated image with five letters and numbers. I dutifully typed them in and hit enter.

Instead of taking me to the hacking tool, or to a request for money, the site loaded a second captcha. This was one of the picture-based ones, like "click everything that's a stoplight" or "click all squares with a bus in them." I was a little annoyed, but I figured that maybe I'd entered the last one wrong, so I was getting challenged again. Maybe it had wanted the letters to be in caps or something.

The instructions on this one read:

Click all letters which are not in the English alphabet. Continue until none are left.

It showed me a grid with sixteen squares, of which maybe nine contained standard letters. The rest had weird shapes that could have been letters in some other alphabet. Russian, maybe? They didn't look familiar, but then again I can't read Russian. Whatever the case, I started clicking.

Each time I removed a false letter, it was replaced by something else. Sometimes it was a normal English letter. Sometimes it was another strange symbol.

I found that I didn't like looking at the curves and angles of the fake letters. They caused a distasteful sensation, like looking at food covered in mold or maggots moving in meat. They made me feel unclean.

I clicked them again and again, making them disappear one by one. When only English characters were left, I hit "OK" with relief.

The screen loaded up yet another captcha. This site was clearly just wasting my time. I didn't know what they were getting out of it; maybe they were using my CPU cycles to mine bitcoins while I had their page loaded or something. Whatever the case, it clearly wasn't actually going to take me to any sort of hacking tool. The whole thing had just been spam for suckers, like I should have known from the beginning.

Disgusted, I was about to close the window when the captcha instructions caught my eye.

Click all squares which contain a childhood memory. Continue until none are left.

My eyes widened as I looked at the grid. There, mixed in with other random pictures, were things I knew from my life. Not major stuff, but the important little things. My favorite stuffed animal, the one that I'd dragged around until it wore out. My first skateboard. My lucky shirt. My old phone number. A picture of me and my mother making ridiculous faces at the camera.

I had no idea how they could possibly have these. Sure, it was a hacking site, but I hadn't given them anything about myself yet. Or had I? Were these pictures on my computer? It was possible, I supposed. I'd had this computer for a while, and there was a lot of weird stuff saved on it. More if they'd gotten access to my Dropbox, which was linked.

Hesitantly, I clicked the stuffed animal picture. It disappeared, replaced by a Hot Wheels car. It might have been mine. I'd certainly had Hot Wheels as a kid. But it could just as easily have been a random picture from anywhere. I moved the mouse over to my lucky shirt and clicked.

Image after image vanished under my mouse. New ones appeared, and I clicked or ignored them in turn. I wasn't sure why I was doing it anymore. This wasn't about getting into the website. It was a compulsion. The instructions had told me to click until all of the memories were gone. I had to obey.

Despite this, I didn't realize what was happening until an image of a stuffed elephant appeared. It was raggedy, with patchy fur and a missing eye. It had clearly been someone's favorite toy, but I knew it hadn't been mine, because mine had been on the screen earlier. My toy had been....

I couldn't remember. Alarm began to bubble up deep within me as I sat there, staring at the screen, that beat-up toy elephant staring back at me out of its one button eye. My favorite toy. I had carried it everywhere. I had known what it was minutes ago when it had first appeared on the screen. Why couldn't I think of it now?

Click all squares which contain a childhood memory, the instructions said. *Continue until none are left.*

Until none were left. What had my lucky shirt looked like? What color had it been? Was it a team jersey? I knew I'd had one, knew I'd just seen it in the captcha, but the memory was gone. Childhood friends, elementary school teachers, card collections— everything I had clicked on was missing from my mind. I couldn't remember the state I'd grown up in. I couldn't remember my own mother's face.

And yet still my hand moved, the mouse gliding forward as if of its own volition. *Click.* My siblings—had there been two, or only one? *Click.* My dog's name. *Click.*

And then I was staring at a grid of sixteen unfamiliar images. With a trembling hand, I slid the cursor to the "OK" button. I gave it one last click.

Congratulations! read the screen. *Account successfully hacked. Spread the good word!*

The words echoed in my head, bouncing back and forth and growing louder and more insistent with every pass. I knew what it wanted me to do. I resisted at first, as well as I could. But those words grew louder and brighter, screaming around inside my brain like a comet, until they were drowning out all other thoughts and causing physical pain.

Spread the good word
Spread the good word
SPREAD THE GOOD WORD
It felt like someone had lit a literal fire in my skull. I squeezed my eyes shut, but the light was coming from inside and my eyelids offered no defense. I felt something wet running down my face and for a moment I was convinced that it was blood, that my eyes had actually popped from the strain. It was only tears, but I wasn't sure how much longer that would be true.

I pressed my palms against my ears, but that was no more effective than shutting my eyes had been. I could feel my eardrums throbbing under my hands. My pulse was racing, pounding to the beat of the words. I felt like my heart was going to burst. I screamed, but although I could feel the vibration scraping my vocal cords raw, I could not hear a sound over the noise in my head.

In terror and fear, I surrendered. Head pounding from the phantom noise, eyes blurred from the pain, I navigated back to YouTube and loaded up a trending video. There was already a message promoting Siczine in the comments. I knew what I had to add to it.

Checking it out now. Looks great so far.

The shrieking in my head stopped immediately. The thought was still there, but it was a whisper now, no longer an insistent demand but just an occasional suggestion: *spread the good word.* I could feel it building slowly again, but I'd bought myself some time.

The sick thing is, it did work. I know what's in Ariel's Facebook account. I know everything she's written in there since she blocked me. Every inconsequential word, every stupid pet picture. None of it was even about me, but it's all in my head now, taking up the space where my memories used to be. I even know her password, for all the good that'll do me.

Those who say that curiosity killed the cat lack imagination. There are things worse than death.

There's Siczine.

You can find it on Google if you care.

WHAT THE RAIN BRINGS

I love forests. I love the color of sunlight through the leaves and the muted sounds of animals going about their lives. I like to flip over rocks and look at all of the teeming life underneath. Most of all, I love the smell. A healthy forest just smells so fresh, so alive. Breathing deeply in a forest feels like becoming a part of nature.

I'll go hiking in any season or time of day. Crisp fall evenings, humid summer nights, brisk spring mornings, even blustery winter days—they all have their own charm, and I love to experience them all.

When thunderstorms threaten, though, you'll find me inside. I don't go hiking in the rain. Not anymore.

Everyone knows you're not supposed to be in a forest during a lightning storm, of course. Generally speaking, it's a pretty bad idea to stand next to tall things when electricity is looking to ground itself from the sky. I hadn't meant to be out there when the storm hit. My weather app had claimed that I had several hours before rain was likely, though, and I had wanted to believe it. Work had been ugly all week. I'd just gotten back at 6 PM from a Saturday shift that was supposed to end at 4, and all I wanted to do was to go burn off some frustration on a long, relaxing walk.

Honestly, I knew the app was wrong. I could smell the eagerness for rain in the forest. The trees knew it was coming. I just didn't want to believe it. I told myself that it was only a couple of hours until dark, and that the worst that could happen was that I might get a little bit wet.

The woods were quieter than usual. All of the animals were hunkering down in anticipation of the coming storm. They didn't have weather apps telling them that there was only an 11% chance of rain in the next hour. All they had were instincts, and years of knowledge, and fur and feathers that could feel the static electricity gathering in the air.

It was still an amazing day in the forest, though. The blue-black clouds shimmered like ink behind the thick green foliage. The wind rustled the tops of the trees back and forth, sending errant leaves fluttering to the ground. Everything was vibrant and beautiful. The woods drank in my stress, absorbing it into the ground like it was nothing. I felt light and calm. I told myself I had another hour before the rain arrived, at least.

I was half an hour from home when I could no longer lie to myself about the impending storm. Those inky clouds were pressing heavily against the trees, blotting out the evening sun and ushering in an early night. The gently rustling trees were now swaying back and forth, creaking and muttering to each other. I could hear the first fat raindrops spattering against the canopy overhead. I turned for home, but it was obvious that I was going to get drenched.

Rain in the forest is a wonderful thing. The smell of the rich earth being refreshed rises up from everywhere. Even in heavy downpours, the trees mitigate the worst of it, and on such a warm day there was no real discomfort in being wet. I'd have to hang my clothes up to dry when I got home, but that was all.

As the rain began to make its way through the trees, I raised my arms up to meet it. I felt like a plant unfurling its leaves to gather in the moisture. I wanted to embrace the sky.

The first grumble of thunder reminded me that I should really be moving forward. Lightning would not care about my poetic impressions of nature. I reined myself in and resumed my journey home.

The storm moved far faster than I did. Flashes of lightning began to illuminate the sky at regular intervals, with thunder following faster and faster on their heels. The rain moved from a light patter to a steady drumbeat, crashing down around me. A light mist rose up from the forest floor as the cold rain sluiced into the warm soil. It gave everything a slightly ethereal quality.

All of a sudden, the sky directly above me lit up, white-hot fire blasting the edge of my vision. The thunderclap that followed it was so intense that it sent me stumbling forward. I felt it as a physical slap across my back. I looked back, expecting to see a tree on fire, but everything seemed fine.

The smell was wrong, too. It didn't smell like ozone, or the charred scent of burnt wood. Instead, there was a faint stench of overheated rubber. It somehow managed to both be subtle and yet completely overwhelm the other smells of the forest. It was not intense, but it was everywhere.

Lightning struck again. This time I saw it. The bolt arced toward the forest, scalding a line across my vision, but it grounded itself just above the treetops on nothing at all.

The air coruscated where the bolt struck, tiny sparks crawling out across an unseen surface. For just an instant, it described the outline of something titanic standing among the trees.

I should have run, of course, but I was too confused to be frightened. What I'd seen didn't make any sense. Lightning didn't just stop right before reaching the ground. Air didn't shimmer like that. There had to be a reasonable explanation.

As I peered into the rain, I swore I could see several hollows in the mist. It could have been eddies caused by the precipitation and the rapidly dropping temperature. Or it could have been swirling around something hidden.

I couldn't be certain from where I was. I walked toward the oddities to find out.

The next lightning strike might have saved my life. It blasted into the non-presence again, limning it with crackling energy. Most of the shape made no sense. It towered over the trees now, over-topping them by dozens of feet. It had too many legs, too many heads. There was no symmetry or design to its pattern. It unfolded at the tops into great waving petals. It bloomed like a root vegetable abandoned in a cellar.

The only part that really made any sense to me was what looked like a tremendous grasping hand. In the brief instant that the lightning struck, I saw it raised high, taloned finger outstretched to ensnare. Even in the split-second it was lit, I could see it moving downward at high speed, heading directly toward me.

I leapt backward, more from surprise than fear. I was about to chastise myself for fleeing what was clearly some sort of meteorological optical illusion, when suddenly the earth in front of me exploded in five equidistant spots.

Fully invisible again in the absence of the lightning, the only indications of that massive hand were the furiously swirling mists, and the clawed furrows carved into the dirt before me. I had no idea where it was, but I was desperately afraid that it was rearing back for another strike. Like a frightened rabbit, I ran.

Lightning crashed again behind me, deafeningly loud. I could smell the hot rubber stench of the thing, hear its heavy tread as it shouldered its way through the trees. Dirt fountained behind me as its hand raked the ground, grabbing wildly at me. I ducked and dodged as I fled, trying to use the trees to separate us. The sounds of splintering wood warned me of the futility of this plan.

An unseen tree root sent me sprawling, skidding painfully across the muddy forest floor. I scrambled to my feet, terrified to be losing ground, and as I did, I saw lightning strike my invisible pursuer one more time.

It had grown larger somehow, significantly so. Each of its dozens of feet was as large as an elephant's. Its spreading petals spanned dozens of feet, interweaving like kelp. That hand, that terrible crashing hand, was the size of a city bus. It plummeted downward like a meteor, slashing through branches to slam into the ground all around me.

Clods of dirt and debris shot from the ground as the unseen fingers drew together at frightening speed. I made a panicked leap forward and collided with something firm yet spongy, like a mushroom the thickness of an oak tree. I did not stop to analyze it. I bounced off, caroming off a similar one to my side, and squeezed between their closing grip.

I don't know how I escaped. At some point I realized I could no longer hear the sounds of pursuit, but my ears had been ringing from the nearby lightning strikes and I had no idea when the other noises had stopped. I certainly had no intention of slowing, in any case.

I ran until I reached my house, and even then, I flung myself into the basement and hid there, shivering in my wet clothes, until I could no longer hear the storm outside. I eventually made myself a small place to warm up and get dry with some old blankets I'd been storing down there. They were musty, but it helped cover up the scent of heated rubber that was clinging to me.

Dawn broke before I finally had the courage to go back upstairs. The storm had long since passed. The field behind my house was misty in the early morning sun. I thought about the swirling holes in the forest mist and shuddered. At least I knew that monstrous thing wasn't simply standing in my field, waiting.

As the fog burned off, doubts began to creep in. Nothing about my experience made any sense. It was insane from start to finish. I wouldn't believe anyone who told me that it had happened to them. Why should I be the exception?

I didn't want to, but I knew what I had to do. If it had really happened, there would be proof. I had to go back.

The sun shone down warmly. I could hear squirrels scuttling around in the branches. Birds called back and forth to each other. Everything was so pleasant, so normal. My doubts grew with every step. Had I imagined it? Had it all been some odd delusion?

I smelled it first, that rubbery scent overlaying everything else. It was faint, but unmistakable. My eyes darted around, and my heart began to race, but I could see no other sign of it. There was only the smell. I moved cautiously on.

Not too much further along, I found what I needed to see: a star-shaped pattern dug into the dirt, five lines eight feet long and over a foot deep, as if an immense hand had reached down and tried to pluck something from the ground. I could see more of them further along the path, stretching back into the woods as far as I could see. Snapped and shattered trees stood alongside, a cenotaph to some gargantuan force passing by.

I thought about following the path back to where it had started. I wondered what I might find there. I decided I could live without knowing.

I still love the woods. I still hike in all seasons, at all times of day. But when there's even a chance of rain, I draw the curtains and I stay indoors.

THE SCENT OF BONES

"Saddle up. A bigwig's missing."

That was my partner, Gabriel. He was the senior ranger in our small park, having been hired nearly two weeks before me back in 2006. I felt that now that we'd both been there for more than a decade, it was perhaps time to consider each other equals. Gabriel disagreed. We mainly got along anyway, so I never bothered to press the point. He was welcome to believe that he was in charge, as long as he never expected me to follow his orders.

"What's the deal?" I checked the time as I started to gather up the necessary gear. It was still before noon, which was a relief. It meant that we'd be doing at least the initial search during the day. Daytime searches had a much higher rate of success. Also a much lower rate of tripping over tree roots in the dark.

"Governor's cousin went out for a hike yesterday and never made it back."

"It's still early. No chance it was an overnight and he's still on the trails?"

"She, and no. Didn't bring any camping gear, apparently. Car's still at the trailhead, cell phone goes straight to voicemail."

"Well, trailhead gives us a starting point, at least." We'd had worse beginnings. Oftentimes when someone went missing, the person calling it in didn't know any more than that they had been heading to our park. Although our park was considered small, that was only a relative term compared to the other national parks. It still covered over ten thousand acres. Given that amount of ground to search, it was nice to at least know what path our missing person had started on.

"Forward the office phone to your cell and let's get going," Gabriel instructed me, as if I didn't know how things worked. I forwarded the calls to his cell instead.

Minutes later, our jeep was bumping along the dirt path that led back to the main road. Gabriel's cell phone rang. He gave me a dirty look as he answered it.

"Ranger station. Uh, yes, sir! We're already on it. Twenty minutes, maybe. Well, but—"

He pulled the phone away from his ear and showed it his middle finger. I couldn't make out what was being said, but the speaker sounded insistent. Gabriel put the phone back to the side of his head.

"Fine, then we'll wait. But as senior ranger, I want to point out—"

He was cut off by another staccato burst of words. I saw him mouth something at the phone. I couldn't make it out exactly, but I was certain it was rude.

"Understood. Sir."

Gabriel hung up the phone and glared at me. I kept my eyes on the road.

"I told you to forward the calls to your phone," he said.

"I must've hit the wrong button."

"Yeah." He snorted. I said nothing. We rode on in silence for a moment before he continued. "Well, anyway. They've got some tracker coming in. We're supposed to wait for him at the trailhead."

"For how long? If we don't get started soon—"

"Yeah, what do you think I tried to tell them? The governor was clear. We wait."

"That was the governor?" I was legitimately impressed. I didn't think the governor knew the name of our park, let alone the number to reach us.

"Yeah, you'd think he'd have people to call for him, right? I guess he must really like his cousin." Gabriel laughed. "Kinda wish she'd gone missing years ago. Maybe we could've gotten some funding out of it."

"Hey, if he calls back, you can bring that up. Better make sure we can find her at that point, though."

"Ah, we've got like an eighty percent recovery rate. Those are good odds. I'd extort a public official with that chance of success."

I get that this banter sounds a bit dark, but it sort of comes with the territory. Fact of the matter is, most people who go missing in the parks show back up on their own. They find their way back to the trails, get their bearings and make their way back to civilization, or at least to other hikers. The ones who are truly lost, off-the-trail lost—we might find ten percent of them. Even fewer if you're only counting the ones we find alive.

Ten thousand acres is a lot of space, is my point. So, it helps to make jokes about the search. Humor distracts you from dwelling on the numbers. It keeps your mind off of the fact that a person's life is on the line.

In this case, we were also trying not to think about the fact that we were being asked to delay the start. Minutes can matter in rescues. We were already maybe a day behind, and now we were going to have to cool our heels in a parking lot instead of getting on the trail. For hours, probably, unless for some reason they'd called the tracker before calling us. Even if he was local, it was a long drive from pretty much anywhere to the park.

So, you can imagine my surprise when, not more than fifteen minutes after Gabriel and I got to the trailhead, we started hearing the heavy *thwap-thwap-thwap* of a helicopter overhead. We both stared up at the sky and watched it rapidly approach.

"They can't possibly be planning on landing here," Gabriel said, looking doubtfully around at the tiny gravel lot.

"I think they are," I said, scrambling off of the back bumper. "Quick, back in the jeep!"

We dove inside and slammed the doors as the helicopter settled down less than twenty feet away, kicking up a massive cloud of dust and tiny rocks. We listened to them ping off the jeep's metal frame as the rotors slowed to a stop.

"Nice," said Gabe. "Think the governor's gonna pay for a new paint job?"

"Quit whining and look professional," I told him. "We've got people to meet."

Two men climbed out of the helicopter, wearing more-or-less matching jumpsuits. They were the same color and had the same company logo stitched on the chest, but they wore them very differently.

The first man's clothing fit him well, looking like the comfortable and athletic outfit that it was. He wore a backpack covered in pouches and snugged it correctly around his shoulders and waist. He was clearly no stranger to hiking.

The second man was practically lost inside his jumpsuit. The collar sat high on his neck, while the sleeves hung past his thumbs and the legs were bunched up at the ankles. The wind from the slowing helicopter blades pressed the loose fabric against his body, revealing him to be disturbingly thin. "Emaciated" might have been the right word, even. His face was gaunt as well, and the dry skin stretched over his bald head looked as if it might crack at any moment, freeing the bones within.

"You two the rangers?" the athletic man asked as Gabriel and I clambered out of the car. "I'm Mr. Davis."

"And I'm Byron," said the thin man, walking up behind him. I saw Davis suppress an eyeroll, which I found odd. Byron hadn't done anything other than introduce himself. Still, I'd certainly rolled my eyes at Gabriel enough times over our careers, so I assumed I was just missing some key backstory here.

"How well do you know this park?" asked Davis.

"Better than anyone," said Gabriel. I didn't roll my eyes, but only because I was used to his bragging. I was better on the searches than he was and he knew it. That was all that mattered.

"And you?" Davis continued, turning to me. "The governor's sister is depending on us. I need a straight answer, no vanity."

"I thought it was the governor's cousin?" I asked.

"Sorry, I misspoke. How well do you know the woods?" Davis's gaze drilled into me, frighteningly intense.

"Well enough. We'll find her if anyone can."

"Oh, don't worry about that. Byron here is a tracker. We just need you to keep us on the trails."

I cast a doubtful glance at Byron. His pallid skin certainly hadn't seen the sun recently, and his eyes looked watery and weak. Besides, what sort of tracker couldn't follow blazed trails?

Gabriel spoke, and the skeptical tone in his voice revealed that he shared my misgivings. "Well, we'll take point, and your man can show us anything we missed. Do you know how long until the other volunteers get here?"

"No other volunteers. This'll just be us."

"Impossible!" Gabriel said. "Do you understand what size we're talking about here? Over fifteen square miles. More to the point for our method of progress, almost fifty million feet. You know how little space a fallen human takes up? Even with a hundred people, this would be a crapshoot, and you want to do it with four?"

Davis wasn't listening. He had turned to Byron and was unrolling a long leather cloth, the sort of thing an old-timey craftsman might have kept his tools in. This one just contained dozens of what looked like white toothpicks, each carefully pinned to the leather beneath an emblazoned number.

He selected one of the toothpicks and held it out to Byron. "Smell it."

"I know her," Byron said, turning his face away.

"Smell. It." The threat of violence was clear in Davis's clipped words. Reluctantly, Byron leaned forward and smelled the proffered sliver. He closed his eyes as he inhaled deeply. Weirdly, I saw a bit of drool gather at the edge of his mouth before he licked it away.

With his eyes still closed, Byron pointed. "There."

Gabriel and I both turned to look, but he was just pointing at a random tree. Davis seemed satisfied, though.

"Come on, let's go." He rolled up his toothpick collection as he headed for the woods, Byron close behind.

Neither Gabriel nor I followed. After a few steps, Davis stopped and looked back. "Daylight's burning. Shake a leg."

"You want us to follow you into those woods based on some sort of psychic nonsense?" said Gabriel. "Absolutely not."

"I don't care if you believe me," said Davis. "I only care that you come with me. If you stay here, you won't have a job by the time I hit those trees. And you'll drastically reduce the chances of us finding our missing person alive."

The matter-of-fact manner in which Davis delivered the ultimatum made it clear that it wasn't a threat. He was simply stating what would happen. Given the resources that had been mobilized to bring him here, I had no reason to doubt it.

Gabriel and I exchanged an unhappy look and started forward.

We hadn't gotten more than a hundred feet down the path when we heard the helicopter starting up behind us.

"Is he going to go search from the air? Not much to be seen through these trees, I'm afraid," Gabriel said.

Davis just grunted, his focus on Byron. Byron, for his part, still had his eyes mostly closed. He was moving forward at a steady pace, clearly untroubled by the roots or even trees in his way. Davis steered him gently around the obstacles, guiding him on the path even as Byron kept his head aimed in a direct line to his goal.

"Looks like you two have your shtick down pretty well," Gabriel said. "What do you need us for?"

"To tell us if the paths are wrong," Davis said.

"You seem to have a clear idea of where you're going."

"Not 'wrong' as in 'leading the wrong way.' 'Wrong' as in 'incorrect.'"

"What's that even supposed to mean?" asked Gabriel, aggrieved.

"Stop asking questions and open your eyes. You'll understand when you need to."

We walked along in silence for a while after that. I tried to keep an eye out around me, but my gaze kept drifting back to Byron. He still had his eyes shut, and he was drooling again. He wiped it away as I looked.

"I'm sorry about that," Byron said. It was the first thing he'd said since we'd left the parking lot.

"Sorry about what?" I was five yards behind him and, as mentioned, his eyes were closed. There was no way he was talking about what I'd seen.

"The drool. I can't help it. I don't notice it a lot of the time, but I notice when others are looking."

"How could you possibly know I was looking?"

"I know," said Byron.

Gabriel snorted. "Got eyes in the back of your head, huh?"

"Something like that."

"How many fingers am I holding up?"

"Four," said Byron. I looked back at Gabriel and saw him holding up four fingers. He appeared as surprised as I was.

"One. Five," said Byron, responding as Gabriel raised and lowered fingers. He never paused in his forward movement. Davis regarded the entire situation with detached amusement.

Gabriel grunted and moved his hand behind my back, completely hidden from Byron.

"None. Four again. One," said Byron.

I could no longer see the number of fingers, but from Gabriel's reaction, Byron was still guessing correctly.

"How are you doing this?" I asked.

"I'm good at knowing where—things are," Byron said, with a slight but noticeable pause before the word 'things.'

"Enough games," said Davis. "Eyes on the surroundings."

"If you're so sure Byron knows where she is, why do we need to keep an eye out?" asked Gabriel. Davis ignored him.

We'd gone a couple of miles when I noticed Byron starting to flag. As I'd expected, he wasn't built for sustained walking.

"Hey Byron, when's the last time you had some water?" I asked, unlimbering my backpack. "Something to eat?"

"No!" shouted Davis.

Byron whipped around, his eyes squeezing shut so tightly they were nearly crushed in their sockets. His skull seemed to pulse under his thin skin. His teeth were bared, and saliva ran freely from his mouth, cascading down his chin in a terrifying gush.

He took a single step toward me and something white flared on the side of his neck, bright enough to shine through the tall collar that had previously hidden it. It was no shape or symbol I recognized, but whatever it was had an immediate effect on Byron.

His eyes flew open. His jaw snapped shut. He stumbled and would have fallen if Davis hadn't caught him.

"Easy," said Davis. "Easy. You still got her?"

"Yes." Byron swallowed thickly. "Yes."

He resumed moving forward, his eyes mostly closed again. Over his shoulder he said, "I would like some water, if you don't mind."

I tossed the bottle to Davis. Staying a few feet away from Byron felt prudent.

We walked on in silence for a while, listening to the sounds of the forest. Gabriel was staring at Byron as if convinced that he could sort out his sightless vision trick through sheer force of will. For my part, I looked anywhere but at the tracker. His reaction to the offer of food had shaken me in a way that I couldn't recall ever happening before. I'd faced down bears and hadn't ever felt afraid for my life on such a fundamental level.

Maybe it was because I was paying extra attention to the path that I started to notice the small oddities. Small things at first, like the path going straight ahead for too long. Nothing anyone new to the park would notice, but like I said, I know these trails. They twist and curve wherever the landscape leads them, and the terrain here is anything but straight.

Every time I was about to remark on it, though, we'd come up on another curve. I told myself that I was just imagining things, and I kept quiet about it. The honest truth is that I really didn't want to do or say anything that would bring Byron's attention back to me. He'd been nothing but quiet and complacent since the incident, walking calmly ahead while Davis kept him from running into obstacles, but my heart rate was still higher than our activity level implied and I couldn't get his feral transformation out of my mind.

Then I saw something that I couldn't let pass without comment. "Gabriel! Look. That's Jeroboam."

The tree I was pointing at was an impressive sight, with a trunk twice as thick as my outstretched arms and branches that seemed to climb up into the sky itself. It was the oldest tree in our park, predating the founding of our country by a few hundred years.

Gabriel barely glanced at it. "So?"

"So? Where did we come in? There's no way we're at Jeroboam."

"There's some way," said Gabriel, nodding his head at the giant tree. "Here it is. Here we are. QED."

Davis, strangely, was much less dismissive. He halted Byron with a firm hand on his shoulder. "Stop. You're certain?"

"Positive. We would have had to diverge a half-mile back to get to Jeroboam."

"Don't be stupid," said Gabriel.

"Shut up," Davis told him. Gabriel closed his mouth out of surprise. "Byron?"

"We're close. Under a mile. Stationary. Crouched down. Either hiding or asleep."

"Let's hope for the latter," said Davis. To me he said, "I want you to look down at the path for the next ten or twenty steps. Focus on where you know we are. Don't look at anything other than your feet and the ground in front of you."

Confused, I did as he said, counting my paces. I was at fourteen when I heard Gabriel swear.

"The tree's gone! I was looking right at it, and it's different trees now!"

I looked up. Jeroboam was indeed gone.

"Good work," said Davis. I had no idea what I'd done, but I was glad that whatever it was had been successful. "Now, stay on your guard. She's twisting things. Even with Th—with Byron here, it's going to get tricky."

Byran opened his eyes long enough to glare at Davis, presumably for whatever he'd almost said in place of "Byron." Davis met his glare with a challenging stare of his own, and after a moment, Byron closed his eyes again and continued forward.

After that, the paths started to get weird. There wasn't any other word for it. They curved in ways that should have led us around in circles. We started to see the same tree repeatedly, though not always on the same side of the path. Once, I looked over my shoulder and saw Gabriel, Davis and Byron following me, although when I looked back, they were still there ahead of me.

Each time it happened I'd drop my focus to the path in front of me, looking at nothing but the dirt and leaves directly under my feet as I stepped forward. After a dozen steps, I'd look back up and the trail would behave again—for a little while, and then I'd be back to staring at the ground. I started to feel like Byron, walking without seeing, following the path that I knew was there.

"A hundred yards," said Byron. He swallowed, a sound so wet that I heard it clearly from twenty feet away. "Still not moving."

"She's not dead, is she?" asked Davis.

"I would know if they were dead," said Byron.

"They?" asked Gabriel. "Thought we only had one missing hiker here."

"Two hundred and six," said Byron dreamily. He laughed, then licked his lips.

"Focus," snapped Davis. "Sounds like we lucked out. She's asleep."

He looked at me and Gabriel and sighed. "I think we ought to split up, come at her from two directions. It'll pin her in place if she wakes up."

"You're sounding like she doesn't want to be found," said Gabriel.

Davis ignored this comment and pointed to me. "You, go with Byron. Don't let him walk into any trees. You, come with me."

"Let Gabriel go with Byron," I pleaded.

"No."

I wasn't usually so easily cowed, but something about Davis's tone brooked no argument. I reluctantly moved up behind Byron and put a hand on his shoulder. There was no fat at all on him, and barely any muscle. Through the fabric, it felt like I had laid my hand on bare bone.

"Not far now," said Byron. He stepped off of the trail, and I attempted to guide him back. "No, no. It's okay now. They're just up ahead."

The trees stretched and warped around us, reaching and changing overhead. Byron moved on in steady steps and I guided him between the dancing trunks, gripping him as much for my own safety as his. I was terrified to be lost in this writhing forest.

Suddenly, there was a young woman ahead of us, curled up among the spreading roots of a tree. She wore a drab grey jumpsuit marked with the number 60 in several places. Her face was hidden by a wild tangle of black hair, and she did indeed appear to be asleep.

"Wake up!" Byron hissed. At the sound, the woman startled awake, fear in her eyes. "Hurry! They fo—"

"*Still*," said Davis, or something like it. The word he said was not that, but it meant that, in a deep and primordial sense. A symbol blazed black out of a nearby tree, and suddenly Davis was lifting a knife away from carving it, as if he had always been there.

I did not have the ability to consider how he had gotten there, or when. I was focused on the fact that I could not move my body, not even to blink my eyes or draw breath. Byron and the woman appeared similarly afflicted, and even the trees had stopped moving—both their unnatural twisting and their normal rustling.

"You'd been doing so well, Thirty-One," said Davis. He walked toward us, moving normally. I struggled for breath, black spots starting to dance in my vision. "Only to spoil it all right at the end. Well, it was a good experiment, in any case. You'll obviously need more safeguards to be allowed out in the future.

"And you, Sixty." Davis turned his attention to the woman on the forest floor. "We've already fixed up your escape route. Your new cell has angles even you can't distort. You won't be getting out again."

My vision began to narrow, darkness closing in. My lungs wanted to heave, but even that motion was denied to me.

"I'm sorry to leave things like this," Davis said to me. "You'll be all right once the sigil fades. Accept what you're told happened today, and things will work out well enough. Don't dwell too much on what you think you remember. Memories are faulty things."

That was the last thing I heard before I blacked out. When I woke up, only a few minutes had passed, but Davis, Byron and the woman were nowhere to be seen. The tree that had held his sigil was nothing but a pile of cold ashes. There was no sign of other fire damage anywhere around it.

Gabriel was missing as well. I shouted for him to no avail, and eventually I gave up and made my way back to the trailhead, hoping to find him at the jeep.

He was not there, nor was he back at the ranger station. His cell phone went straight to voicemail.

The governor called later that day to thank us for the safe return of his sister, and promised anything we wanted in return. I told him that Gabriel was missing.

"Do you need helicopters? Dogs? Say the word, and I'll send them."

"We could use the tracker you sent earlier," I said.

"Tracker?" He sounded confused. "I'm sorry, I have no idea what you're talking about."

I didn't take him up on the helicopters or the dogs. I did look for Gabriel, for days afterward, but I was unsurprised not to find him. The ones who are truly lost, off-the-trail lost—we very rarely find them. And I had the feeling that Gabriel, wherever he was, was farther off the trail than anyone had ever been before.

PASSIVE

The house is burning. Only two of us made it out. There were six at the start of the evening. Seven, I suppose. That was the entire problem.

I don't know when the seventh arrived. Deena and Angelo showed up first, while I was still putting out snacks. It must not have been there before them. I recall them being the first. It can't hide in nothing.

Kay showed up next. I know she was alone, because I've been trying to figure out the right time to ask her out. If she'd brought someone, I definitely would have noticed.

When Christof and Marina got here, Angelo called out, "It's about time you two made it!" He specified two, I remember that. That's five arrivals, and of course I was there all along. Maybe the door was opened at some other point.

It might not matter now that it's all over. I feel like it does, though. I need to understand what happened. I owe it to my friends.

We were playing cards when we noticed. It was a six-handed game, and Angelo was dealing piles in front of each player. One, two, three, four, five, six, and the seventh to himself.

"You've got too many piles," Deena said.

Angelo looked at the table in confusion. There were cards in front of each of us. There were seven separate stacks.

"Weird. I don't know what happened there," he said, gathering up the cards. He dealt them out again. One, two, three, four, five, six. One to each person, but he had not yet put a card in front of himself.

With a nervous chuckle, Angelo said, "Okay, what am I doing wrong? Six of us, yes?"

We all agreed. There were clearly six.

"Everyone put your hand on your card," he said.

All six cards were covered. Angelo still did not have one.

"All right, one more try," said Angelo.

"While you're sorting this out, I'm going to go to the bathroom," said Kay, standing up. She left the room. Angelo dealt the cards. One, two, three, four, and a fifth to himself.

"Kay, how many people are you?" he shouted.

"Very funny," she called back. We heard the bathroom door close.

"Just deal six hands," I told Angelo. "There are six of us. It'll work out. Everyone will pick one hand up and play it, and no one will be left out."

"You'd really think so," he said. "But why was I getting to seven before?"

"You're bad at math," Deena told him.

"Better not let you keep the score," Christof chimed in.

Kay's chair was scooted back up to the table. Angelo dealt the cards. There were six hands this time. Everyone picked one up. No one was left out.

"Weird," said Angelo, shaking his head.

Despite the rocky start, the game went well. Christof won, so as punishment we sent him to the kitchen to fetch more drinks. Just after he disappeared into the other room, I heard a startling noise, a sort of quick choking gasp followed by a loud bang. I was just getting up to see if he was all right when the wine was brought to the table, and I busied myself pouring everyone a fresh glass instead.

I noticed that Kay's glass was still untouched from earlier.

"Hey, where's Kay?" I asked.

"She went to the bathroom," said Deena.

"What, again?"

"I guess."

I leaned my head around the corner to see down the hallway. The bathroom door was closed. I supposed Marina was right.

"Shall we deal another hand?" I asked.

"As soon as Christof gets back," said Marina.

I looked around. Christof wasn't here.

"Where did he go?"

"The kitchen," said Marina.

"The wine didn't bring itself in here," I pointed out. "And all five of the new glasses have been moved."

Marina gasped. "Are you suggesting that someone—is drinking Christof's wine?"

We all laughed. I did wonder where Christof was, though. And Kay, for that matter. She'd been in the bathroom for a very long time.

She couldn't have been, though. We'd played the game six handed. She must have been here. Maybe she just wasn't drinking.

"Quick round of spades while we're waiting for those two to get back?" asked Angelo, dealing out the cards.

"You've dealt five hands," Deena pointed out.

Angelo slammed the cards down on the table. "Okay, something is going on here! Everyone, hold hands."

We all looked at him quizzically, but he was serious. We reached out and took each other's hands, forming a circle around the table.

"Now, in order. Everyone say the name of the person to your left."

My name was said. I looked left and said, "Marina."

"Deena."

"Angelo."

"And I'm next to Scott," Angelo said, nodding at me.

"Wait," I objected. "My name was already said."

"Let's go to the right," he said.

Angelo's name was said. He followed it with "Deena."

"Marina."

"Scott."

"And Angelo," I said.

"No, I was named first," he said.

We looked at each other. I could feel his hand in mine. I could see him next to me.

"Look at the table," Angelo said. "Why is there an extra glass of wine in between us?"

"Let's take a photo," said Marina. "Then we can see everyone at once."

She put her phone on the table. We all backed up, put our arms around each other and smiled. The photo snapped. We gathered back around the table to look.

"It's you, me, you and you," said Marina, pointing. "Four of us. No one else."

Angelo studied it for a moment. "It's not a selfie. Who took the picture?"

"Christof," said Marina.

"Kay," I said in the same moment.

We all looked around the room. Neither one of them was here.

"He must still be in the kitchen," said Marina. "I'll go see."

"I think we should all go together," said Angelo. "Come on."

We entered the kitchen as a group. It was empty.

"Do you smell gas?" asked Deena.

My attention snapped to the stove. Two of the knobs for the burners were snapped off. I spotted them tucked under the cabinets nearby, as if someone had pushed them out of the way so as not to be noticed. There was a dent in the metal of the edge, too.

"Christof must have dropped something on the stove," I said, heading over to see about turning off the gas. "Nice of him to mention it."

The knobs were broken too far down to turn. The gas was starting to give me a headache. I grabbed hold of the stove to pull it out from the wall and shut off the line behind it, but it was surprisingly heavy.

"Did I leave something in here?" I asked, opening the oven door.

Christof's body was crammed inside, the limbs bent and folded back on themselves in order to make it fit. A gory pool of blood filled the bottom of the oven, sloshing distressingly back and forth from my attempts to move the appliance. Most of it seemed to have come from his head, which had been violently crushed. His eyes bulged outward, staring at me.

I screamed, of course. We all did. I turned away—to run, to find a weapon, possibly just not to see it anymore—and Deena died.

Her throat was ripped open. It wasn't when I turned back, and then it was. Nothing did it. It just happened. Her hands flew up to clasp her ruined neck, but it was far too late to hold anything in. She collapsed to her knees. Her hair was held back as she died, keeping her upright and facing forward so we could all see the panic and despair.

We were all frozen for a second. Angelo moved first, diving for her, but by the time he wrapped his arms around her she was slumping forward, already gone. He screamed, a raw caterwaul of rage and pain. After a moment, he focused it into words.

"Where is it? What did this?"

I grabbed a knife and put my back into a corner, looking around frantically. Marina was gone. I hoped that she had run. I didn't like that I didn't know.

"It's been here all night," Angelo hissed. "Among us. Playing with us. Where's Kay? Where has she been all night?"

The bathroom, I thought, but I pictured Christof's broken body in the oven, and I knew that I did not want to open the door to check.

Angelo continued his rant, his voice cracking in his fury. "We can't see it. We can't know about it. You and I thought we were holding hands when it was between us. This is all a game to it. We don't know how to play. We can't even see the board!"

"We've got to get out, Angelo," I said. "It's not safe to be in here. Even without whatever's happening, the stove's still leaking gas."

"It is," he said, and his voice was suddenly eerily calm. "Everywhere. And you know, that's an awfully good way to deal with something you can't see."

"What are you doing, Angelo?"

He fumbled in his pocket and pulled out a lighter. "The back door's right there, Scott. Run, and close it behind you. Don't stop running when you're outside."

"Angelo—!"

"I'm sorry about your house, Scott. Run."

I took a step toward him, but he pulled the lighter in toward his body. "Go. If you don't go now, I'll do it while you're still in here. I probably ought to anyway. It's a better way to be sure."

He flicked the lighter. It sparked. I fled for the door. Behind me, I could hear him flicking the wheel again.

I made it outside before the kitchen exploded. I had my hand on the knob pulling the door shut, when a roar of heat and light slammed the door closed and flung me down the stairs onto my back lawn. The windows erupted in gouts of flame, pelting me with burning hot glass.

I scrambled along the grass, desperate to get further away. My back was burning, and I rolled to put it out.

The house is clearly a loss, but I called the fire department anyway. I didn't know what else to do. I don't know what I'll tell the police when they find the bodies inside. I don't even know how many they'll find.

If Angelo got it, whatever it was, then there'll be at least four bodies. Him, Deena, Christof and the other. Probably five, assuming it got Kay early on. Maybe six, if Marina didn't make it out.

One of them must have, though. I'm not alone out here.

My hand is held tightly as I watch the house burn.

THERE'S SAFETY IN CIRCLES

When I was a baby, I had a mobile that hung over my crib. I remember the shapes, the circles with their patterns of dots and the wires connecting them to each other. It had a motor that made the branches swing around, and the circles would twinkle and wink in the moonlight that came in through my window at night. That mobile is one of my earliest memories, maybe even my first. I can remember lying there looking up at it and feeling warm, safe, and content.

As soon as I was old enough to start holding a marker, my parents taught me to draw the circles. They'd hold my fat little hand and help me trace the loops over and over. I learned their patterns before I learned the alphabet. I could draw the circles in perfect curves long before I could write my own name.

My mother made up names for the circles, silly things to help a child understand them. There was Chubby, the collector. He was the big one, with the little families inside. Three circles in a little triangle, for mommy, daddy and me. One big circle on the far side of Chubby's tummy, for love. And three little circles outside on sticks, for body, mind and soul—if there was time. They were important, but not as important as the major circles. They didn't do as much.

Below Chubby was little Oliver. He was plain, just a little circle with a tiny baby circle right in the middle. He was called Oliver because he looked like he was saying "Oh!" My mother would always make a surprised face when she told me this, with her eyes open wide and her mouth in a little tiny O. I always giggled. I liked Oliver.

And off to the side of both of them was Jerry, the joiner. Jerry had a double wall, and double lines connected him to both Chubby and Oliver. He had three dots inside in a diagonal line, for ready, set, go! The "go" dot was circled, to make him go. He had a chair, a quarter arc outside of him that he could sit in while he did his work. Like Chubby's little stick circles, the chair was only if there was time. Jerry liked his chair, but he didn't need it.

When I outgrew my crib, my parents bought me a real bed and retired the mobile. They painted the circles on my wall, and I got to paint little Oliver. I labored over that simple circle for an hour to make sure it was right, and when I was done, it looked every bit as good as the ones my parents had done. It might have just been two simple little circles, but I was incredibly proud that my parents didn't even have to go over my lines to straighten them out.

I was eight when my dad died. Still young enough to think of him as daddy, but old enough that mom was willing to tell me a little bit about what had happened. She told me that daddy had been caught outside of the circles, and he hadn't been able to draw them in time. She told me that I couldn't tell anyone that he was gone, and that we were going to have to move. The way I understood it at the time was that the circles weren't working anymore, and we needed new ones. While my mother painted over every wall of the house with plain white paint, covering up all of the old circles, I laid on the living room floor and drew two dozen new sets. Chubby with his families, surprised little Oliver and Joiner in his chair. I drew big ones on posterboard to hang on the walls, and little ones on post-it notes to carry with us.

I asked my mom if Chubby still needed three circles since daddy wasn't coming back, and tears spilled from her eyes as she explained that daddy was always with us in the circles, that was part of what they did for us. They would always keep us safe, even after we were gone. I don't know if she actually believed that or if she was just saying it to make me feel better, but I believed it at the time, and it helped.

We moved to a new town, another small town, and I made new friends. I didn't want any of my friends to be caught outside of the circles, so I started drawing copies for everyone I met. I knew I wasn't allowed to explain the circles to anyone, so I just told them that it was a design I liked. My teacher asked if I wanted to be an artist when I grew up, and I said yes.

As I grew older, I learned that giving everyone the same geometric design was weird, and that kids would talk about me behind my back. Kids stopped taking the circles from me, but I still wanted them to have protection, so I started incorporating them into other pictures. I'd draw alien solar systems, waves topped with sea foam, marbles in a bucket—anything where I could hide my circle design. Everyone still thought I was weird, but artsy weird is better and more interesting than just regular weird, so it was okay. I'm sure that most of the kids tossed the drawings at the end of the day, but I felt better knowing that the circles were out there.

Mom died when I was seventeen. I'd expected it by then—not when it happened, of course, but I knew that it would happen some day. She'd explained everything to me once she decided I was mature enough to handle it. Dad had died on a farm, shot by a farmer. He'd been in control of himself enough to stay away from people, which Mom was proud of him for. When the farmer heard the frantic lowing of the cows and came running with his gun, Dad had tried to flee rather than kill him. The farmer shot him in the back, killing him.

I was furious at the farmer when I first learned this, but Mom told me not to be. The farmer was just defending his land, and Dad had done right to give up his life rather than take the farmer's. We are born to die violently, she told me. We can delay it, but we cannot prevent it. And in the end, our greatest triumph will be how few people we've hurt before we fall.

Dad was only twenty-five when he died. Mom made it almost to forty. It was bad luck, a pileup of really lousy events. She had gone out of town for work, a weekend business conference. On the way back, the bus broke down, smoke billowing from the engine and filling up the passenger compartment. The bus driver ordered everyone off, and Mom couldn't find her purse. Someone had taken it, by accident or on purpose. It had her traveling circles in it, her protection.

She tried to sketch them in the ground outside, but everyone was confused and milling about, and they kept stepping on her diagram. Frantic, she started drawing on the side of the bus, but the bus driver yelled at her and came running over to stop her. Realizing it was too late, Mom snatched a cell phone from another passenger's hand and sprinted off into the woods.

I know some of this from talking to people who were on the bus, and some from the final phone call I got from her. It was an unknown number, and I didn't pick it up, so I only heard the voicemail later.

"Honey. I love you. Everything's gone wrong and I'm caught outside the circles. I need you to come find me. I need you to make me safe."

It took weeks, but I tracked her down in the woods. She hadn't even managed a partial circle, not like Dad, and she'd been lost longer. I trapped her like a common animal, and I killed her there in the woods. I buried her along with the hikers she'd found, and all of their equipment. On the top of the grave, I picked out the circles in pebbles, then topped it all with a huge flat rock, sealing the circles beneath. It was only symbolic; the curves were broken and the lines didn't match, but I had to mark it somehow for my own sake.

I packed up the house that time. I didn't tell anyone she had died. I sold the house and moved, forging her signature on anything that needed it. When I got to a new town, I told everyone that I was twenty-two and fresh out of college. Some folks have asked about my parents, but when I tell them I'm an orphan, they don't pry further.

I live alone now. I tattooed the circles on my stomach, and I thought I'd found a way to beat it, so that I'd never be caught outside of the circles. But skin is a shifting, unreliable thing, and I can't depend on those lines. I realized that when I started to have dreams. Nothing solid, nothing definite, just flashes of hunger and bone and fear. I'd wake up with the smell of blood in my nostrils, my jaw clenched, my hands knotted into fists. When I painted the circles on the door to my house, that all went away again.

I used to wonder why my parents even had a child. Don't get me wrong, they were great parents. They were good to me; they raised me well. They loved me. But they knew what they were bringing into the world and what that meant. And for a long time, I wondered why they were willing to do a thing like that.

The thing is, though, even with what I am, with how I know things will end eventually, I'll never end it. I'll never kill myself. I like living. I have friends, a good job, freedom. I like being alive. And that means that at some point, someone's going to have to put me down. I can't blame my parents for not wanting to trust that to a stranger.

Living is good. Living with a mate would be even better. I think it's time to go exploring, to find someone else to share my circles. And in the end, I hope I'll have someone who will do what needs to be done, and make sure that I die in a way that would make my parents proud.

DARKNESS FOR DARKNESS

Both parents bolted awake at the cry of terror from their son's room. Their adrenaline-fueled fear shifted into exasperated anger when they made out the words: "Monster! Monster!"

Grousing, the father lurched out of bed and pulled on a robe. "That kid. I swear."

"Don't yell at him, honey." The screams were continuing and growing even more shrill.

"I thought it was a real problem. You know, like I'm going to have when I fall asleep at work tomorrow." He shuffled down the hallway and pushed open the door to his son's room. "Okay, wha—"

He froze mid-sentence, his mouth hanging open in shock. His son was crouched in a corner of the room next to his paltry night light, pressing himself against the wall hard enough to crack it. Tears poured from his face as copiously as the blood from his torn ankle, but the boy seemed not to notice either one.

"Monster!" he gibbered, pointing frantically toward his bed. His panicked brain had no room left for any other concepts. "Monster!"

There was no other word for it. Something utterly inhuman was attempting to pull its way free from under the bed, clawing desperately at the shadows of the room. It moved in a snarl of teeth and rage. It looked, not like a nightmare, but like the very concept of nightmares itself. It was built of fear made sharp and weaponized, and it was coming closer with every passing instant.

In shock and terror, the man almost closed the door. Almost, he left his son to face the horror alone. Then an instinct almost as deep as self-preservation roared up to defend his family, overriding his traitorous right arm and shouldering the door fully open.

The thing could not exist in the light. It did not flinch back as the hallway light flooded the room. It simply was no longer in those spaces. And the man was directly next to the switch that controlled the lights for the room.

One flick, one instant, and it was gone. For a brief second it poured out of the crack in the closet door, infinite eyes dripping to the ceiling as claws scored the woodwork, but the father ripped the door open to reveal nothing but clothes and piles of toys.

He ran to his son, scooping him from the floor, heedless of the blood and urine now soaking his robe. He screamed for his wife as he ran for the front door of the house, only to stop dead as he saw the night peering in from outside. The dark, forbidding night.

His wife found him huddled in the hallway beneath the chandelier, cradling their crying son.

"What happened? What was it? Is he okay? What happened to his ankle?"

Her husband answered none of her rapid-fire questions. His gaze was fixed on the chandelier. One of the bulbs was burned out. He seemed unable to tear his eyes away.

The scene was playing out all across the city. 911 was alive with calls. The hospitals were flooded with people nearly catatonic with shock, except that they screamed endlessly if they were taken away from the light.

Gunfire sounded as police were dispatched. They had not even made it out of the station parking lot. Something disjointed was creeping under the cars, scuttling from shadow to shadow. In the flash of the gun muzzle, it was not there, but the darkness flowed with fangs as soon as the brief light passed.

Floodlights blazed, and the lot was empty except for panicked policemen. Those who had not seen it questioned their colleagues' sanity. Those who had seen it knew that it was more real than any terror they had ever experienced before.

All around the city, lights sprang to life in houses and apartment buildings. Even the offices downtown lit up as night workers flipped switches in fear, desperate to expand the areas of light around themselves. The central power station, unprepared to cope with the unprecedented load, stuttered and failed. In a horrifying cascade, the city went dark.

Chaos erupted. Families fled to their cars for the safety of the dome lights, only to see razor fingers whispering at them from inside of the air vents. Wisps of agony brushed across their heels from beneath the seats. Many drivers crashed, unwilling to put their feet down long enough to operate the brakes. Car horns blared from hundreds of wrecked vehicles, adding to the discord.

Fires began to burn as thousands of panicked citizens all feverishly sought any source of light. Even those fortunate enough to have fireplaces did not make use of them, unwilling to lean in beneath whatever terrors might stretch down from the blackness of the chimney. Furniture was set alight: sofas, armchairs, anything that would catch fire easily.

Unfortunately, the fires produced more than light. The burning substances gave off a thick black smoke that roiled with torment and bones as the shadow monster tried to pull free. Those who had set the fires fled, leaving them to spread and consume entire houses, even neighborhoods.

There were too many for the firefighters to stop, even had they been allowed to. Instead, the responders were attacked as they began to spray down the fires, beaten and bludgeoned for reducing the light. They retreated to safety as the flames raged. A pall began to form over the city, a grey film that blotted out the stars and tasted of graves.

Darkness spread. The monster occupied every shadow, every sunken doorway, every alley. It ripped from ten thousand locations at once, bursting forth in a pustulant, tarry tide. It tore through metal and stone as easily as flesh, leaving shrieking devastation in its wake. Nothing stopped or even slowed it except for the light. It could not be where the light was, but it was everywhere else.

The monster poured forth as the city cowered before it. It was the promised loss at the end of all things. It was the failure of life given rotting flesh. It was fear.

And it was afraid.

It slaughtered heedlessly as it ran, as mindless as any cow in a stampede. It burned through its reserves of energy, stolen and hoarded from billions of human lives across tens of thousands of years, throwing it all away in a frantic attempt to escape. It rammed itself into any space it could find, pulling itself free from every shadow, nails and spikes attempting to anchor itself to reality, to stab into the light itself and tear free of its shadow dimension.

Behind it came something else, something worse. Where the monster fled, he moved calmly, smooth and deadly as a shark. He carved off pieces like a butcher flensing a carcass. He ate the nightmare raw and hungered for more. Every exposed piece was in danger, and to the hunter, everything in the shadow was exposed.

Larger and larger the monster made itself, forcing its way through. It had always before confined itself to flutters in the darkness, slivers seen through darkened forests or distant doors. Now it held nothing back, crashing through every shadow imaginable. As the smoke embraced the city, it reached through the cracks in the skyline itself, looming over the buildings in a terrifying apocalypse. It was tenuous and shot through with holes as various lights stabbed into it, but it drove the smoke before it and used it to blot out the offensive light. It flowed into the city in a cataract, wrapped in darkness and smog, crushing cars beneath its bulk. The city screamed.

It was not enough. Knives stabbed at it from behind, unmaking and unraveling it. The more energy it expended, the more the hunter drew from it. No size was large enough, no space safe.

It wailed, a sound that shattered minds like they were glass. Cornered, it turned to fight, but the hunter was inside of it. It tore away its own substance, and the hunter fed on the damage it did to itself, growing stronger with every cut.

Sinew and tendons and blood fell away beneath the hunter's knives and ravenous mouth. The monster died as it had existed: in terror and darkness. The shadows in the city ceased to pulse with horrible motion. The fires and fear and madness still raged, but the thing that was causing them to spiral was gone.

Elsewhere, a thin, impossible distance away, the hunter flexed his fingers experimentally. He could feel where he needed to be. He was almost strong enough to tear the hole open. Like the beast, it would take everything he had gathered to break through, to make even the tiniest pinprick. But once he had achieved that, he would have it all back and more.

"Home," he whispered, thinking of the limitless energy that awaited him, of what he had once been.

The sound drifted over the city, a soft susurrus that briefly drowned out the sirens and blaring car horns. The moment of deadly calm was, somehow, worse than the noise.

HAPPY BIRTHDAY

Today's my birthday. That's not generally something I bring up. I don't celebrate it. Almost no one knows when it is, and I like it that way.

I don't like being put on the spot. I don't like the falseness of people wishing me a happy birthday because Facebook told them to. The whole thing just feels like an obligation. So, the fewer people who know about my birthday, the better.

All that said, I went out for a birthday dinner treat last night. One of these years, I'll forget about my birthday entirely, and that'll be perfect—but in the meantime, it feels weird to just let it go by like any other day. I didn't invite anyone else along. I didn't make a thing out of it. I just went out for sushi at a place I like that's a bit more expensive than my average.

It was pretty dead in there, which was perfect. I had an entire section of the restaurant to myself. It was just me and a frankly unreasonable quantity of sushi rolls, but I'd ordered while hungry and I was prepared to face my mistakes.

About three-quarters of the way through my food, I was starting to slow down significantly. I was still determined to finish it all, but my hunger had long since been sated and my attention was definitely wandering. That's when I noticed the music that was playing over the restaurant's speakers.

Restaurants always have some kind of music going. It's usually just something inoffensive to serve as background noise, to make it less awkward when conversations stop because everyone's got their mouth full. It's like the music in elevators. It's designed to be bland, something that no one cares about.

Usually, anyway. This song, though, first caught my attention because I thought it might be the tunnel song from *Willy Wonka and the Chocolate Factory*. You know, where the boat's sailing through that psychedelic darkness while Wonka's chanting that weird dirge about how "the rowers keep on rowing"? Super creepy scene.

Anyway, this was sort of like that, though I can't say exactly how. It was discordant, but not unpleasantly so. It was being played on some sort of stringed instrument, but not one I could name. It nipped at the edges of my consciousness, demanding attention. When I finally started actively listening to the song, the words were even stranger than the tune:

every day a gift of time
growing older, aged like wine
a taste for flavor will be fine
we celebrate your birthday

At first, I just thought it was an odd coincidence. It's not like anyone knew I was out for my birthday, and no one in the restaurant was saying anything or paying any attention to me. So, I just wrote it off and kept eating my sushi.

The song didn't end, though. It must have looped somewhere, because it just kept playing. I couldn't make out all of the words, but of those I could, every verse was weirder than the last.

though you may wish it to wait
there's one cause to celebrate
don't you think it's getting late
we celebrate your birthday
taste of blood it may be yours
tearing wishes to their cores
time at last to settle scores
we celebrate your birthday

And on and on like that. It must have gone on for ten minutes or more before the waiter happened by and startled me out of my fascination.

"Can I get you anything else?"

I blinked, trying to refocus on the restaurant around me. "No. No, I'm fine. Hey, is it someone's birthday?"

He looked around at the mostly empty restaurant. Only two tables were filled aside from mine. There was an older couple over against the far wall, and a quartet of teens in the back corner. Neither of these groups looked particularly party-like.

"Not as far as I know. Why?"

I gestured at the ceiling. "The music."

He tilted his head, listening. After a moment, he shrugged. "Yeah, the chef's got it set to some J-pop station. They play all kinds of weird stuff on there."

"Yeah, but—have you listened to the lyrics?"

He shrugged again. "The translations aren't always the best, either."

"Okay, but why is it looping?"

He grinned uncertainly at me, as if I were playing a joke on him. "I don't think it is. I mean, I guess maybe the station could be doing that? I just don't think they would."

"But—" I realized that short of making him stand there for another ten minutes to prove that the song wasn't changing, there wasn't any way to convince him. Also, why did I even care? It was just an odd song. I could solve this by leaving the restaurant.

"If I can get my check, please."

"Absolutely." He bustled away, no doubt glad to be done with our strange conversation.

The song warbled on as I signed the check and gathered up my belongings:

sinew muscle blood and bone
these are things you call your own
but you'll find they're just on loan
we celebrate your birthday

I shouldered my bag and hurried out of the restaurant, the song vanishing as the door closed behind me. Once free from its clutches, I shuddered. Remembering it felt worse than listening to it the first time. The words seemed to slide around in my mind, forming unsettling patterns.

My mind worried at the song like a tongue probing at a loose tooth, rattling it back and forth. I tried to think about something else, anything else, but the song just kept creeping back in. I think I was starting to puzzle out some of the verses I hadn't heard the first time. Certainly the words didn't seem familiar.

born to fight and to compete
do you think that you're complete
walking rotting bags of meat
we celebrate your birthday

The tune jangled in my mind. My mouth ached. I realized I was clenching my jaw and forced myself to relax. The words kept unraveling inside my head, though, spilling out into some sort of bridge. The stress crept back as the lines intensified.

happy day of elevation
looking upward to salvation
reaching far above your station
can't you see the consternation?

dark, foreboding constellation
spells out your determination
but despite your fascination
all will end in ruination
JOYFUL DAY GRATIFICATION
HIDES THE FILTHY DESICCATION

The song was at a fever pitch, shouting in my head. I lurched against a wall and leaned there, letting it hold me up as I frantically dug through my bag. I found my headphones and slammed them into my ears. I pressed play on my phone, not even caring what song I heard.

Through my earpieces came the tinkling string notes of that terrifying birthday song.

far too late now to forget
tiny little mind upset
you'll have time left to regret
we celebrate your birthday

I tore my headphones out and stared at them in horror. My phone claimed it was playing one of the songs from my library, but when I raised the headphone to my ear again, I could hear the birthday song buzzing inside like a struggling insect.

I disconnected the Bluetooth, thinking that maybe something had hijacked my headphones, but I almost dropped the phone when the song started spilling out of its speaker. Frantically, I mashed the stop button.

For a moment, things were beautifully quiet, nothing around me but the sounds of the city, of people going about their lives. Then, like a relentless itch, the song started up in my head again.

you have had your time to grow
enjoyed your little puppet show
come and join us down below
we celebrate your birthday

I shoved my fingers into my ears, as if that would help. I hummed, sang, anything to drown out that taunting song. No matter how much noise I made, though, it was always there, lurking, waiting for a moment of silence to reassert itself.

My apartment had never been so far away. I ran up the stairs when I reached my building, bleating to myself. I burst in the front door, raced down the halls, fumbled my keys into the locks and slammed the door behind me. Grunting, shouting, I ran for the bathroom, for the medicine cabinet.

There, top shelf: the zaleplon I'd been prescribed last year when I was fighting with insomnia. It always knocked me out within minutes. I ripped open the cap and scrabbled for the pills inside.

I threw three into my mouth, then added a fourth one just to be sure. I cupped my hands and gulped directly from the faucet, letting the water wash the pills down into my stomach. For a moment, the rush of the water seemed to drown out the song, and I almost relaxed—until I started to hear plucked strings within the white noise, and I hastily turned the faucet off.

I huddled in bed after that, waiting for the pills to kick in. The song gnawed at my mind, daring me to listen. I fought it with snorts and gasps and swallowing noises. Anything with a pattern, anything with a melody, it could find its way in. I must have sounded like a dying animal, but it kept the song at bay.

At last, I slept. If I dreamed, I don't recall it. It was dark, silent, blissful.

I awoke some time in the middle of the night. My mouth was dry, my body ached, my bladder throbbed. I was still in my street clothes. Half-awake, I stumbled to the bathroom to relieve myself.

As I flushed the toilet, I heard the song again. I plugged my ears, expecting the gesture to be futile, and the song stopped.

Cautiously, I lowered my hands. There it was, soft string notes just above the threshold of audibility, insidious lyrics sneaking their way along. I crouched down, and the volume raised ever so slightly. The song was coming from the sewer.

I left the bathroom and shut the door tightly behind me. Still I could hear the notes, seeming to drift in from everywhere. My kitchen sink echoed with the distant song. The notes dripped gently from the air vents. From outside, unseen singers carried the tune.

no one gets to live forever
though you may be strong and clever
no one has escaped us ever
we celebrate your birthday

I looked outside. From the shadows of trees, bushes and parked cars, shapes shuffled forth. Each one held a candle which only defined the darkness of the creatures holding them. They slowly drew closer, encircling the building, softly singing. When they reached the walls, they began to climb. The candle flames burned before them, drifting upwards as the shadows rose.

come at last where you belong
join our ever-growing throng
sing our never-ending song
we celebrate your birthday

I've tried calling for help. Any number I dial just plays that song at me. If there's anyone on the other end, I can't hear them.

The singers are pressed up against my windows. I can hear them in the hallway, rustling against the door. There's a slow and steady pressure. I just saw the first pane of glass crack.

I think it's time to just let them in. After all, it is my birthday.

Time to celebrate.

THE OLD GRAVE

I've read that your hair and fingernails keep growing after you die. Then again, I've also read that's stupid, and that actually what happens is that your skin contracts, making your hair and nails look longer. That one always seemed more reasonable to me. Dead is dead, after all. You don't keep going after you're dead. You just go in the ground.

I've had a lot of time to think about what happens when you're dead. I used to work in a graveyard, doing groundskeeping stuff. That's everything from mowing the grass to filling in the graves to picking up the trash people leave behind. You'd think people would have more courtesy than to litter in a graveyard, right? But you'd be wrong. People have no respect for others.

It was mainly just me and JR working Ever Rest Hill. It wasn't that big of a place, so the two of us going full time kept it under control. I didn't see him much during the days, since we'd be off at opposite sites trimming the bushes and what have you. But I saw him pretty much every night.

See, me and JR didn't have a lot going for us. The job paid minimum wage, plus a quarter an hour for every year you'd been there. So, JR was making eleven bucks an hour, and I was pulling in just over nine. Take out taxes, and that leaves me pretty firmly in food stamp territory. Heck of a place for a guy with a full-time, no-breaks job to be.

People don't care about each other, like I said. So, when people came to the cemetery to cry over poor dead grandpa or whoever, no one stopped to think twice about whether the guy who kept everything looking nice was doing okay. If I'd screwed up and let vines grow over the grave, I guess they would have thought about me then, and I would've heard about it for sure. But as long as it was all kept up, they were more concerned about the dead than about the living.

But JR, he saw a way to turn that around. You've heard the phrase "you can't take it with you," I'm sure. Doesn't mean people didn't try, though. The way some of these people were dressed, you'd think they were going to a red-carpet gala instead of a hole in the ground. Morticians dressed them to the nines and decked them out in gold and jewels and stuck them in boxes that cost sometimes more than I made in a year. Then it's *boo hoo hoo* at the church, quick trip in the back of a hearse, one last cry at the graveside and boom, the whole thing's under a few tons of dirt never to be seen again.

Mostly never, anyway. See, JR figured that if we could bury them, we could dig them up again just as easy. It's the same backhoe either way, so it's just a matter of whether you're putting dirt in or taking dirt out. And yeah, it was rough the first time we cracked open a coffin. I saw that body lying there all stiff and rotten and I about backed out.

JR, though, he just grinned up at me and said, "Jackpot, man!" Then he held up a watch worth more than my car, and I figured I could just about do this.

After a while, it was easy. It was a real victimless crime, too. We took stuff that nobody ever knew was missing, and it made things a little bit brighter for us. I got a car that could pass inspection without me bringing the mechanic a case of beer. JR got himself a real nice grill, and we'd cook out some nights and toast to our luck. We still weren't getting rich, neither of us, but we weren't going begging either.

Thing is, though, we started to get kind of used to the extra money, and Ever Rest was only so big. We didn't have but so many new people every month, and JR and I were going through them faster than they were coming in.

We started doing stuff to stretch it, to get more value. We cut off fingers when we needed to get rings free. JR started checking the old folks for gold fillings. We even started taking the coffins when they were fancy enough. My plan had just been to strip off the bronze and copper fancy fittings and see what we could get for the metal, but JR went and had a quiet word with the funeral home. Turned out we weren't the only ones looking to make a little extra profit. They bought the coffins off of us at 20% and sold them again at full value. The 80/20 split ticked me off a bit, since we were doing all the work, but JR pointed out that it was way more than we'd get for the metal. So, I shrugged it off and kept going.

Even stretching it like this, though, we kept working our way farther and farther back in the cemetery. The older graves were less likely to have good loot, but when they did, it was a total haul. We'd have to dig up sometimes twenty or thirty graves before we found one that wasn't just bones, but that thirty-first one would be like someone had just dumped a jewelry box onto a skeleton.

That stuff wasn't always easy to sell, though, and so where this used to be a once-in-a-while thing, to get some extra cash, eventually I was seeing JR every night, like I said. We had to keep at it because we never knew what nights would be busts and what nights would be earners. And we went farther and farther back, digging up older and older graves.

We were back in the oldest part of Ever Rest when things went wrong. I'd just dug out the dirt, and was climbing out of the backhoe to hold the light for JR. He was climbing down into the hole to clear away the final dirt and open the lid. He seemed gung ho like always, but as I walked over, something felt wrong.

Fresh graves smell a bit like mud, a bit like rot and a bit like medical stuff, the way hospitals smell. Old graves just smell like dirt. But this smelled like something rank wafting up from the open mouth of a cave, something whispering to your nose about living and dying forever in the dark. It stopped me in my tracks for just a second, and I think that pause saved my life.

JR either didn't smell it or didn't care, because he was down in the grave and prying the boards off of that coffin. I heard the boards crack, and I heard JR say, "The hell?"

Next thing I heard was screaming, an awful blood-curdling yell. "Get it off me!" JR shouted, and I saw his hands scrabbling at the top of the grave. I started to reach for him, I swear I did, but then something dark whipped out of the grave behind him and lashed around one of his hands.

I heard his fingers break as that thing ripped his hand backward, and his screaming pitched even higher. I held my light up as high as I could, and for just a second, I got a clear view of what was in that grave.

The only thing visible of JR was his hand, the one that hadn't been grabbed. That was still reaching for the sky, fingers grasping frantically at nothing. The rest of him was just lost in a tangled, seething mass of bloody, filthy, matted hair.

It was hair, I know it was. I've tried to tell myself it was anything else, some kind of animal or anything, but I know what I saw. It was hair, a giant, writhing ball of it, moving all on its own. It grabbed JR and when it saw me looking, it sent tendrils out to grab me, too.

I yelled and hurled the light at it, and then I did what I had to do. I leaped back into that backhoe, and I shoveled every pound of that dirt exactly back where it had come from. I poured it all back in, slammed it all down tight and then drove the backhoe back and forth over it a few times to be sure. Then I sat there, panting, until my heart settled back down to normal, and I was sure there was nothing moving in that grave beneath me.

I quit the job after that. I worked odd jobs, moved a few times, generally just kept changing stuff about my life until I finally quit waking up with nightmares. I always sort of hoped I'd get to a point where I could tell myself that I'd imagined it all, that maybe I was drunk or high or something. But there's just too much reality in that image of JR's hand desperately reaching out for help, and I don't think I'll ever get it out of my head.

I've been settled down for a few years now. I've got a little one-bedroom apartment that I rent, walking distance from my job at the gas station. It's a nice enough place, and the landlord cares about it, so there aren't a lot of issues.

So, I wasn't real worried when the drain started backing up the other night while I was taking a shower. If it was anything major, I knew he'd be out in a day or so to fix it. But I stuck my fingers in there to feel around, see if I could save him a trip.

I've been in this place for a few years, like I said. I live alone, and I've got short hair. The shower's never backed up before. But what I pulled out of the drain was a thick clog of long, tangled hair.

The shower was backing up again last night. I think it's time to be moving on again.

WITNESS

The date had been going well. Not only was she clever, interesting and pretty, but she was laughing at my jokes and responding in kind. The connection was palpable. We were both enjoying letting it build over the course of the dinner.

Then I felt that old familiar urge. My heart sank.

I pretended to check my phone. "Hey, something's come up."

"What?" Her expression told me that my ruse was transparent. I pressed on regardless.

"This is terrible timing, I know, but I can't put this off. I'm so sorry."

"What's going on? Is everything okay?"

"It's—private. It'll be all right in the end. I have to take care of this now, though."

I stood up to put on my coat. "I'll grab the check. Can I text you tomorrow? I'll explain a little better then."

She nodded, still confused and more than a little annoyed. There was about a fifty percent chance that my apology text tomorrow would go unanswered, I figured. I'd have a story to tell her by then at least. Maybe a drunk friend that I'd had to bail out of jail, or suspicious activity on the home cameras. Something hard to verify and easy to keep controlled. Something that wouldn't come up again later.

Who was I kidding? There wasn't going to be a later for us. Even if she did respond tomorrow, even if I got another date, this was going to happen again sooner or later. I couldn't bring someone else into my life, not in any permanent way. I was called away much too often for that.

I don't know why I have this affliction. I don't think I did any-thing to deserve it. I almost hope that I did; no one should suffer like this for no reason.

I am called to witness violence.

It happens at irregular intervals—sometimes several times a week, occasionally nothing for months. It just began one day when I was out walking. I suddenly felt the need to go to a specific place downtown. It was an odd, insistent desire, and I remember wonder-ing where the abrupt impulse had come from. It wasn't far out of my way, so I decided to indulge my whim and see what was there.

The spot that I reached was an unremarkable intersection, like any of a thousand others in the city. I looked around, trying to see if there was a shop here whose name I had seen on a billboard or something. I could find no reason why this spot was different from any other in the city.

There was a screech of tires. Metal tore and glass shattered. I hadn't seen either car enter the intersection. I didn't know which one had run the red light. All I saw was a dynamic moment of wreckage and blood. One car flipped onto its side, its passenger door bashed in. I saw the driver of the other flung into his wind-shield, his face contorted against its smashed surface.

A horn blared in the aftermath. The windshield wipers of the upright car flicked comically back and forth, as if attempting to clear away the damage. People were already running to help the drivers, but I just stood still in shock, the image burned into my brain.

I couldn't explain what had happened. I didn't know how I had known to be there, or why. It haunted me.

A few weeks later, at home one evening, I felt the need again. It was farther this time, but drivable. The issue was not getting there in time. I could feel that I would be able to. I also felt a deep terror that I was going to see another car accident when I arrived.

I resolved to ignore the urge. I settled deeper into my chair. I turned the volume up on the television. I covered myself with a blanket and arranged a pillow behind my head. I poured myself a glass of wine.

Despite all of these distractions, the itch grew stronger. It was a biological need, something I could no more ignore than the need to go to the bathroom. It grew worse and worse, until finally I flung off the blanket, grabbed my keys and ran to my car.

The sensation did not lessen as I drove. If anything, it grew worse as I could feel myself running out of time. I sped up, racing an invisible clock. I was almost there.

A light in front of me turned yellow. I considered running it. Then it struck me: was I about to *be* the next car accident? I slammed on the brakes, coming to a halt at the light just as it turned red.

Movement in the alley to my right caught my eye. I glanced over in time to see a man stagger back against the wall, hands clutching his stomach. For an instant, I thought he was drunk, until I saw the other man leap forward and stab him again.

I called the police. I hoped they would somehow be in time to help, but the victim had fallen to the ground after the second stab and hadn't moved since. His assailant had long since run off. I steeled myself to go into the alley.

I told myself that maybe I was supposed to help. This could be some kind of a gift, an opportunity to save someone who otherwise wouldn't make it. I hadn't acted at the car accident, but I could now.

It was already too late. He was dead before I ever reached him. I had his blood on me from kneeling next to him and checking his pulse. I didn't want to get back into my car like that, so I just waited next to him, holding his limp hand until the police arrived.

They questioned me and let me go. It was clear I hadn't been involved.

Clear to them, anyway. I was significantly less sure. If I'd ignored the desire to come, would the mugging not have happened? Had I played a part?

I promised myself that whatever this feeling was, I would reject it the next time it came. I remembered the irresistibility of its pull, but I swore I would hold strong.

The opportunity arrived two days later. I was at a table in a restaurant when it came over me. I gritted my teeth and steadfastly stared at my meal.

The feeling ballooned inside of me. I wrapped my fingers tightly around my fork and shoveled in bites of food, trying to tamp it down. I only succeeded in nauseating myself.

It continued to intensify. I felt feverish. I gripped the table to press myself into the chair. My legs burned. There was a sensation of pins and needles all over my entire body.

Then, in an instant, it all stopped. Relief washed over me as I was blissfully returned to myself. I had outlasted it. It could be beaten.

At the same second, back in the kitchen, the fryer exploded.

The cooks burst through the doors, screaming. Thick black smoke billowed out with them, but even through the cloud I could see their horrific burns. Their skin had bubbled and dripped onto their stained shirts. Their hands were bloody claws.

They shrieked for help, but the restaurant was bedlam. People stampeded for the doors, knocking chairs and tables into others' paths as they did. I saw a man trampled underfoot. I tried to help him up, and was nearly knocked down myself. I gave up and ran for the exit like the rest.

The restaurant burned to the ground. Five people died, including the cooks.

I searched the news for the place I should have been. It was a baseball field at a public park, and there had been a scuffle between an enraged parent and an umpire. Punches had been thrown, but that was the worst of it. The parent had gone to the hospital with a broken knuckle from punching the umpire's mask.

This is how it's been for years. I never know what level of violence I'll witness, but if I don't make it there in time, something far worse will happen. The original event will still occur, mind you, so it's not even like I can save whoever's there.

I've tried to lock myself away from everyone, thinking that if there's nothing to see, then nothing can happen. There are many ways to witness, though. I've heard vicious beatings. I've heard people beg for their lives. I've had bullets come through the walls. One time I hid in a sewer tunnel, certain that no one could be nearby to be hurt then. The gas explosion above crumbled the street and dropped eleven bystanders almost on top of me in a violent tumult. I huddled there, trapped, and watched them die in the rubble.

I'm far from unscathed from these incidents. I have scars, burns, broken bones and more. There always seems to be more for me to witness, though. I always walk away.

This time, I have found myself downtown again. It is packed with humanity, thousands upon thousands of people going about their lives. I like watching them in these peaceful moments where nothing is going wrong. I have seen too much death and destruction. I have witnessed too much.

There is a low rumble, a sound rising up from the earth itself. It is all around us. The buildings are starting to sway. The peaceful moment is over, and now the air is filled with panicked shouts. No one knows what to do. People are running for their cars, running from their cars, simply running.

I see it all. Cracks are appearing in the street. A tree is slowly toppling, its roots severed. Windows are shattering. Everywhere, everywhere, the screaming.

Let this be my final witness. Please, let it be done.

WITHIN

Four men sat around the dining room table. Three of them were laughing and joking, easy banter reflecting years of familiarity with each other. Their similarity of looks and tone suggested that they were brothers. The table was bare of food, but their words and manner made it clear that they were content to wait.

The fourth man did not resemble the others, either in looks or in attitude. While they chattered, he only stared hollowly forward, eyes fixed on the window opposite the table. His cheeks were sunken. His skin was sallow. He did not seem to hear the jocularity around him.

At one point, his eyes fluttered shut. He slumped to the table, only to be caught halfway there by the man next to him.

"Careful! You cannot simply lower yourself to the plate. There are words to be said, permissions to be given."

"Besides," added another, "would you fill your own plate before that of your guests?"

All three cackled at this witticism. The emaciated host shook his head slowly back and forth before leaning back against his chair. He still said nothing.

"If you are too tired, this can all end in a moment," said the guest who had caught him. "You know this. You have but to fulfill your obligations as host and we will be on our way."

"I can out-wait you," muttered the man.

"Though it hurts me to disagree with you in your own home, you will find that you cannot. You have perhaps two meals remaining in you, I think. I have become quite a good judge of this. And then we will have a meal in us."

"He has lost hope," said one, studying their host's face. "Determination goes next. And then—the left arm, I think? So, he can still cut the meat."

"The host must serve, of course! We would never presume to take what is not offered. For though it is rude to make guests wait, it does courtesy no service to be rude in return. We are unfailingly polite. We know you will come around."

The doorbell rang. The host's eyes flickered toward the hallway, his missing hope glimmering in their depths. The three guests exclaimed in delight as they piled out of their chairs and charged for the door, jostling to be first to open it.

"Another comes! What charmed lives we lead."

"Shush, brothers. Comportment!" The tallest of the three opened the door. His brothers elbowed in behind him, all three grinning maniacally in anticipation of what was shortly to come.

The man on the front steps was an almost parodically generic white male businessman. He smiled pleasantly as the door was opened, but one eyebrow quirked slightly in surprise.

"Things are not as they seem here," said the new visitor, looking over the three guests with interest. "This is not your house."

"Correct!" beamed the leader. "We have but stopped by for a meal. Our gracious host is unfortunately indisposed, but we will take care of him!"

"Will you, now?" The man on the steps peered past the three brothers in front of him, attempting to see further into the house. He seemed to regard them as no more than obstacles, no more worthy of his notice than a pole blocking his vision at a sporting event.

Nonplussed at the lack of reaction or contribution to the conversation, the leader of the guests pressed on. "Perhaps you would like to bring him a dish to aid in his recovery? Forgive my presumption for the prompt, but we all let our manners slip and need reminding from time to time."

"Speak and I will hear," said the man on the steps. His voice was not loud or resonant, but it settled into the bones like a command. The three brothers took a step backward as one.

From the dining room, the host's voice croaked out weakly: "I, as the duly appointed representative tasked with the preservation of this home and its contents, hereby invite Grey Michael inside."

"Ah," said the newcomer, offering a genuine smile. "You see? I am expected."

Grey Michael stepped into the small space vacated by the brothers. Confused but still anticipatory, they fell back another step. The new arrival nodded politely and closed the door behind himself.

"What an interesting presentation," he said. Previously he had been looking past the three guests, dismissing them as mere impediments. Now that he was inside the house, his gaze was locked on them, studying them. The expression on his face was one with which they were very familiar: hunger.

"You cannot—" began the first brother.

"Did you not hear your host?" Grey Michael cut him off. "I have been invited. Clearly you know the power of such an offer."

The brothers spread out as Grey Michael walked forward. They scattered apart to slowly surround him. He was unperturbed. He walked between their fixed smiles and into the dining room to address the starved man sitting at the table.

"Prepare your defenses now. I am intrigued to see where this goes. I will consume what I have been called here to remove, but I am not fooled."

"Alas, there is little to consume in this house!" called the first brother. He was now leaning casually in the doorway to the kitchen, despite not having moved through the connecting room.

"Tsk." Grey Michael turned his attention back to him. "Such parasitic guests that bring not even a single gift to enrich their host."

"It is the place of the visitor to be treated, not to treat! We do not create the rules. We merely abide by them."

"You take advantage of them," said Grey Michael. "You twist words and abuse intent. You pretend ignorance when it suits you, and insist on compliance from others to the letter of a law that they did not know existed."

Suddenly he was behind the guest, looming out of the darkness in the kitchen to clamp heavy hands onto his shoulders. "My invitation, by comparison, was extended with full knowledge and intent. I will show you the weakness of your paper-thin technicalities."

Grey Michael reached up and seized his captive by the cheek. His fingers punched through skin and muscle, but no blood flowed.

With a vicious pull, Grey Michael ripped the lower jaw away entirely.

With the smile torn from the guest's face, nothing remained. There was no exposed muscle, no writhing tongue. Behind it was pure emptiness, a flowing blackness that dripped from the upper half of his face.

The guest spun away, torn flesh flapping. He attempted to say something, but the words were swallowed up by the void. He retreated back through the dining room to the safety of his brothers. They were no longer smiling either. All three crouched, preparing for a fight.

"I will show you," Grey Michael said. "You will see the error of assuming you are the largest monster in the night. But you will not have a chance to learn from this mistake."

The lead guest hissed something past his curtain of darkness. All three brothers leapt to attack.

They moved as a pack, fanning out around the dining room to split their opponent's focus. One took cover behind the table, while another sprinted up the wall, lightning fast. The leader charged directly at Grey Michael, but it was only a feint, a distraction to catch his eye.

The one who had run up the wall vanished, disappearing between scurrying steps to reappear behind Grey Michael's legs. He struck out with clawed fingers, raking deep furrows from calf to ankle. An unearthly cry rang out as fabric and skin split, letting billowing blackness spill forth—for Grey Michael was no longer there, and it was his own brother's legs he had torn open.

"Little famines," said Grey Michael, seated calmly at the far side of the table. "You are too driven by your hunger. I understand your need, but if—"

All three brothers were suddenly at the table, hands seizing cutlery and plates to fill the air with a vicious barrage. Even as the missiles leapt from their hands, though, the lights shut off and the room was plunged into darkness. Despite the open curtains around the picture window, no light penetrated the room. Odder still, there was no sound of the thrown objects landing. The brothers could hear themselves panting, but nothing else.

"—if," Grey Michael's voice suddenly sounded from all around them, "you are not the master of your need, then you are merely a slave to it."

The lights blazed back to life. The brothers and their host were alone in the room. The table was set as if they had not touched a thing.

The window had become a mirror. So had both of the open doorways. Each showed a reflection of the dining room instead of the space that should have existed beyond. Through the doors and windows in those mirrored spaces, the dining room reflected endlessly.

As the brothers looked around, they became aware of a distant screaming. Far off in the most distant reflections, things were beginning to go dark. Door by door, window by window, their images screamed, ran and were snuffed out.

The destruction grew closer. The source became clear. Unhurried, unbothered, Grey Michael stepped methodically through each doorway and window and ripped each room's occupants to shreds. He tore them limb from limb and crammed each piece into his distended jaw, somehow even managing to make this ungainly act look casual. As each trio died, the image of Grey Michael consumed the lights and set his sights on the next passageway closer.

The brothers fled, or tried to. The mirrors were implacable beneath their flailing fists, showing only their equally panicked reflections smashing back against them, each as desperate to escape as the other. They hurled chairs and even the table, but were unable to create even the tiniest chip in the impassable surfaces before them. And still Grey Michael advanced.

At last he stood before them, tearing the last chunk of darkness from their final reflections to feed his insatiable appetite. From three directions he looked at them, staring pitilessly from doors and window. The brothers flinched together at the center of the room, each trying to hide behind the others, wondering which image was the true one and from which direction he would attack.

Grey Michael stepped through all three portals at once. The barrier that had imprisoned the brothers was not even an inconvenience to him. Each of his three selves seized a different one of the guests, fingers sinking in to fix a hold. Then, as one, they ripped the brothers apart.

Although it looked like a feeding frenzy, Grey Michael moved more methodically than any shark. The brothers stayed alive even as pieces were ripped from their bodies, their hands and legs and even torsos torn away. They died only when there was nothing left to consume. Their eyes were the very last thing to go, forced to watch as Grey Michael ate everything that they were.

When the very last bite was gone, Grey Michael was one again. The other two copies did not vanish. They simply ceased to have ever been there. The window looked out upon a quiet suburban street again, and the doorways led to a hallway and a kitchen. Grey Michael straightened his suit and turned to his host.

To his surprise, he found the man dead. There was no mark upon him. He was simply slumped on the floor, fallen where the brothers had stolen his chair in their doomed attempt at escape. His chest was still. The room was silent. There was no life within it.

"Unusual," said Grey Michael. He touched the corpse as if feeling for a pulse, and held the pose for a long moment. Finally satisfied, he straightened and walked to the front door to open it.

The door no longer led to the street. Instead, it opened to the kitchen. The house had been bent inward on itself in an impossible topology.

"What remains?" asked Grey Michael, stepping through. He tapped the counter, opened the refrigerator, satisfying himself that he was indeed where he appeared to be. "What else is in here? Come. I would like to meet you."

He opened the small window over the sink. Although the image through the glass was that of a small backyard, through the opening the basement of the house was visible.

Experimentally, Grey Michael shattered one of the glass panes. The image of the backyard fell away with the shards.

In one smooth motion, Grey Michael slid through the window to stand in the basement. The space he had entered through was a small hopper window near the ceiling of the unfinished room. Light spilled in through it from the kitchen. The others along the wall, still closed, looked out into the yard.

"I have been called," Grey Michael said. "Can you say the same? I have eaten the famines, which you allowed to persist. If you could not harm them, you can do far less to me."

The basement was silent. Nothing answered his challenge. He could see no movement in any of the hidden corners.

"This is not the end," Grey Michael offered. He moved slowly up the basement stairs, alert for anything out of place around him. "All that I take will be remade once my place is restored. We do not belong in this dying universe. I will open a way back to where things do not cease. I must take from you now to do that, but it does not have to be an act of destruction.

"We can rise above the death of this place. We can simply join."

The door at the top of the stairs led into the hallway, as was normal. Ahead, however, the front door still stood open, revealing the kitchen beyond. There remained no way out.

"Cease this game," said Grey Michael, his voice growing angry. He climbed the interior stairs to the top floor. The doors in the short hallway above all led into small bedrooms. The windows, when opened, provided passageway only to each other in a complicated knot.

Grey Michael moved through the house with increasing urgency, his tone shifting from cajoling to threatening and back. No matter what he said or where he looked, he found no occupants of the house other than himself, and no way out.

Minutes spilled into hours. Hours collapsed into days. Days bled into weeks. Grey Michael did not sleep. He did not eat. He did not quit searching for an exit. But bit by bit, slowly but inexorably, he slowed.

Finally, an untold amount of time later, he stopped. Only for a moment, only long enough to sit and rest his legs. His eyes closed for the merest fraction of an instant.

Confinement, blazed the air before him. Grey Michael's eyes flashed open at the burning sigil. He attempted to leap to his feet, but the weight of the word pressed down on him, binding him.

Humanoid figures in blank masks barged into the house, flowing freely through the doors that had kept Grey Michael trapped for so long. They bore more symbols in place of faces. *Command. Consume. Erase.*

Grey Michael raised a hand, but the figures lashed out with ropes of rubber and metal, binding him in planes far beyond the physical. Their ceaseless assault rolled over him in a wave, overpowering his exhausted resources. In seconds, Grey Michael was hooded, bound and being transported from the house.

In the dining room, two of the figures bent over the dead host.

"I haven't got a pulse. How long has it been?"

"No more than a minute. Start chest compressions! We can still get him back."

The man's sunken chest did not look like it could hold up to the pressure of CPR, but the figure above him set to it with a will regardless. Each punishing stroke seemed about to cave his ribs in entirely, but suddenly the man on the ground began gasping for air on his own.

"Korneli! Korneli, thank God. You're still with us."

"I… feel like I've been hit by a truck," said the man on the floor feebly.

"Well, you were dead for a minute. Longer in here, I suppose. Glad life didn't hold that against you," said the one who'd been doing the compressions.

"Don't worry, you came back with good old-fashioned science," said the other man. "Nothing in you that shouldn't be there."

He reached for his radio. "Lie still. We need to get you on IVs as soon as possible. I'm sorry you had to suffer through that. We never thought it would take Grey Michael that long to come."

"He suspected something," said the recently revived man.

"Much good it did him. We got him all the same."

Lying on the floor, wearing the body of the dead man named Korneli, Grey Michael smiled to himself. If they believed a trick as simplistic as bending spacetime could capture him, then he had nothing to fear. It would be worth discovering the capabilities of this group before moving on, though. They clearly knew of his activities. It would behoove him to learn more of theirs.

Let them search his molt for answers. Even as they studied it, he would be studying them.

THE PUMPKIN BRIDE

His name was Piotr Petrovich, but we all called him the Pumpkin King. He lived alone on a sprawling farm outside of town. It had been in his family for generations, but it seemed like Piotr was going to be the last scion of the Petrovich clan. He had never married, and although he worked the farm diligently, he had no one to pass it down to.

What a farm it was! Acres upon acres of corn, which he turned into a tremendous corn maze every fall. Fields of wheat, barley, all sorts of grains. And above all else, the pumpkins.

His pumpkin patch was a sight to behold. It was visible from the road and went on for miles, a sea of green vines studded with bright orange globes. They grew in all sizes, from little round gourds all the way up to behemoths as big as Piotr himself. He sold them by the truckload, shipping them all over the country, but he still always had plenty left to populate his stand at the farmers' market in town. All through fall it would be piled high with pumpkin pies, pumpkin bread, pumpkin soup—every pumpkin-based food you could imagine. No one had any idea how he had time to cook so much while maintaining the farm on his own, but he managed it.

People in town used to joke that Piotr wasn't tan, his skin was just orange from all of the pumpkins he ate. They said that you knew he was nearby when it suddenly smelled like you'd just started carving a jack-o'-lantern. It was all in good fun. He was a local legend, which meant that he was larger than life in all dimensions.

Piotr leaned into it, especially in the fall. He spent weeks every year reshaping the corn maze, making it better and more complicated than the previous one. Folks came from hours around to find their way through it. He let folks set up food trucks, carnival games, the whole nine yards. And of course, he had his pumpkin treats out there for sale as well.

Part of the fun of the maze was that it wasn't just about finding your way to the exit. Piotr hid strange things throughout the maze, totally unexpected stuff like a giant metal insect built out of a scrapped car, or a row of skeletons digging their way up from the ground. Those things were never on the direct path out of the maze, so only those who were lost got to see them. It was a consolation prize of sorts, and gave us something to talk about with our friends when we made it back out. It wasn't just about who got through the fastest, but also who had found the neatest things inside.

Piotr changed the decorations up regularly to keep them from becoming boring. The only one that was there every year was the Bride.

The Bride was a pumpkin-headed scarecrow that stood way out in the center of the maze, placed on a metal pole that was twenty feet high or more. It was dressed in a tattered wedding dress with long, flowing sleeves and a train that hung more than halfway down to the ground. When the wind picked up, that fabric would flow and flutter, beckoning people toward it.

Not that you could get to it. You could see the Bride from a good chunk of the maze, but none of the paths ever led there. It just scowled down from its post, the fearsome expression carved into its pumpkin face getting ever more gruesome as the season wore on and the pumpkin started to rot and fall in on itself.

I don't remember exactly how it started, but one year the kids in town were determined to get the Bride's head. Just one of those things that someone challenged someone else to do, probably. It didn't seem like a big deal, until the first guy to try reported back that he'd tried to sneak through the corn to get to the Bride, only to find that there was a chain-link fence hidden among the stalks.

We went out to investigate, more than half expecting him to be lying or wrong, but sure enough a fence blocked access to the Bride. It wrapped all the way around with no gate or break, closing off an area maybe thirty feet on a side all around the scarecrow. Strands of barbed wire ran along the top, too, and we dared each other to touch it to find out if it was electrified. It wasn't, as we found out after one of the guys pushed another into it.

The idea of getting the Bride's head had just been a passing thing before, but now it was a matter of pride. Piotr had anticipated us. We couldn't let him win. We were going to have that pumpkin.

We came back with gloves and leather jackets to drape over the barbed wire, and climbed the fence. The first one to jump down on the far side immediately sank into mud past his knees. It took two of us to pull him out, and we retreated in confusion as we considered this new wrinkle. The mud didn't extend outside of the fence. It was clear that this was another intentional barrier.

We tried again with tall rubber boots and wire cutters to snip a hole in the fence. We cut the wire where we could put it back if we had to, which turned out to be a good idea after we crept through the mud to the base of the Bride's pole and found out that the metal was greased. If we jumped, we could just about touch the trailing fabric of her wedding dress, and we discussed whether claiming a piece of that would be enough.

It would not, obviously. We had come for the pumpkin, and we would not let Piotr keep it from us.

Fifteen of us sneaked in the next night. This was no longer a challenge for individual bragging rights, but a team effort. It was all of us versus him.

It took hours. We climbed on each other's shoulders and slipped and fell a hundred times. The flooded ground cushioned our landings, but we were all rapidly covered in mud and filthy grease. The Bride's fluttering dress coaxed us onward, though, promising that the goal was just ahead.

I was the one who finally made it to the top. I was at the top of a chain three teenagers high, with others buttressing the bottom and encircling the pole to provide support and grip. The Bride's dress whipped all around me, threatening to knock me from my precarious position on my friend's shoulders, but I could see a small metal platform just above me.

I brushed it with my greasy fingertips, testing it. It felt solid enough to hold my weight. Taking a chance, I leapt upward and grabbed on, muscling my way up and through the enveloping white fabric of the dress.

Finally I was there, standing next to the Bride. I could see my friends staring up from below me, grins on their faces. In triumph, I lifted the pumpkin from the Bride's head and held it high.

All of their expressions turned to shock. Beneath the carved pumpkin was no scarecrow, but an actual woman. Her skin was sallow. Her cheeks were thin. Her hair was matted with pumpkin guts. Her head lolled to the side and did not move when I removed the pumpkin covering it.

I was sure it had to be one more joke, one final oddity hidden within the corn maze. I placed my hand on her neck to confirm that it was only plastic, but she was warm to the touch.

Suddenly, her eyes fluttered open. I jerked backward and fell from the platform, my carved pumpkin shell prize tumbling along with me. It shattered when we landed, but although the wind was knocked out of me, the sodden ground saved my life.

The police rescued the woman and took Piotr into custody. The raid of the farmhouse uncovered evidence of dozens of missing women, including pictures of each of them wearing the Bride's dress.

It had never been a scarecrow at all. Every year it had been the latest of Piotr's victims, drugged and left to die out in plain view of us all, hidden away by the cruel pumpkin mask.

Piotr raved that it was necessary, that the sacrifices fed the farm. He swore that without the ritual of the Bride, nothing would grow. He had only done what was necessary, he said—what had always been done in his family.

They locked him up and sold the farm off. It never did seem to produce as well as it had when Piotr was there, though. Eventually, they redeveloped it into warehouses, which was just as well.

To this day, I shudder when I see a pumpkin.

SOUHAIT

I'm an artist. Not one you've heard of, though that may be changing soon. Being an artist is about creation, not about commercial success. I wouldn't mind getting the occasional acceptance mixed in with the constant stream of rejection, of course, but it's a process.

A long process. They say that most artists don't become famous until after they're dead. I'd always hoped that I'd make it slightly before that.

I graduated last year with an MFA from a relatively prestigious institution, along with a dozen other folks who convinced themselves that an insurmountable pile of debt was the best way to jump right into the starving artist lifestyle. We were, as mentioned, a small class, so we all went to each other's showings and were generally supportive, but I was only really friends with two of the others, Jerrod and Albina.

The three of us ended up rooming together for the last year of the program, and we kept that going post-graduation. Having other folks in the house who look through the mail with the same mix of hope and trepidation is surprisingly helpful. Alone, it's easy to simply look at everyone else's filtered life and assume that you're the only one failing. When you come down in the morning to find your roommate crying in her cornflakes because her last eleven submissions haven't even gotten the courtesy of a rejection letter, it's a little easier to see that this is just how life goes sometimes.

One of our favorite Friday night activities was going to local galleries to see who they had on display. There were a few reasons for this. One, it gave us a good idea of what they liked to show, helping us hone our own submissions. Two, it was very cathartic to be catty about what had been picked. Three, a lot of the galleries had free hors d'oeuvres and wine.

I guess four, we liked art, but honestly it was hard to remember that sometimes. Sometimes looking at other people's finished canvases just made me angry. What made them able to decide that they were done? What made other people agree that they were worth hanging on the wall? What justified the astronomical price tags next to them?

I'm not saying that this was anything but jealousy. I'm just saying that art and I are in a complicated relationship.

About a month ago, we went to a newly opened gallery, Souhait. It was the usual setup: tall glass windows in front showcasing the art placed strategically on bright white walls within. It had the standard mix of oddly angled separators allowing the patrons to wander slowly through the room and discover the paintings one at a time. Basically, it looked like every other gallery, but as it was a new opening, it had better wine than most.

I was taking a casual tour of the perimeter when Jerrod appeared at my elbow.

"Hey, congratulations!" he said. "You weren't going to tell us? I can't believe you managed to keep this a secret."

"Sorry, what?"

"Oh, yeah, 'what' indeed." He steered me around several corners to where Albina was admiring a painting. "'There's a new gallery opening, we should all go, no reason.' Congrats!"

I stared at the painting in disbelief. It was one of mine.

I was certain that I hadn't submitted to this gallery. I hadn't even heard of it until Albina had mentioned that it was opening. I would have remembered receiving a letter of acceptance, and I definitely would have remembered delivering a painting. None of these things had happened.

And yet there my art was on the wall. It had my signature, and my name displayed next to it on a card. I knew the piece. I'd done it two or three years ago. It was good, very representative of my style at the time, but I'd moved on and had stopped trying to get it displayed a while ago. The last I had seen it, it was six or seven canvases deep in a stack of pieces that I had nowhere else to put.

It was fairly obvious that was not the case now. The proof was on the wall in front of me.

Albina and Jerrod were both praising me, so I just smiled and made vaguely humble comments. I must have submitted it. It wasn't like someone had broken into our apartment and stolen a single piece of my art. It was both confusing and concerning that I couldn't recall offering it to this gallery, but it was the only explanation that made sense.

I was still trying to puzzle this out when another familiar piece caught my eye. I nudged Jerrod. "Oh, so I'm the one keeping secrets?"

He raised an eyebrow at me, and I pointed across the floor. His eyes widened as he saw the same thing I had: one of his paintings neatly framed and prominently displayed.

"I didn't even know you'd finished that one," I said. "I swear I saw you working on it like two days ago."

"Yeah," he said, sounding a bit lost. "I was."

"How'd you get the gallery to take it before it was even done?"

"Oh my God, look!" said Albina.

In the back corner of the gallery, occupying an entire corner, was a small collection of Albina's work. It was expertly curated. I'd watched her develop her style for years, and the eight paintings chosen here perfectly encapsulated the entire range. Clusters of people kept gathering in front of them, and I saw more than one slip off to speak to the gallery owner about purchasing a piece.

"Albi, these are amazing," I told her after we finally managed to get close enough to see them all properly. "This—some of these are absolute perfection. I don't think I've even seen all of them."

"Seriously, when did you do all of this?" asked Jerrod. "Some of these are definitely new. Unless you have a secret studio you've been hiding from us?"

He narrowed his eyes at her in mock suspicion. She laughed, shoving him lightly, but behind her smile I saw the same confusion that I'd heard in Jerrod's voice, the same that I'd felt myself. None of us knew that our work was going to be on display here. Something was very odd.

We didn't talk about it then. Oddity or not, our art and our names were on display, and there were free drinks to toast with. We refilled our glasses, congratulated each other effusively, wandered the gallery for a bit and then did it all again. By the time we were walking home, all concerns had vanished from all of our minds. We were successful! We could figure out how and why later.

The next morning, Albina was dead.

I woke up late with a hangover. Jerrod woke up later, looking even rougher than I did. There was nothing resembling breakfast anywhere in the apartment, so we sat and sipped our coffee silently. Albina's door was open, and I think we both hoped that she'd gone out to get bagels or something and that we would shortly be provided for.

She wasn't answering texts, and Jerrod and I were just starting to get concerned when there was a knock at the door. We opened it to find a policeman asking if we knew Albina Shevchenko, and if we had contact information for her family, and if we could come identify the body.

It had been a hit and run. She'd been dead by the time witnesses had gotten to her. No one had seen the car's license plate. The police didn't even pretend that there was a chance of justice.

They gave us her effects, including what remained of a bag of bagels. Somehow that was the worst part for me. She'd gone out to get something to celebrate with us. It made us complicit.

At the funeral, the priest spoke about her giving spirit and her wonderful personality, but most of all, he spoke about her massive artistic talent. He went on at length about what she could have created if she had not had her span cut short. The entire gathering nodded along with him.

Jerrod and I exchanged looks. It wasn't that he was wrong. She was amazing, and eventually the world would have known about her. It's just that it hadn't happened yet. The three of us were, as far as we could tell, the only ones really aware of how much potential we had. If everyone knew this about her, why had she been scraping by in a dingy apartment with us, trying to get enough money together to buy more art supplies?

"We should go back to Souhait," Jerrod said after the funeral. "The gallery owner probably doesn't know. We'll need to get her pieces back before he trashes them when she doesn't respond."

Our trip was unnecessary. The gallery owner had Albina's obituary blown up to large size and prominently displayed next to a tremendous collection of her work. It covered entire walls of the gallery, each piece with an explanatory card discussing when and why she had painted it. Where the prices had been on the cards, every single one was marked "SOLD."

I was looking around for the owner to ask where he was sending the money when Jerrod grabbed my arm.

"Look," he said, half-whispering.

Arranged in a neat circle on one wall were a dozen of his paintings.

"I don't know that I want to be on display here," he said. He sounded frightened.

"Then take them back. They're your pieces."

"Are they?" He pointed. "I never finished that one. That's how I wanted it to look, but I couldn't get it right. I swear I never completed it. And there! I never painted that. I thought of it, I knew it in my head, but I have never put brush to canvas for it. Not even to start it.

"How could they have any of this? How could anyone?" His voice was rapidly rising toward hysteria.

"Hey, let's get you out of here," I said, putting an arm around his shoulders. "We'll come back tomorrow and get them taken down if you want. We're all running on fumes right now."

Privately, I thought again about the piece that Souhait had of mine. I'd never gotten around to looking for it at the apartment. Things had been a blur since Albi's death. I wondered how this gallery had so much of our stuff. I wondered what else had been taken.

Back at home, Jerrod rummaged through his artwork, hunting for something.

"See?" he said finally, holding up a canvas. "I told you. It isn't done."

He was holding up something that could have been an early attempt at one of the pieces we'd seen in the gallery. It was the same general idea, but the colors weren't right, and the composition didn't gel. Also, as he'd said, it was clearly incomplete. Parts of the canvas still showed through in some areas. It wasn't what was hanging on the walls.

"I told you," he repeated. "How can they have art I never finished?"

I tried to get him to calm down. I sat him down on the couch and poured him a drink. We'd go back in the morning, I said. We'd find the owner. We'd sort all of this out. It was a problem for tomorrow, not for this evening. Not right after a funeral.

I thought I'd gotten him to agree with me. I poured us both another drink. Somewhere in the middle of that one, I fell asleep on the couch.

When I woke up, Jerrod was gone.

Just one of those things, the police said. Wrong place at the wrong time. He'd been mugged. His credit cards and phone were gone. He'd bled out in the street. He was almost halfway to Souhait.

I went there to get his art taken down, like he'd wanted. They'd already expanded the collection. His photo smiled down at me from the main wall, next to an obituary lauding his talent, his bold innovation, his novelty. The rest of the gallery was plastered with his work. I recognized some of the paintings he'd been rifling through at the apartment the previous day. Most had already been sold.

And on the back wall, in a small but well-lit section by themselves, hung six of my paintings. The one that I'd seen the first night was there, along with two others I was particularly proud of. If I'd been asked to pick three pieces to best represent who I was and who I had been as an artist, those might have been them.

The other three bore my signature, but I did not paint them. Not yet. Like Jerrod, I knew the subject matter in them. I had thought of them, conceived them, and even made some attempts to put them to canvas, but they had never come out like I'd imagined. I'd set them aside to try again later, when I had better supplies, when I was better.

Yet here they hung, complete and perfect, exactly as I had pictured them. It was a triumph of my craft.

It was beautiful to see what I could become, given enough time.

It's just too bad that I don't have it.

Most artists don't become famous until after they're dead.

EXCERPTS FROM A NOTEBOOK FOUND ON A DEAD BODY

[The body of Velia Albert, 36, was recently discovered on a local playground. It bore no signs of trauma or indicators of cause of death. Her backpack contained a journal, from which the following passages have been taken.]

I'm sitting here with a dead body. I don't know how to feel about this. I should feel something, I think, but I don't think I do. Or maybe I'm just suppressing it.

I found him in the woods, not three days into my trip. It's Daniel. It's clearly Daniel. He looks good, even great. Aside from being dead, obviously. But it's been a year since he disappeared, months since we gave up looking. Not gave up entirely, obviously. I came hiking with a vague idea that I might find something. I knew it was a delusion, though.

Only it wasn't. I found him, found his body. He looked just like when I last saw him, and for just a second, I thought maybe he was okay, that he was sleeping. There was no pulse, though. And he was light when I moved his head, so light. It's like all of his insides were gone. He didn't look emaciated, but he must have been starving.

He's been lost in the woods for a year. How could he not be?

He still had his backpack. It had all of his things in it, even his cell phone. It's dead, of course. He must have tried to call for help so many times. There's no service out here.

There's no blood, no signs of any wounds, not even any discoloration of the skin that I can see. I've only looked at the parts that aren't covered. I carried him back to camp, and I know I felt things rustling in his shirt. I don't want to see the bugs eating him.

I put my sleeping bag over him. I didn't know what else to do. I suppose I'm sleeping on the tent floor tonight. I hope it's not too cold.

This is a ridiculous thing to be worried about. I'm clearly redirecting.

I don't know how I should feel.

***

This is terrible.

He must have died yesterday or the day before. Right before I found him. If I'd come out here a day earlier, I might have found him alive, found him in time.

I took the sleeping bag off of him this morning and gagged. His body collapsed overnight. His face is sunken like something pulled the skull out and left the skin intact. It's sagging in on itself like a rotting jack-o'-lantern. His chest is the same. His arms look shriveled. I can't see his legs beneath the pants, but the fabric is sitting more loosely than yesterday. I'm sure it's all the same.

His skin is pebbled with tiny greyish-white dots, like the heads of pins. They're clustered together by the hundreds, taking up huge swathes of what I can see. Are they eggs? I thought about scraping one off, but I don't know what I could do with it if I did. I don't know how to identify an insect egg.

I can't carry his body back with me now. I don't know how I was planning to in the first place, but now I'm afraid he would fall apart if I tried to move him.

He smells, but not like I would expect. He smells like an old basement, damp and earthy. I'd put it down to the rain, but it didn't rain last night. It did two days ago, before I found him, but he didn't smell yesterday.

It suddenly occurs to me that if this is contagious, I'm screwed. I carried him yesterday, had him draped over my shoulders.

I think I'm fine. He didn't look like this yesterday. This is probably just something that happens to bodies in the woods.

I'm never touching that sleeping bag again. That's for sure.

****

I'm in the tent. Something's wrong with Daniel's body.

I had a coughing fit at the fire. It was like I'd breathed in smoke, only the smoke was blowing away from me. There was something in the air, though, some particulate matter. That was what I'd choked on.

It was all over Daniel's body, hanging over him in a big cloud. I thought it was bugs at first. A swarm of something come to eat him. It only drifted on the breeze, though. I think it was rising up from him. I breathed in whatever it was.

I ran for the tent. I don't know if it's sealed against the outside. I suppose it can't be, or I'd suffocate in here overnight. It's better protection than nothing, though.

I can still see the cloud drifting outside. It's thick enough to cast a faint shadow in the light of the fire.

I have no idea what to do now. I'm going to stay in here until the cloud goes away. Or until the fire burns out and I can't see it anymore, I suppose.

****

The cloud was gone this morning. The air smelled fresh in that forest way. I don't seem to be having any residual effects from breathing in whatever that was.

Daniel's body is gone. Or rather, it's there, but it's erupted entirely into mushrooms. They look like fingers coming off of him, or toes. Some of the fatter ones look like noses. It looks like someone ransacked a morgue and threw all of the little extremities in a pile. They're not all flesh-colored, though. Some are the same blue as his hiking jacket, some are grey like his pants. The big patch down by his feet even looks like his backpack. I suppose it's some sort of protective coloration, mimicking whatever they're growing on.

I wouldn't know it had been a person if I hadn't seen him two days ago. It's just a riot of fungus now.

***

Daniel's backpack is gone. His body I can understand, but not his pack.

I wanted to get his cell phone. I thought he might have recorded a message on it for us or taken pictures or something. I figured I could charge it when I got back home, and even without his body it would prove that I'd found him. If I did. I'm starting to wonder.

I got a stick to brush the mushrooms away from his backpack, but underneath the mushrooms were just more mushrooms. They grew in striated layers, different colors like cutting open a fancy cake, but all the same spongy texture. They broke apart under my stick, falling away in chunks.

I saw his phone in there. I know I did. But when I tried to fish it out with the stick, it broke apart too. It crumbled into broken chunks just like everything else.

I took a photo of one piece to prove I wasn't crazy. It has SAMS printed on it as clear as day, where the A is like an upside-down V like it always is in the Samsung logo. It's an insane thing to be on a mushroom, but I crumbled it in my hands, and it was definitely organic.

I probably shouldn't have touched it. I had to know.

I'm getting out of here. I'm leaving my sleeping bag and my tent. I'm sorry to litter, but they were sitting out in that brown miasma. I can't take chances.

***

It's pouring rain tonight. I wish I had my tent.

***

I found Daniel's body. Again.

It was at the base of a tree, laid out on the damp ground and looking just like it had before. No damage, no blood. Practically peaceful.

I thought I was going crazy. I touched it, rolled it over, opened the backpack. All just like before.

He was light, though. That must have been what made me think to do it.

220

I squeezed his arm as hard as I could. There was resistance at first, and then all of a sudden, the skin just popped like the casing of a sausage and my fingers sank in.

There wasn't any blood. There wasn't anything. Inside was just a uniform spongy texture.

I ripped his arm. It tore like foam rubber. The insides broke into clammy chunks that I could crumble in my hands.

The backpack was the same. So were the contents. I found his phone again. I took a video. It looks just like a phone, but when I bent it hard enough to break, it snapped to reveal that same featureless interior.

It's mushrooms. It's all mushrooms. I don't know how, but it is.

***

Rained again last night. Saw Daniel's body twice more today. I ignored it this time. There's nothing else to learn.

I'm only a day away from getting back home. I don't know if I should go, though. Woke up this morning to find my hand and arm pebbled with tiny greyish-white dots. I scraped them off, but the skin was red and itchy where they had been. I've had to scrape it several more times today. They keep growing back.

My throat feels scratchy when I breathe, too. I don't think I got to the tent soon enough. Or it didn't help enough.

Maybe a hospital could help me. Or maybe I'd just be bringing this back to expose more people to it.

I'm going to camp out tonight. I'll see how it looks in the morning. I'll make a decision then.

***

They're growing. My arm was covered this morning. What's worse, I recognize things in the mushrooms. They're tiny, poorly formed, but they're mimicking things I brought with me. My phone. My keys.

I took another photo for all the good it will do. There's a section right by my elbow that has my own words. Words I wrote yesterday. It's growing a copy of my journal.

I feel feverish. Things look blurry. Even this page.

I'm not going back. With any luck, this dies here with me.

[The morgue drawer that should have contained Ms. Albert's body was found, on subsequent inspection, to contain only a liquefied mass of an unidentified organic substance. The evidence bags with her personal effects likewise held nothing but slop.]

TOUCHING INFINITY

This is the story of how the world almost died. It is a tale of unlikely saviors and untrustworthy heroes. It is the story of Dinesh Singh, and the birth and death of DREAMS.

Dinesh Singh was a mid-level bureaucrat of no particular note, and an occultist of only minor talent. He was destined to go nowhere particular in life, a fact which irked him greatly. He saw the power around him, both the bludgeoning force of the government and the nimble persuasions of magic, but he was constantly thwarted in his attempts to harness either for himself.

Sometimes, one very bright idea is all it takes to change destiny. In Dinesh's case, the idea was this: use the power of the government to capture the power of magic. From such a simple concept, DREAMS was born, and through it the Facility.

DREAMS was one of those delightful backronyms of which the government is so fond. It stood for the "Department of REality Assertion and Magical Suppression," a full name which would have gotten it rejected had anyone actually read it. It took only the lightest of magical touches to encourage a bureaucratic committee to skim past the details of a small line item on the budget, and with the stroke of a pen, DREAMS moved from concept to existence.

Dinesh knew that his fledgling department was only as strong as its ability to avoid an audit. His first move was to seek out more sources of power, ostensibly to safely contain them. He and his eager team began to collect magical books.

Some of these fit the classic description of a spell book, tomes bound in stained leather and filled with strange symbols and rituals. Others masqueraded as mathematics texts, atlases, or even children's books. In all cases, their effects were the same: lives ruined, people driven mad, the world warped in their wake.

Dinesh knew he could use them to further his own ends.

The custodians of DREAMS pried these books from the hands of those who had been afflicted by them, but were then left with the problem of what to do with the users. Many could no longer exist in the world now that the curtain of reality had been ripped away. Some had absorbed the power from the books and were now bound to them. Others had simply seen too much and had become a danger to themselves and those around them. In either case, they could not be left where they were. And so, the Facility was created.

The official motto of the department is *Vires in Tenebris*, "strength in darkness." However, the unofficial motto swiftly became *Fines Iustificare Significat*: the ends justify the means. Many of the books of power had the potential to be great assets in the collection and suppression of other supernatural items and agents. Officially the books were destroyed or buried. Unofficially, of course, Dinesh began calling upon their power to strengthen his department.

He used them with caution, of course. They were shielded and sealed away when not in use, watched over by a guardian known as the Librarian. His real name is not recorded anywhere, even in the Facility's secret files. Most believe he was a contemporary of Dinesh's when the department was founded. It is amazing the lies people will tell themselves to avoid seeing the truth.

The Librarian lives deep in the Facility, in what would perhaps be the basement if the building had use for such spatially distinct terms. His domain is bright, cheerful and clutter-free. He never ages. As far as the Facility knows, he never leaves.

When a custodian comes seeking knowledge, the Librarian dangles the book they need before them, while speaking cautions of the price the book will exact in return. He lends out his books with a smile that hides too many teeth. He knows his warnings will go unheeded. It brings him joy.

Unlike the Librarian, Dinesh's name is well known. It appears on memorial plaques on benches and water fountains throughout the Facility. Pictures of him labeled "Founder" hang on the walls near conference rooms. He is in every part of the Facility— literally.

Large portions of the Facility are occupied by cells designed to contain various beings with reality-warping abilities. Dinesh knew that no standard prison could contain people who could walk through walls, reverse time or otherwise flout the laws of physics. Something dynamic was needed to stop this sort of threat. Something intelligent. And so, with knowledge borrowed from the Librarian, Dinesh sacrificed his humanity to become that thing.

It is said that Room 1 contains the remnants of Dinesh himself, the quivering, uncovered nerve center laced into the very cement of the walls. No one has gone to check, nor can name anyone who has. It is simply known.

None of the custodians know every part of the Facility. It shifts and changes as needed. Its security system is agile and aware. The custodians' job is mainly to bring in new threats to be contained from the outside world. Once inside, the Facility takes over.

It is not infallible. The people and powers it contains are strong and clever, and many do not wish to be confined. But the Facility does not tire or sleep or feel pain. It cannot be blinded or distracted. It watches everywhere within itself all at once, anticipating and defanging threats before they can even materialize.

Over the years, DREAMS's mandate has slowly expanded. The Facility allows the custodians to safely close away darker and more dangerous beings. The Librarian's books give them the powers necessary to approach these creatures on their own terms. They sell their humanity a piece at a time, sacrificing themselves as surely as Dinesh did. They tell themselves that they can handle it, that they will not end up residents of the Facility as many of their colleagues have in the past. They go to the Librarian for just one more protective sigil, one more word of power, and they ignore the mocking glee of his smile.

For decades, this was good enough. The Facility had the occasional breakout, but the damage was always limited and containable.

This was not that. This was something new. This was me.

Grey Michael.

They caught me, the eater of the supernatural, and brought me into the middle of a buffet. Truly, I should have asked to be caught. I had spent years hunting, fighting and using my own carefully hoarded power to snare my victims. I could have simply strolled through the Facility and plucked them from the vine.

They did not know what I was, of course. My mask of humanity did not fool them, but they might have believed that I once had been a man. They did not know what I did with the power I consumed. They only knew that I was growing ever stronger.

Humans fear what they do not understand, and the custodians of DREAMS more than most. They hatched a plan to catch me, to contain me before I surpassed their Facility in power.

At one time it might have worked. My hunger was driven by a need to restore myself to my former glory, after all. Had they caught me soon enough, they truly might have been able to contain me.

Instead, they only alerted me to their existence. Curious, I allowed them to bring me in. Once I saw what the Facility held, I was breathlessly pleased that I had.

It had everything I needed. I could feel it as soon as I passed through its doors. Here at last was power enough to complete my goal, to force a hole between this degraded, dying universe and my own. My beautiful home of limitless power.

I let them bring my molt into the Facility, the cast-off thing that they thought was me. In the guise of one of their custodians, I logged its entry myself. It amused me to toy with them, to balance on the cusp of triumph and hold myself back. There was nothing they could do to stop me now, but that was no reason to leave anything to chance.

I started with the Facility itself. When it opened its mind to allow the knowledge of the newest prisoner, I was there, waiting. I tore into its psyche and ripped it away in chunks.

Alarms sounded. Custodians panicked. I stripped the protective sigils from those in the room with me and watched them collapse, crushed by the bargains they had made for power. The runes crunched lightly between my teeth.

I reached for another piece of the Facility's power, but it had gone, fleeing from me. I had expected this. The final game had begun.

I slowly stalked the hallways, watching the tiles beneath my feet wither and flake away like dead skin. Doors bled lubricant from hinges and knobs as I touched them. They twisted painfully in their frames after I passed through, hanging like dislocated fingers.

I expected to encounter the custodians as I walked, but to my surprise the Facility hid them from me. There was nothing they could have done in any case, no preparation that would have been sufficient to inflict even the most minor of damage, but I had thought the Facility would sacrifice them to buy itself a few more moments.

Instead, I had unfettered access to the residents. They knew I was coming. They could feel the Facility's terror, its impotence in the face of my onslaught. They banged at the edges of their enclosures and shrieked for the Facility to free them, but it was afraid to allow even so small a piece of its mind near me. I watched their cells melt before me, heard their final pleas, and absorbed them into myself.

Step by step, my deliberate progress carved pieces away from the Facility. I would find where it was hiding its custodians sooner or later. I would make my way to its heart, and fully, deliciously consume every piece of this magnificent building. It was only a matter of time. The end was no longer in question.

I could hear reality singing so softly that no one less attuned than I would have been able to hear it. I drifted through the dying rooms listening to the soft notes. It sang of thinness, of captured potential waiting to be released. It promised fulfillment at last. It spoke of home.

It was an almost physical sensation, the song. It vibrated within my body. The universe of limitless energy from which I came, to which I had been striving so long to return, was a paper-thin distance away. Just a touch more power, and I would be able to pierce the separation between them.

It would take everything from me, every scrap of strength I had been able to gather. Years of grubbing for power in this entropic paradigm, where energy constantly bleeds away instead of replenishing. Years of consumption and effort and death, of carefully managing resources to spend the minimum necessary in order to miserly hoard as much as possible. All of that, and I would still only be able to make the merest pinprick between the two worlds, a single subatomic hole joining them for the slightest fraction of an instant.

That was all I would need. In that moment, I would again have access to my unfettered power. I would rip it from the true universe in a tidal wave, tearing that microscopic hole open wide enough to serve as a portal for his return. That action would cost me nothing. My realm has no concept of cost, of diminishment. Everything is available for the taking without ever being lessened, as it should be.

This universe—I had no idea what would happen to it. Perhaps it would benefit from the roaring influx of infinite power. Or perhaps it would collapse entirely under the weight of a burden its limited physics were never designed to support. I did not care. It did not matter. Once I was restored to my full mantle, once I had reclaimed my birthright, I would be able to create a thousand universes like this, and destroy them just as easily.

Somewhere in this dying building, the Facility still hid power from me, power which I needed. It called out to me, begging me to take it, to draw it into myself. I drained it from the corridors as I walked, leaving stone sagging like rotting flesh.

The Facility's heart was near. I did not mind its final, panicked flight. It gave me an opportunity to savor the exquisite inevitability of my ultimate success. My time in this world taught me the virtue of patience. Anticipation makes the reward sweeter.

Suddenly, a demand was placed upon me. A spell of summoning whipped from the floor to wind its way around my body, coercive and insistent. The strand was thin but tenacious. It was rapidly joined by another, and another. They wove together in a razor-edged net, pulling me painfully toward their creators.

It would take almost no effort to sever the bindings, but almost was not quite the same as nothing at all. I was reluctant to relinquish even the slightest amount of power unnecessarily with victory so close at hand. I allowed the hooks to remain, tugging me along new ethereal pathways until I stood in the center of the room with the summoners themselves.

Sixteen of the custodians were gathered in a circle, standing shoulder-to-shoulder and facing away from me. They held thin leather tomes in their hands, all open to a page with the forgotten rune *Compel*. The syllables spilled from their tongues to fill the room with thick, stifling magic. The circle formed by their bodies seethed with it. None turned to look as I was drawn up from the depths to stand behind them.

More custodians lined the walls, forming a living barrier between me and the torn remnants of the Facility. They, too, held copies of that leather-bound book. I watched their fingers compulsively trace the three linked circles stamped into the cover, sketching the shape over and over. Their mouths uttered dark truths that reshaped reality, even beyond what the Facility was normally able to do. They fed the spells with their life force, their minds, their very beings.

They had abandoned all safeguards. Perhaps they understood what my departure might mean for their universe. Perhaps they were simply fighting back like any cornered animal.

It hardly mattered. The spells meant to trap and reduce me merely fascinated me. I ran my hands through the magic, letting it sift through my fingers. I peered into the structure to see how the bonds were made. They thickened and settled around me until I may have looked bound to an outside eye, but they were as tenuous as tissue paper compared to my strength. I knew the spells would hold only until I applied resistance.

As I examined the spells, I saw that a common thread ran through them all. It was a simple, repeating pattern upon which every one of these spells was built. Distilled down to a word, it was this: *Know*.

I picked the spells apart, pulling this word out to look at it more closely. It was built upon smaller structures as well, but upon examination those structures too were merely *Know*. It was a fractal concept, infinitely created upon itself.

I put the word into my mouth to feel the shape of it. I did not bite down upon it as I had the previous sigils. I merely felt it, tasted it, considered it.

It wanted to be said.

I said it.

Know.

The Librarian stood before me in the circle, a wolf's grin upon his lips. The room was silent and still. The magic still flowed almost imperceptibly around us, coiling like frozen smoke, but time had stopped to allow this meeting.

The Librarian spoke.

"Grey Michael." Laughter danced behind his words. He used my false name, the one which could be said without invoking power, but his tone said that he did this by choice. It was possible that he was bluffing. I did not yet know.

I could feel his power and the potential threat, but I was certain that I could consume him when I needed to. For now, curiosity still held, and the desire to conserve power. I opted to converse.

"Who are you?"

"You pulled me from the spell. What better answer could I give than that?"

"You have what I need to leave."

"More than you know."

"I can take it." I probed him, testing for weakness.

The Librarian still smiled. "I will give it freely, a statement which I rarely make. I much prefer to trade."

"Then why make an exception?"

"The only thing that you have that I need is a realization. And for you to have that, I must first give it to you."

"What if I refuse to accept it?"

"None of us have that luxury. We can, if we are fortunate, choose the time and place of our realization. This is the gift I offer to you today."

"I need nothing from you. Your paltry sorcerers have not bound me."

"Nor were they meant to. I depended on your curiosity to bring you here. Had it not, I would have had nothing to give you after all."

"Very well." Despite everything, I found myself interested in what the smiling creature before me had to say. "What is this realization?"

"You need this world."

I laughed in genuine surprise. "This broken, bleeding place? You would not say that if you knew where I was from. When I swallow your magicians here, I will be able to reach it again at last. I will swing wide the gates and let infinite power flood this universe. All of the science, all of the tiny magics they have ever known here will be swept away in an instant as every being becomes a god all at once, to create and destroy and revel forever in the constant joy of being."

"And then what?"

"Then—anything. Everything. Eternal, unending power."

"You are not what you once were, Grey Michael." The Librarian spoke my true name this time, one not fully heard in this dimension since I had first been invoked. "You think that you have been lessened, and it is true. But you have also become more. You have facets you did not have before. You have curiosity. You have patience. You have desire. None of these things can be fulfilled in your home. And so, you will learn a new sensation, the creeping destructive seed of this universe: boredom.

"All of your infinite power will not be able to fix that. Things will always be too easy. You will never again face a challenge. And it will eat you alive."

I considered this for a long moment. The eddies of nearly frozen magic moved subtly against me. Was the Librarian right? Had this universe altered me so? I, who had always been unchanging. I, who had always been omnipotent. Had it made me something I had not been before?

Finally, I shook my head.

"No. When I am as I was, I will be as I was. Undiminished, unbroken. And if I am not, if you are somehow correct, I can simply rebuild this. So, there can be no loss."

"There is still one possibility for loss."

"What is that?"

The Librarian grinned. His teeth were sharp and white. The rows seemed to go on much farther than his mouth should allow. "I could kill you."

I wanted to laugh again, but instead I felt a flash of fear. "Impossible."

"Perhaps. But are you certain? Certain enough to risk the loss of infinity?"

"I have eaten entire dimensions of magic. There is nothing you could do to me."

"But are you *certain*?"

I was not. I stared at the Librarian, at the laughing look in his eyes, at this thing that was both a spell and a man, story and reader, more than either and more than anything else besides. I felt him. I knew him. And I was not sure.

"This is what I propose," said the Librarian. "Take the last of the power you need. There is enough in the magics of these attempted bindings. Open your pathway to your universe of infinite power. And run."

"You would let me regain my full self?"

"I would let you leave. Leave this world without further disturbance and go back to where you came from. If you find that your acquired traits—your curiosity, your desire—still bother you, then you can diminish yourself from time to time and return to receive a reminder of the delight of having everything.

"And if I am wrong, and they no longer trouble you, then come back in glory to face me. If, that is, you are certain you will win."

"I will do that." I still did not truly know if his proposal was a bluff. With all I had gathered, surely he could not have stood against me. Certainly I should have been able to consume him. His name was already in my mouth.

Yet the risk was too great. His smile told me that he knew I would not call the bluff.

I offered the Librarian a smile of my own, and my hand to shake. "I will see you again, in one capacity or another."

He accepted my handshake, a gentleman graciously accepting his win. "May you wear your realization in infinite health."

I opened my mouth then, letting the Librarian see the roiling darkness inside, studded by distant stars. With one inhalation, I drew all of the magic in the room into myself. It flowed in effortlessly, leaping free of the frozen casters, sliding past the Librarian like he was a rock in a stream. He did not move or flinch. His smile never slipped.

I felt the magic join the ball of power inside. I condensed all of that potential energy into a single, sharp point and, with all of my will, pressed it against the darkness inside, the barrier that blocked me from home.

For an agonizing moment, the barrier held. Then, as soft as thought, I felt a pinprick of light flare within me. At last. At last! Home.

I do not know exactly what I left behind me. Grey Michael as he had been was gone, and I was returned in all of my majesty. Yet he still persisted inside of me, changing my aspect in subtle ways. Never before would it have occurred to me to wonder about things outside of myself. Never before would I have thought to guess.

I imagine the Librarian greeted the custodians, his devoted sorcerers, with words of reassurance. I imagine that he told them that they had succeeded, that they had driven me from the realm of man. I imagine that he helped them protect and repair the Facility as it restored itself, as they attempted to resume their interrupted lives.

I am certain that he did not tell them the cost that they had paid, and that the books would continue to take. Just as I am certain that he did not warn me about the consequences of placing his word upon my tongue. I do not know how much of this he orchestrated, but I know that he took full advantage.

I carry his true name inside of me now, as he carries mine. We will meet again someday, as I promised. We will see who has more fully subsumed the other. It will not be a battle, precisely, but nor will it be a joining. Worlds will be altered in our wake.

For now—it is enough to be home, and whole, and renewed.

May your world turn smoothly. May the degradations of entropy sit easily upon your shoulders.

And if you should encounter the smiling thing that saved your universe, offer him Grey Michael's regards.